SOUTHERN CRIMES

BY
PAMELA GULLEY

Southern Crimes
-written by-
Pamela Gulley

Published by Bright Beginnings Publications
www.brightbeginningspublications.com
brightbeginningspublications@gmail.com

This novel is a work of fiction. Any resemblances to actual events, real people, living or dead, organizations, establishments or locales are products of the author's imagination. Other names, characters, places, and incidents are used fictitiously.

Cover Design: Dottie D'Zigns
Editor: Artessa La'Shan Michelé

ACKNOWLEDGEMENT

Writing has always been a hobby of mine that I kept to myself as a personal getaway from life's situations. I had never planned to display my works to anyone before my daughter encouraged me to give it a chance and see how far it will take me. I want to start out by thanking God for blessing me with the gift for writing and the courage to overcome my fears by giving me the strength to complete this book despite all the obstacles that were placed in front of me in this past year. I would also like to express my appreciation to my daughter Rayauna for giving me the push I needed to pursue my dreams as a writer and now publishing my first book. Without her valuable input and assistance, this book may have never been completed. I would also like to thank my husband Raymond for supplying the materials needed to help me get started on this new path in my life and my son Lee for giving me ideas for this book and providing me with the equipment needed to get me one step further to accomplishing my goals and sharing my excitement through it all. My dear friend Angela Johnson for helping me to understand that what I am doing is a blessing sent directly from God to me and that I am to embrace this new journey with all my heart. I can't forget one of the most important people that helped me make my dream come true. I want to thank Candice Glover, for all the time she spent helping me with this project. Finally I would like to thank LaTrice Allen with Bright Beginnings Publications for giving me the chance of a life time to express my artistic talent through my writings. She believes in me as a writer and gave me the opportunity make my writings truly come alive. I hope you all enjoy my debut book and please look out for more of my books to come. Thank you

DEDICATION

This book is dedicated to my mother Lilly and my son Lee. Last year was the most difficult year I have ever faced by almost losing two of the most important people in my life. My mother suffered from colon and breast cancer and now battling a brain tumor and my son was shot seven times. They were both expected not to make it but by the grace of God, they are both still with me and getting stronger each and every day. It has been hard, but they are both strong and have the will to live. We are faced with difficult times but the love I have for my mom and son has made me focus on my dreams as they encourage me to follow my heart and dreams. I can't thank God enough for allowing me and my family to still have my mother and my son and that is why this book is dedicated to the both of them because I saw firsthand the blessings of God.

CHAPTER 1

Marlie sighed wearily as she watched her six-month old son sleep peacefully on the cardboard and blankets she had prepared for him and carefully placed in a dark corner under the *Talmadge Memorial Bridge*. "How could this have happened? Who were those men? Oh John, my love. I can't believe this," she said to herself. She bowed her head to pray. "Dear God," she said in her soft southern accent, "what great joy I know you have for me at the end of this journey. Please give me the strength to endure all evil things that may come my way. In Jesus name, Amen."

MARLIE JEAN COOPER was a thirty-one-year-old homemaker, wife, and mother of six-month old son John David Cooper Jr. She stood about 5ft 10inches, slender in the waist, and long legs. Her milky white skin made her long red hair look as though the sun kissed it. She had all the grace and elegance of a true southern bell. Looking out beyond the train tracks, surrounded by broken glass, old tires, and empty box cars that were once occupied by vagrants and some small animals, Marlie could see the sun begin to rise, as it reflects off the waters of the Savannah River. She thought back to the night her husband was murdered. She could almost taste the lemonade that was made of fresh lemons and sugar cane straight out of the fields that they were sipping on that fateful, hot, summer evening in 1997. (two nights ago).

Cradling her baby in her arms as he slept peacefully, she looks at her husband, who was holding her, and said, "I love you John Cooper," as she leaned back to kiss him.

"You are my world, forever I am yours," he spoke softly to her as they embraced each other. Sensations of passion began to overtake them both.

"Let me put the baby to bed. I think he will sleep through the night, then we can finish what we are starting."

"Hurry back, my darling, I need you now," he replies, as he started to unbutton his shirt and unzip his pants to indicate that he was in the mood for love. And with that, Marlie gave her husband a long sensual kiss and then got up and turned to go in the house to lay the baby down for the night.

As Marlie began to lay John Jr. in his crib, she heard the sound of a car pulling into the driveway and turns the ignition off. The sounds of three car doors slamming shut moved through the air like a swift summer breeze. She placed the baby in the bed and covered him with the blanket that had a design of Big Bird from Sesame Street in the front, rubbed his head, and said goodnight. The sounds of men's muffled voices moving towards the back of the house where John David was waiting for her to return caused Marlie to take notice. She walked over to the window, slightly opening the curtain to see who the strange voices belonged to. Suddenly, shots rang out like fireworks on the Fourth of July. Marlie jumped backwards and fell to the floor, startled by the sounds of the blasts. Terror overtook her instantly, covering her from head to toe like a heavy blanket and making it hard for her to move briefly. She quickly rose to her feet and ran to the window, just in time to see John fall to his knees and then face down on the grass in front of the hammock they both shared just moments earlier. Death overtook him before his body hit the ground.

JOHN DAVID COOPER SR was a tall man of 6ft, brown hair, with locks of curls throughout his head. Deep blue eyes that we so deep, it seems the ocean would even be jealous. He had a muscular physique that sent chills through Marlie's soul, even when he was fully dressed. A very upstanding man in his community and also a well-respected attorney. A sudden rush of panic came to Marlie. "Oh my God, my husband, they killed him." The shock of what she just witnessed made her gasp loud enough to cause one of the men to look up in her direction. Quickly, she ducked back in the shadows, clasping her mouth with both hands so that she would not be heard again, trembling as she tried not to scream.

"Let's move out!" one of the men yelled from the driver's side of the car he was driving.

"But, I just saw something!" the man yelled back, then looked in Marlie's direction.

"Dame it Rick, let's go man." A stronger demand was given and just like that, they got back in the car and were gone back into the night. Silence came like a rush of wind blowing at hurricane speed. Marlie stumbled over one of the baby's stuffed animals that was still in the middle of the floor, almost hitting her head on the corner of the changing table her father-in-law had made for his first grandchild.

"Shit!" she yelled, rose to her feet, and continued down the stairs and out the back door to where her husband lay. She cried out as she picked his head off the grass. "Oh God, someone help me!" she yelled over and over again.

CHAPTER 2

The sound of the passing train's horn startled her back to reality, causing her to take notice of her surroundings. *Bum Heaven,* she thought to herself, as she gazed in the direction of a homeless man lying on a slab of cardboard that she assumed that he picked out of the trash bin of the local grocery store, wondering what could have happened in this man's life that would cause him come to a point in his life where he has nothing except for the clothes on his back and a few items in a garbage bag. Saddened by her thoughts, she took a deep breath, only to be welcomed by the horrible smells that engulfed her nose and briefly took her breath away. She was amazed that she braved the night amongst all the broken glass, trash, and the wretched smell of urine that penetrated the morning air from all of the other unexpected quests she discovered lived under the Talmadge bridge that she made her temporary residences for the night.

Marlie rubbed her eyes as she looked around, making sure no one had noticed her sitting in that dark corner with her baby lying next to her. The sun was completely up and she could hear her baby begin to stir on the soft pallet. She wiped the tears from her now rosy red cheeks then reached for her child. "Good morning sweetheart, I bet you're hungry." Being that John Jr. was only six months old, feeding him came pretty easy, given that she was still breastfeeding. She gently cradled her child to her left breast to feed him while trying to think of her next move. The first thing that came to mind was to get her son somewhere safe. She thought of her in-laws, Bob and Mary Cooper, but quickly thought against that for fear they may ask too many questions that she didn't have the answers to at this time. Then, the thought of Evelyn came to mind.

EVELYN HERSHER, an old college roommate and her best friend. They were close like sisters. Evelyn was one of the most prominent attorneys in Atlanta. She passed the Georgia State Bar exam on the first go round. Graduating Summa Cum Laude from Georgia State University, specializing in criminal law, and second highest in her class. Many law firms were after her from the start, but she chose to open her own law practice and it became a success in a very short time. She was well known all over town as one of the fiercest attorneys in the Atlanta district, but had the looks of a supermodel with blonde hair and green eyes that looked as if they could see though your soul to find the truth. At the age of twenty-seven years old, she was already a threat to other prestigious law firms in the area.

She was what you would call a "hot commodity" in Atlanta. Engaged to Charles Malone, a pediatric medical doctor in Atlanta's Children's Hospital and well known for his research in juvenile diabetes and helping to find a cure for the disease. He was five years her senior and also deeply in love with her. Marlie and Evelyn kept in close contact over the years, since they first met in college, almost living similar lives. Evelyn knew Marlie like the back of her hand and vice versa, as sisters would.

Marlie finished feeding her baby, gently burped him, and changed his diaper. Bundling her child and working his little body into the straps of the carrier, Marlie left from where she rested and headed towards Lane Street to hail a taxi. *I need to get to Evelyn's house*, she thought, as she directed the taxi driver to go to the Greyhound Bus Station in downtown Savannah.

****

"Your case is being investigated as we speak sir; we should have some information for you in a couple of days. I will contact you soon as it hits my desk," Evelyn told her client as she sat behind the big mahogany desk in her lavish office located on the 15th floor of the Springhill Business Center in downtown Atlanta. Tall buildings and lavish four and five star restaurants surrounded the business center, which also has theaters and nightclubs that gave the district a healthy nightlife. Evelyn and her employees frequently visited an Italian place famous for their Calzones and Lobster Ravioli, which is what Evelyn ordered most.

"Ms. Hersher, you have a call on line one. It's a Marlie Cooper, she says it's quite important," the voice of her receptionist called out.

"Put the call through please," Evelyn replied, surprised that it was Marlie, thinking that she was calling her to talk about the wedding fiasco that happened when Debbie Cook married

Bret Hartford at the Country Club of the South last weekend. Excited to hear from her friend, she quickly picked up the phone. "Well, I'm sure you calling me to talk about Debbie's wedding and I have been dying to tell you the latest scoop that's going around town about her new husband," Evelyn expressed with joy.

"Hi Eve, sounds interesting, but that's not what I'm calling you for-" Her words were cut short by the announcer stating that the bus headed to Atlanta was now boarding and would begin seating passengers with last names beginning in A-G.

Evelyn, becoming concerned for her friend, began to speak, "Marlie, are you alright?"

"Listen Evelyn, I'll be in Atlanta in the morning and I need a ride and a place to stay. Can you meet me at the Greyhound station at 9am tomorrow?"

"What's going on? Is everything alright?" Evelyn's concern slowly turned to worry when she heard the sound of Marlie's voice, in an almost crying tone with a touch of fear and regret all rolled into one.

"Please don't ask questions over the phone, no time to talk. My bus is boarding. I'll see you in the morning and I'll explain everything that I know, ok?" she replied and hung up the phone. She looked around, making sure she was not being followed, before heading to the terminal to board the bus headed to Atlanta.

Evelyn stared at the phone for a few seconds before she hung up the receiver. Fear was now full blown for her friend. Not really sure how to react to the brief conversation she had just had with her friend, she buzzed for her assistant. "Anna, please call the limo service and have them be at the Greyhound station tomorrow morning at 9am. They will be waiting for Marlie Cooper."

"Right away, Ms. Hersher," Anna replied. After that, Evelyn called her fiancé Charles, who was unavailable at the time due to patient scheduling for the day. Evelyn left a message for him to call her as soon as he could, but left no other details of what she was calling for.

"Anna, clear my schedule for the next two days," Evelyn had instructed her assistant; she gathered some of her files together and placed them in her briefcase, grabbed her coat and car keys, and headed towards the elevator at the far side of the building. She was wishing she had changed her mind and brought her tennis shoes with her today, knowing she has to make this long journey to the elevator and then through the parking deck, which seemed like a ten-mile hike through a cold, wet basement. She hated that walk.

CHAPTER 3

Marlie tried to sleep on the bus ride to Atlanta, but images of that fateful night kept playing over in her mind. Who were those men that came to her house and killed her husband? What did they want? What did John know that got him killed? Visions of the man that looked up at her came to her mind; she remembered the scar that ran across his face like the Joker from the Batman movies. She could remember hearing their voices, which they had Italian or maybe New York or some Upstate area accents. Why would they come all the way from New York? Was it just to kill John? Are they looking for me next? These are questions that ran through her mind. Chills went down Marlie's spine like a jolt of electricity had just struck her.

She opened her eyes and looked around. John Jr. was sleeping ever so comfortably in the carrier strapped to his mother's chest. She held her baby closer and closed her eyes again and tried to rest as much as she could, but not dream. She knew tomorrow would be another hard day. The bus pulled into the station at 9am promptly as scheduled. The driver announced that they had arrived in Atlanta and would be exiting people off shortly and to gather any of their belongings and make sure not to leave anything behind. The bus driver finished the announcements with, "Thank you for traveling Greyhound."

Marlie stood and stretched, feeling stiff from the cramped seat she sat in all night. She grabbed her things from the overhead compartment and her baby and left the bus. As she got off, she noticed a driver standing by the entrance holding a sign that read: *Marlie Cooper*. She slowly walked up to the driver and said, "I'm Marlie Cooper."

"My name is Max; I'll be driving you to Ms. Hersher's house." The driver took her bags and proceeded to the car. It was about a twenty-minute drive from the bus station to Evelyn's house. They pulled up to the gate of what looked like something from an old southern movie with willow trees that stretched across six acres of land. Beautiful white magnolias lined the front lawn bringing a sweet smell that complimented the summer breeze that lightly blew. The house sat on an old plantation that once belonged to her great uncle who helped to hide many slaves that were headed north to freedom. Legend has it that the curse that was placed many years ago has damned the land from having any profitable crops or producing any fruits from the trees on the property. As they approached the front of the house, a butler opened the door and greeted Marlie as she got out of the car.

"Good morning Mrs. Cooper, right this way," he said and led her through the foyer and down to the parlor, where Evelyn was sitting reading the morning paper and having coffee with Charles.

"Guess who's coming for breakfast?" Marlie said as happily as she could, entering the parlor.

"I'm so glad to see you finally," Evelyn said, as she jumped to her feet to greet and hug her best friend she hadn't seen over a year. "John Jr. is getting so big," she said, as she leans forward and gives the baby a kiss on the head.

"Well, come on in here lady. I'm family too, you know," Charles joked, as he walked towards Marlie.

"It's really good to see you guys and thanks for having us," Marlie replies humbly.

"May I get you a bite to eat ma'am?" the servant asked.

"Yes, please," Marlie replied. Charles instructed Marlie to have a seat at the table as Evelyn helped her get the baby out of the carrier. A distraught look came to Marlie's face.

"What's wrong dear friend, from the look on your face, it's serious?" Evelyn asked.

"I think someone may be trying to kill me because of John," Marlie began to say as the servant walked back into the parlor from the kitchen to serve Marlie her breakfast. As the servant finished, she collected the used dishes from the table and left the room without turning to look back at any of them, as if not at all interested in the new houseguest.

"What the hell!" both Charles and Evelyn said at the same time, with expressions of terror on their faces. No one spoke for a few minutes, not sure what to say. Tears welled up in Evelyn's eyes as she just stared at her friend.

"Haven't you guys heard the news yet? She asked, looking at both of her friends. She took a couple bites of her food, drank some of the orange juice that was in front of her, took a deep breath, and started to explain the events that had taken place the last few days.

CHAPTER 4

"What's up with you Rick? You got a look of either worry or you got to take a dump," Mo chuckled, as he sped up interstate 95 back to New York.

"I can't stop thinking about that hit the other night you know. I swear I saw something move in the window back at that house. I know I was a little wasted, but I swear I saw something," Rick replied, obviously in deep thought.

"So, what you saying, man?" Mo asked, in his own personal dumbfounded way.

"I'm thinking, he was married with a kid, right?" Rick responded

"So," Mo replied, almost visibly confused at what Rick was talking about.

"So, maybe she was there, in the house I mean, and if so, maybe she saw something or least heard something," Rick answered.

"You think she saw us? Not good Rick. Leave no witnesses right?" Mo said in a childlike tone of voice that sounded almost as if he was a kid asking for an ice cream cone and not getting it. Silence fell in the car as they both pondered the thought of "what if". The radio interrupted their thoughts as it announced the death of *John David Cooper Sr.*

'A very prominent attorney in the upper class area of Savannah. Shot four times in the chest while sitting in his backyard with his wife and son a short distance away in the house. His wife called 911, who rushed him to Georgia Regional Hospital thirty miles from his home, where he was pronounced dead forty-five minutes after his arrival. Police are investigating the case, but have no leads at his time. John Cooper's wife was also at the hospital, but comments were declined at this time, due to Mrs. Cooper was too distraught for comments. More information will be released at a later time.'

Mo and Rick turned and looked at each other as if they knew what each other were thinking. Without saying a word, Mo made a sharp U-turn and headed back to Savannah. "I told you I saw someone. The wife, it was her, she saw us man. Shit, I knew it!" Rick yelled, throwing his hands up in a rage.

"Calm down buddy!" Mo yelled back. "We'll just have to kill that bitch before she sings to the cops." Mo pressed the gas pedal a little harder and the car took off like a bat out of hell, slamming the two other hit men in the backseat into each other, as if they were a teenage couple about to make out.

*****

Detective Raymond Mitchell sat at his desk going over photos, evidence, and reports of the Cooper case when his phone rang. The person on the other line gave him a bit of information, which would hopefully help get his first lead on the case. "Ray, we just got the lab results of the tire prints that were found on the Cooper Property, the night of the murder." The person begins to tell the detective as he listened and took notes at the same time.

Detective Raymond Mitchell was a decorated officer of 25 years in the Homicide Division of the Savannah Police Department, serving 10 years in the department's gang unit. He was a tough but gentle man of 5ft 10in with the build of a well-developed body builder. Both massive and sexy all rolled up into one. He was the kind of man who took his work seriously, sometimes spending weeks focused on one case and wouldn't rest until he caught the suspect he was in pursuit of. He seemed almost to be married to his job; maybe that's why he never married or had a serious relationship with anyone for that matter. "It seems the tire prints came from a Lexus SUV," says the caller. "One of the neighbor's claims seeing a black Lexus SUV parked in front of the Cooper home two nights before the murder."

"Did he happen to notice the license plates on the SUV?" Detective Mitchell asks before hanging up the phone. He leaned back in his chair, tapping his pencil on his desk. Who the hell were those men and why were they parked in front of Attorney Cooper's house? What did they want with him? It didn't quite make sense to him but he vowed to himself and Attorney Cooper's now widow that he would find out what happened here. After all, Savannah is a quiet, peaceful place where hardly nothing happens here, except for the occasional domestic disturbance, where some husband comes home drunk one night after hanging out with his friends and beats the shit out of his wife cause she asked him where he'd been or some hormone charged teenagers partying too wild and loud down by Tybee Island well after hours. Suddenly, he thought of Mrs. Cooper and how she was doing. He hadn't seen her since the night her husband was murdered. *She sure is a beautiful woman,* he thought to himself, as he closed his eyes and took a deep breath. *Wonder how she is in bed?* He smiled at the thought, then felt guilt overcome him for being attracted to Mrs. Cooper when her husband was just murdered. He shook the thought of her out of his head, leaned forward, and began to go over the files again, when his phone rang again. "Detective Mitchell," he says, as he put the phone to his ear.

"Ray, this is Michele, we're out at the Cooper house and we found something we think you need to see. How soon can you get here?"

"I'm on my way," Ray replied and hung up the phone. He stood up, grabbed his jacket off the hook, and headed towards the exit without saying a word to anyone on his way to the Cooper residence.

CHAPTER 5

Charles fixed everyone a drink as Marlie continued to tell the horrific events from two nights ago when her husband was killed, how some guys were lurking around the hospital and followed her home, and how she had to take her baby and get away when they tried to break in her house and that's why she ended up sleeping under the Talmadge Bridge to hide from them. She wept off and on as she told them how, in one minute, she was in her husband's arms about to make love to him and the next minute, she was holding his bloody, lifeless body in her arms. Marlie wiped her tears and took a sip of the scotch that she held in her trembling hands.

"There's something else," she said. Taking another sip of her drink, she started talking again. "About a week ago, John David gave me a key. He said it was to a safety deposit box at First Chatham Bank in Savannah." She then handed Charles her glass for him to pour her another drink and continued talking. "He told me that if anything should happen to him, to go to the bank and take everything out of this box and to take the baby and leave town, not telling anyone where I am. But the strangest thing was that he told me not to use any credit cards or checks. Only use cash when buying things."

"Well, what was in the box?" Charles asked, in both a nervous and anxious tone.

"I don't know yet because of what I told you what happened the other night when they broke in my house," she answered.

"Oh yeah, did you call the cops about the break in. Could you tell if they took anything?" Charles again questioned.

"No. I just packed some things in a bag for the baby and me and eased out the house from off the balcony stairs. But before I left, I could hear them talking downstairs. I don't think they even knew I was there, probably thought we was still at the hospital. I heard one of them say that the tapes and files had to be in his office, then I heard one of them call the name *Rick* and that's the second time I had heard that name." Marlie paused and began to sob. Evelyn reached over and comforted her friend. "I left the house with my baby and ran as fast as I could. I was too afraid to get a hotel room because I didn't want to be trace by using my Visa, so we slept under the bridge that night just to be safe, you know?"

"But Marlie, you could have been attacked by some homeless person or something worse," Evelyn said in an almost scolding tone of voice, like a mother would do to her child for misbehaving.

"I wasn't worried about any homeless person. I was more worried about those men who were in my home. I felt safe there for the night, plus I really didn't sleep that much. The next morning, I headed here," Marlie explained.

"Well, what are you going to do now? I mean, are you going to call the police and tell them about the break in?" Charles asked, handing Marlie her second glass of Scotch.

"Yeah, I am, but after I find out what this is all about. I mean, what's inside that safety deposit box?" She paused and put her hand on her head. "Whatever is in that box, was it worth my husband's life? I must find out what this is all about first. What did he know that was so bad, it caused all of this?"

A troubled look came to Evelyn's face as she stared at Marlie. "I really think you should go to the police with this information Marlie; they can help."

"Well, I do have a business card from a detective named Raymond Mitchell. He told me I could call him whenever I needed and he would be there for me. He almost seemed to care about me, but how could he, given we just met. Maybe I will call him, but after I find out what is in that box."

"Whatever you need, we are here for you," Evelyn replied.

Marlie looked at her baby, who was sitting on Evelyn's lap, playing with the pearl necklace that hung from her neck. "I need you guys to keep my son for me, for just a little while, just till I can figure out what happened to John David."

"Of course Marlie," they both said and for a moment, no one spoke a word. Instead, they all sat staring at each other, as if in a silent conversation between the three of them. After their breakfast and conversation, which each vowed to keep between each other, Evelyn showed her friend to her room so that she could shower and get some rest. The maid had taken John Jr. in the other bathroom and gave him a bath so that Marlie could have some alone time. After her shower, she climbed into the big bed of the guest room and cuddled next to her baby, who was already asleep, thanks to the maid. She closed her eyes and slept for the first time in the past few days since John's murder; she slept peacefully as if she was home in her own bed. She dreamed of being home in Savannah with her husband and son, both smiling at her in the glow of the morning sun. She could feel the rays of the sun beaming down on the both of them and smelled the sweet scents of the lilac and magnolia flowers that were in full bloom and waving in the gentle breeze.

Turning into the embrace of her husband, she could smell the scent of his cologne as she pressed her face deep into his chest. The sounds of John Jr.'s laughter came flowing in her ears, as if in approval of his parents as she and John lovingly kissed each other. Marlie smiled and turned onto her other side as she continued sleeping.

Shortly after, Evelyn silently opened the door to the guest bedroom and peeked inside to find her friend resting peacefully and from the look on her face, she seemed to not be thinking of the events that happened a few nights ago, which has haunted her dreams since the beginning. Sadness filled Evelyn and then the thoughts of the last time they were together as couples, hanging out on her patio, enjoying the evening heat on a hot July night when Marlie and John had visited before she gave birth to John Jr. She reminisced on the fun they all had that night while relaxing by the pool enjoying cocktails and conversations, while Charles flipped steaks and shrimp on his new gas grill Evelyn had bought him as a Christmas gift the year before. Evelyn breathed deeply as she smiled and quietly closed the door to the guest bedroom and walked down the stairs to her office to try and tie up some loose ends at work and to inform her assistant that she would be taking a few days off.

Detective Mitchell arrived at the Cooper residence thirty minutes after the phone call. He parked his car on the side of the house by the water fountain shaped like a small child that looked to be holding a water pitcher in which the actual water was coming out of. The attorney had placed it there for his wife some years back. He turned off his car and took a deep breath before getting out of the car and heading towards the house where he met his partner, Michele Brown, standing by the back of the house.

Michele Brown was a twenty-nine-year-old African American woman. She had been on the force for three years now and like her partner, she too was married to her job. No husband or children to worry about, except for her pet bird Riley, who was a three-year-old parrot she had bought when she first moved to Savannah 3 years ago. She was bright for her age and just as tough as any of her male co-workers. She was beautifully shaped for her height of 5ft 5in, with hips that were just right for bearing many children. Detective Mitchell had always had strong feelings for her, but would never act upon them for fear of rejection. Especially given his reputation as a ladies' man.

"Hey Ray, glad you could make it," Detective Brown greeted her partner as he approached. She smiled as he walked towards her, having a quick little fantasy of her and her partner alone together in a room with candles everywhere. She imagined the two of them dancing slowly to a love song playing in the background. They would look into each other's eyes and slowly begin to kiss as passion begins to feel them both like warm water being poured all over them. She could feel herself becoming aroused by her visions as her partner came closer.

"You ok Michele?" Detective Mitchell asked, as he approached his partner.

"Yeah, I'm fine. Look, we found something in the house that we think you should take a look at," Michele said, as she caught her breath and turned to head to the back door of the house with Ray close behind.

Detective Mitchell looked at his partner from behind. *Boy, if I could just once, get between those thighs, I swear she'd be mine. I wonder if she's seeing anyone,* he thought, as he smiled to himself.

"The reason we called you was for you to take a look at these papers we found in Mr. Cooper's office, not my ass. But I must say," she looked Ray up and down for a moment, smiled, and said, "I am flattered, thanks." She smiled and walked into the District Attorney's private office located next to the laundry room on the first floor of the two-story house he once shared with his wife and child. Michele walked up to the desk and picked up a folder. She handed it to Ray, who opened it immediately and read the contents. This was his second lead on the case. It was a letter threatening the attorney's life if he didn't keep his mouth shut about what he knew.

"Well. I wonder what he knew," he said, as he closed the file and looked at his partner who was standing in front of him. He felt a throbbing sensation begin to stir as he smelled the perfume she was wearing. "Does anyone know where this came from?" he asked, trying to get his composure.

"Not yet, but we are about to take this down to the station to see what kind of fingerprints we can get off of it. I just wanted you to see this before we remove it from the premises," she said, as she stepped closer to her partner. "Plus, I kind of wanted to see you." She smiled, as if she was secretly saying something with her eyes.

Ray looked at her confusingly and then smiled at her before speaking. "Well, if you just want to see me, how about after work for dinner?"

"That would be lovely, but I don't think I can. You see, I never sleep with my co-workers, it's not good for business," she said in a sexy tone of voice.

"And what makes you think we would sleep together?" he asked, already knowing the answer to the question.

Michele stepped closer to her partner, where her breasts pressed against his chest. She moved closer to his lips as if to kiss him. "Believe me Ray Mitchell, we would sleep together. As a matter of fact, you would come back for more." She then puckered her lips and kissed her partner, but barely touching his lips, then quickly walked away, leaving her partner dazed, alone, and now horny.

"I got to get that woman," he said to himself, shook his head, and then left the room. He walked out of the back door where two uniform officers were standing. He ordered one of the officers to send him the analyst report from the threat letter as soon as they get word and then turned and headed back to his car. On the drive back to the station, he had a thought of what possibly it could be that attorney John Cooper knew that could have gotten him killed. He's a well-known district attorney, most of his cases have been made famous because of the person he was prosecuting, like crooked politicians, rich scumbags that think their above the law just because they have money. He was always on the news and talk shows discussing how he put another white collar criminal in jail. But there was something different about this. There was little to go on at this time, so connecting the dots on this case was going to be harder than he could imagine. Little did Detective Mitchell know, he would soon see the connection.

He came to a red light on Taylor St. three blocks from the police station. He thought about his partner knowing that she would be there made him smile a little. He remembered the conversation they had earlier back at the Cooper residence. He also remembered how she had made him feel. He began to imagine what it would be like to make love to her. To be between those thick thighs of hers, kissing her soft breast, and touching her in places where treasures are buried. A horn blew from behind Ray's car, which startled him back to reality, only for him to notice his manhood standing at full attention. "Shit. I gotta get that girl before I bust." He said aloud to himself. He pulled into the station's parking lot and turned the car off. He sat there for a few moments, trying to collect his thoughts, which would take a while to do.

CHAPTER 6

Marlie awoke the next morning by John Jr. playing and pulling on her hair. The sun was already high in the sky and the birds were singing their sweet morning air sounding as nature's alarm clock. "Good morning my little one. We've got a busy day today, or should I say that I have a busy day," she said to her baby as she leaned forward and kissed him. John Jr. giggled at his mother and made noises as if he was trying to respond to her. Marlie got out of bed with her son, showered, and dressed the both of them, then headed downstairs. She walked into the kitchen, with John Jr. in her arms, to find Evelyn sitting at the kitchen table talking to someone on the phone.

"Anna, I want you to have all my calls transferred to my home office. I will be working from here for a few days and reschedule any meetings I may have. One more thing, if anyone asks, I have the flu and will be out till next week," she instructed her assistant.

"Yes Ms. Hersher, but I need your signature on the Johnson file, so that they can begin the settlement process," Anna quickly replied to her boss.

"Ok, fax the papers to my office here. I'll sign them and fax them back as soon as possible. There should not be any problems that require me to be there, but if you need me, just call the house. That will be all for now, Anna. Don't bother me unless you really need to; I'll be resting all day."

"Right away Ms. Hersher. I'll fax over the Johnson file for you to sign and fax back to me. If you could handle this before 2 o'clock, then this case can be put to rest. I'll wait for your fax and feel better soon," Anna responded and hung up the phone.

Evelyn turned and greeted Marlie with a big warm southern smile that would make any stranger feel comfortable in her presence. "So, how did you sleep?" she asked, as she took John Jr. from Marlie and began kissing on him as if he was the love of her life, while John Jr. giggled in returned.

"It was a well needed sleep. I felt as if I've been awake for days," Marlie answered.

"Are you hungry? I can have my cook whip up something real quickly for you," Evelyn said, still playing with the baby. "And for John Jr., our cook can make the best organic baby food this side of Georgia."

"No thanks, I'm not up for eating right now. Just some coffee, if that's ok," she replied, as she sat down at the breakfast bar and poured herself a cup of coffee. She gazed out the window as she stirred the creamer into her cup. She had a thousand things running through her head.

One thing that struck out to her most was the feeling of being watched back at the hospital and then the break in at the house that same night. *Who were those men that killed my husband*, she thought to herself, feeling grief overtake her like big waves covering her from head to toe and pulling her back into the deep abyss where sorrow, hurt, and pain lives.

"Marlie, honey, are you alright?" Evelyn asked, walking towards her and comforting her like a sister. She kissed Marlie on the head and hugged her tight before she spoke again, feeling her own throat begin to swell with grief. "I can have all the funeral arrangements taken care of if you want. You are like family to me, so whatever you need, it's done."

"Thank you Evelyn. I knew I did the right thing by coming here. How can I ever repay you for everything you're doing for me?" Marlie asked, as she hugged her dear friend back. They embraced for a few moments then looked at each other with serious expressions. Marlie took a sip of her coffee before she began to speak. "I need to find out what's in that box at the bank, maybe there's some kind of answer to who killed John and why. I got a gut feeling that whoever did this will be after me now because they probably think I know something. Listen, I need to go today. The sooner I get to that box, the more I will know. I'm going to find my husband's killer," Marlie said, looking at her friend.

"What can I do to help?" Evelyn asked.

"First of all, thank you, again, for keeping John Jr. for a few days. You know I hate to leave him, but I know he'll be safe and in good hands here with you. Second, I need a car so that I can drive back to Savannah. This way, if anyone is looking for me, they won't recognize me driving your car and maybe some cash, so I don't have to use any credit cards. And third, I will call you from a hotel. I'll be staying in one, just to be safe. I think I need to stay low for a while. I will only contact you once, for now, till I know for sure I'm safe."

Marlie got up from where she was sitting and walked out onto the patio. She gazed at the garden Evelyn had along the back end of her yard near the willow trees and took a deep breath. *I've got to find out what happened. What was John involved in?* She thought. After putting the baby down, Evelyn grabbed the morning paper and walked out to the garden where Marlie was standing lost in her own deep thoughts, she almost hated to disturb her.

"Marlie, dear, I think you should see this." Evelyn handed the newspaper to Marlie. She read the front page: *Senator Herman Works will not stand trial for rape.* The heading read. "This is the case John David was prosecuting, right?" Evelyn asked.

Marlie shook her head in response. She continued to read on: *The charges against the Senator have been dropped due to lack of evidence and the prosecuting team will need more time to replace attorney Cooper, now that he has been murdered. John David Cooper was preparing to prosecute Senator Works on the charges of raping an underage girl. The law suit also claims that the Senator tried to blackmail a local prominent judge, whose name is being withheld at this time, on alleged claims of child abuse, in the incident where the judge's daughter was admitted into the local hospital with apparent broken ribs and leg. In a brief statement to the press from one of the judge's staff that the daughter sustained these injuries from a fall from her motor scooter she was riding and crashed into the guest house located on the judge's property and nothing more than careless child's play. That claim was being investigating at the time of press release. It was also said that District attorney Cooper had substantial evidence to put Senator Works away for a lot of years and destroy his political career forever. District attorney Cooper was the only one working the case as we know. The police are looking into this case to see if there may be any connections to the Cooper murder case. Senator Works is still being investigated even though the charges have been dropped in connection to another case. There is a strong chance that more charges could be filed against the senator and this case could go to court. It was also said that District attorney Cooper had substantial evidence to put Senator Works away for a lot of years and destroy his political career forever. District attorney Cooper was the only one working the case as we know. The police are looking into this case to see if there may be any connections to the Cooper murder case. Senator Works is still being investigated even though the charges have been dropped in connection to another case. There is a strong chance that more charges could be filed against the senator and this case could go to court.*

Marlie sat the paper down and looked at Evelyn. "So, here's my first clue. I really got to get to that damn box to find out what's in it. I got to go. I need to get back to Savannah today." She turned and walked back into the house. She grabbed an apple from off the table on her way to the guest room to get dressed.

Evelyn just stood there in the garden, mouth open with an expression of both worry and confusion on her face. Not sure if she should follow behind Marlie or just stay where she stood; she chose the first option and followed her friend into the house and went to her own bedroom to dress for the day. Walking up towards the bedroom door, Evelyn could hear Charles on the telephone talking to someone in an almost panicked tone. She could not quite make out the words that he was saying but from the tone of his voice, she could tell that he was having a heated conversation with whoever was on the other line. She continued walking towards the master bedroom but then paused, just as she reached for the doorknob and just listened.

"What is this I hear? They killed him? That was not part of the plan. You said that they were only going to send a message and that's it," Charles said, as he paced back and forth across the bedroom floor in front of the television as the news was reporting what Evelyn and Marlie had just read about moments ago in the morning newspaper. Evelyn listened a few more minutes before opening the door to find Charles standing in front of the window looking out, as if he was looking for someone, as he talked on the phone.

Instead of Evelyn immediately asking questions, she walked over to her side of the room and sat down at her lavished vanity table that was filled with all different types of perfumes and a cherry wood jewelry box that was in the center of the table as the focal point of the entire vanity table. She began brushing her hair as she pretended to not be listening to Charles' conversation. Charles hung up the phone shortly after Evelyn entered the room, trying to act as if everything was alright, but it clearly showed something different on his face. "What was that about?" Evelyn asked, as she continued stroking her hair.

Charles walked over to the closet and opened the door exposing his business suits and began thumbing through them in an attempt to find something to wear for the day, avoiding her question as if he never heard her. Evelyn stared in his direction but didn't push the issue of him obviously ignoring her. Instead, she made a mental note to bring it up again, once he had his shower and dressed for the day. But, she did not forget what she overheard in the hallway a few moments ago about something not being a part of the plan and she wanted to make sure she knew what that plan was, if any plan at all.

CHAPTER 7

The black Lexus SUV pulled halfway into the long driveway of the house where attorney Cooper was murdered in his own backyard just a few days ago. Mo turned the lights off and shut off the Ignition. "I guess the murderer really do come back to the scene of the crime, hey Rick?" Mo says in joking tone.

"Shut up Mo. This is some serious shit here, no time for joking around," Rick says, almost annoyed by the comment made by Mo. "Just shut up a minute." Rick took out a cigarette and pushed the car lighter in. He tapped the cigarette on his knee while he waited for the lighter to pop out.

"What now Rick?" one of the guys in the backseat asked in a deep raspy voice that resembled the sound a bear makes during mating season. "Why we just sitting here, you waiting to get caught or something?" he barked another question out at Rick.

Getting even more annoyed, Rick pulled out his gun and checked the magazine clip to see how many bullets he had left. He snapped the clip back into the gun and turned to look at both Mo and the men in the back seat. "Ok, here is what we are going to do. Mo, you go park the car around the corner or something, but not too far, in case we have to make a run for it," Rick gave instructions and Mo just shook his head in response. "You two come with me," he ordered the two guys in the back seat and they got out of the car.

Mo started the car and made a U-turn back down the driveway to the entrance, turned left, and disappeared. Rick and the other two men calmly walked towards the house up to the police tape that seemed to almost wrap completely around the entire house. Once at the back door, Rick pulled out his gun and with the handle of the gun, broke the glass on the lower window, reached in, and turned the lock to open the door. The three men entered the house and waited for Mo to join them. After a short moment, Mo ran up to the back door and entered the house and shut the door behind him.

"So, what we looking for?" someone asked from behind Rick, who was now on the phone talking to someone he referred to as *Boss*. The other men began to search the house, starting with the downstairs and working their way upstairs. Mo, on the other hand, seemed to make his way to the kitchen to see what kind of food he could scrounge up.

Rick walked into the kitchen still holding the cell phone to his ear. "Ok boss, yes sir, we will look there," he replied before hanging up the phone and placing it back into the lining of his Armani suit he bought just before coming to Savannah. "I want to look good for the job and all those babes I plan on meeting," he once said.

"So, what's up Rick? Who were you talking to on your cell?" Mo asked, still chewing a mouth full of the ham and cheese sandwich he had just made himself from the Cooper's fridge.

Rick looked up at Mo and slightly giggled out loud. "Damn Mo, you're greedy," he said to his cousin.

"Shit man, I'm hungry, haven't eaten since we got here yesterday," Mo answered in defense, but felt no guilt for his actions. "Seriously man, who were you on the phone with?" he asked after taking a big drink of the orange juice he had poured to go with the sandwich.

"That was Boss man," Rick answered. "He's not too happy the wife and kid are still alive. He wants us to find them and take them out, in case she knows something and starts talking." Mo looked at Rick, as if to ask a question, but not quite sure how to correctly ask. He took another bite of his sandwich instead. "Boss wants us to search Cooper's office for some medical records. Says they real important, bout a judge's kid," Rick spoke up. He looked around to see if he could find a flashlight so that he could search the downstairs office without turning on any lights, so not to arouse any attention to the house from the neighbors. He walked back towards the office as Mo followed behind.

They entered the office and immediately began to tear through the desk drawers and cabinets, searching file after file and looking for anything with the name *Walker* on it. For about an hour, they searched the office, turning over bookshelves and computer tables. They even searched the private bathroom that was in the office only John used, only to come up with nothing.

Mo sat down in the desk chair that was now perched in a corner, after one of the men slammed it against the wall to get it out of the way to give him more room to search the desk drawers in an attempt to find what they had come from.

"I don't think anything is here, Rick," he said, sounding exasperated from all the lifting they had him doing, given he was the biggest and the strongest of them all.

"That's the problem Mo, you don't think," Rick snapped back. Mo took a deep breath and huffed aloud, displaying his dislike for the distasteful remark that was just given. He rolled his eyes at Rick and turned the chair in the direction of the door, got up and walked out, snapping back at his cousin.

CHAPTER 8

Marlie tried to stay focused on the road as she drives up the interstate headed back to Savannah in the car she borrowed from Evelyn. She felt a twinge of guilt and fear at the same time. The guilt she felt was from the thought of leaving her son behind and fear for what was to come. Her thoughts got the best of her as she began to think about her husband and the events from the past couple of days. She thought about the safety deposit box John David had instructed her to get to if anything should happen to him. She also thought about detective Mitchell. Wondering should she give him a call when she got back to Savannah? But what would she say to him, she really had nothing at this point, so why should she? Trying to get her thoughts in order, she pressed the gas a little harder. "I need to get home first," she said aloud to herself. "I left the key there that John gave me."

Then, another thought rushed her mind, just as quick as a jackrabbit running in an open field trying not to be eaten by the fox chasing him. "Maybe the police found the key when they searched the house or worse; maybe the men that killed John searched the house and found the key." Marlie began to feel anxious as she pulled off the interstate and onto Gordon Street towards her home. She turned left on East Jones Street and down to Taylor St. where she lived. She decided on the drive there that she would park a few blocks from her home in case she was being followed, hoping that no one recognized her driving Evelyn's car.

She pulled up and parked behind a black Lexus SUV with New York plates and thought to herself, *someone is a long way from home, but city folks come to the south every now and then*. She quickly put that thought out of her mind and focused on the task at hand. She turned the car off and got out. Wearing a hooded sweatshirt and sweat pants helped cover her face so that the neighbors out in their yards and other people walking past would not recognize her. Coming to her driveway, she began to walk slowly, looking back to make sure she had not been spotted. Before she approached the house, her instincts guided her to the back of the house towards the cellar door located next to the back door. Noticing that the lower window on the door was broken, she gasped. "Shit, someone else besides the police was here. They would not have broken the window to get in." She turned and slowly walked to the cellar doors and quietly opened one of heavy doors and slipped down the stairs. Knowing already where everything was located, she reached into the workbench drawer and grabbed a flashlight, but before she could turn it on, she heard the door open from upstairs then heard men talking as they walked down to the basement. Her heart began to race with panic. She looked around and quickly ducked behind the old grandfather clock John David had been working on, but never finished. The two men reached the bottom of the stairs and looked around.

"They got a lot of stuff here. How we supposed to find anything useful, let alone a freaking file?" one of the men asked.

The other man made something like a groaning sound then looked around the room once more, lit a cigarette, then said in a deep raspy voice, "You take that side and I'll take this side. Let's get this over with. I hate basements, they're so creepy."

"What you scared of, big man? I told you about watching too many scary movies, so don't turn chicken shit on me now," the other man snapped back sharply. The two men began to search the basement. They started trashing and throwing things here and there, checking all the cabinets and drawers.

"Hey Mo," one of the men said, "Check out this old clock. Think it still works? Probably worth something." He walked towards the clock, passing boxes and paint cans that were now scattered all over the floor. He stood there for a while, just staring at the clock as if waiting for it to talk or play a song. "Hell, it's not working; looks like it might have been here a long time. I wonder if it got a wind up button in the back." He began to move some of the boxes out of his way to make a path to the back of the clock. Marlie held her breath and closed her eyes as she stood almost two feet away from the gangster who was invading her home. As the man started to reach for the clock to pull it out to check for a wind up button, Mo walked up behind him and startled his buddy.

"Don't sneak up on me Mo. That is a sure way to get killed," the raspy voice man snapped.

"Whatever man, there is nothing down here, let's get out of this dusty, spider infested hell whole. I'm getting dirty and you know how I hate dirt," Mo said. They both turned and walked back to the stairs leading to the kitchen. "Who is the chicken shit now?" Mo asked laughing, as they headed to the kitchen and shut the door.

That was too close, Marlie thought as she exhaled and took a deep breath. She made her way from behind the old clock and looked around. "The dumb ass forgot to cut out the lights," she said quietly, then made her way to the stairs leading to the kitchen. She put her ear to the door and listened, wondering how many more men were in the house. She had already counted two men as she put her ear to the door to listen harder. She heard another man's voice.

"Did you find anything?" Rick had asked as he walked down to the other end of the hall.

"Nothing useful, just a bunch of junk," Mo answered.

"And a really good looking old grandfather clock, but it don't work," the other guy said.

"There's nothing up here either," Rick replied, walking back to the kitchen and sitting down at the table. He pulled out his cell phone again. The other two men followed Rick and sat down at the table. Mo followed shortly with four bottles of Corona beers he had taken out of the fridge. He handed each one a bottle, then sat down and started drinking. "There's nothing here boss. We searched from top to bottom, but came up empty handed," Rick said, trying to stay calm as he talked. "Yes sir, we're on the way now," he said, after a few minutes of listening to what the boss was saying. He hung up the cell and took a drink of his beer.

"Well, what did he say?" one of the men asked anxiously.

Rick took another drink before he spoke, "He wants us to find Mrs. Cooper. She's got to know something."

"How we supposed to do that?" Mo asked.

Rick thought carefully for a moment then looked up at the three men. "Well, I figure she got to come home sooner or later, so I'm thinking that we will come back and we'll get information out of her one way or another. She got to know something. "He pulls out another cigarette, lit it, inhaled deep, and let out the smoke.

"What if she goes to the cops?" Mo asked, almost worried.

"She won't," Rick replied, then took another drink of his beer. "Cause we gone kill her; that way she can't go squealing to no cops." A devilish grin came on Rick's face as he thought of a way to kill Marlie after he has had his way with her. After all, from all the pictures of her and her husband all around their house, he did think she was a fine piece of ass.

"Well, what are we going to do in the meantime?" one of the men asked Rick, as he walked over to the kitchen window and looked out.

Rick took out a piece of paper from the inside pocket of his leather jacket, read it, looked at the rest of the men, then spoke. "We'll stop at the funeral home where her hubby is. Maybe she's there making funeral arrangements. I'm sure they'll be burying him soon and if not, we'll get a hotel room and wait for it to get dark, then we'll come back and get that bitch."

The four men toasted with their beers, finished them off, then left heading for the town funeral home. "Which one you think he's at, Rick?" Mo asked.

Rick shook his head. "Not sure man, so we just have to check them all." The four men walked back down the driveway, headed for the SUV that Mo parked a few blocks up from the Cooper house.

Marlie waited a few minutes before she opened the basement door. Even though she heard them all walk out the house, she wanted to make sure. "Those bastards, I have to stop them before they get me," she said to herself, as she watched the four men at the end of the driveway disappear off to the left. She turned and looked at her home. Devastated by the mess left behind by the police and the goons that were just here, she walked through the mess and into the living room where she sat on the couch and put her face into her hands and sobbed briefly. Thinking of her husband and the life they shared gave her more pain than she could handle at this moment, with just as much anger, hatred, fear, loneliness, and grief all rolled up into one.

She gathered together all the strength she had and left the living room and went onto the front porch, still trying to lay low so that no one would see her. Looking around the porch, she noticed that the potted plants she had placed on the banister's edge for decor were still there. They were white magnolia flowers with yellow lilies as an accent, lined in a beautiful sequence, and the sweet smell of both flowers complimented each other's sweet fragrance. She moved down towards the second to the last magnolia plant on the banister and lifted the entire plant out of the pot. The key was there. Thank God she and John David decided to put it there, both thinking it would be safe there, given no one would ever think it would be there. "Sweet," she whispered, then went back into the house.

Walking directly to her husband's office, she stood in the doorway and looked around. She noticed the picture of her and John David lying on the floor at the foot of his desk. She walked over to the picture and picked it up. It was one of their wedding photos. Marlie frowned when she saw that the glass frame was cracked down the middle and in the upper right corner. She wiped the picture off anyway, as if trying to remove the cracks. "I will always love you, John David Cooper," she said to the picture, as she stared at her husband. She sat the cracked picture back on the desk then sat down in the big leather chair she bought just a year ago when he decided to turn the old storage room into his office.

"What the hell happened to you John? Help me find your killer," she said, looking upward and as if almost in response, the wedding picture on the desk topped over and fell to the floor, breaking the picture out of the frame. Marlie bent over and picked up the picture when she noticed some writing on the back. It read: Case file 426193A Judge Walker child abuse case. *What's this all about and why is it here?* She read the message. *Abuse case, this can't be Grace Walker, the judge?* She thought. Marlie got up from the chair and headed upstairs to her bedroom. She opened the door and looked around. It was a mess in there, just like the rest on the house. She walked over to her bed and pushed all the debris to the floor and lay on the bed, placing her head on her husband's pillow. Smelling the scent of the cologne he used to wear that remained on the pillow, slowly, she drifted off to sleep, but not before she set the alarm clock that sat on the nightstand next to the bed to make sure she would be up and out of there before the bank closed for the day. It was already 8:30am, so she decided to sleep for a few hours.

She woke around noon to the alarm clock ringing. She reached over without looking and turned off the alarm, rolled out of bed, stretched, and headed to the bathroom to shower and change into her own clothes. After her shower, she dressed in a pair of *Donna Karen* jeans and sweater with matching boots that were of the same brand. She also packed a couple more bags for herself and the baby and went back downstairs. She fixed a sandwich and poured a glass of orange juice, sat at the breakfast bar, and ate. After she finished, she placed her used things in the dishwasher so no one would know she was there. She grabbed the bags that she had packed earlier and placed them on the kitchen table. She then went back into her husband's office and took the wedding photo and put it in her purse. She then went back into the kitchen, took the bags off the kitchen table, and headed for the back door. She took one last look at her home and said out loud, "When I come back here, this nightmare will be over." And with that, she locked the back door and made her way back to the car. When she reached the car, she put the bags in the trunk, got back into the driver's side, and started the car. She noticed the black SUV with the New York plates was gone as she pulled out from where she was parked, but quickly put it out her mind as she headed to the *First Chatham Bank* located on Barnard Street, about a 45-minute drive from where she lived in West Chatham County.

CHAPTER 9

Detective Mitchell was awakened by a knock on the door of his one-bedroom apartment, located in *Ardsley Park* in Midtown. It was a modest little bungalow made for a single person. The apartments drew in young professionals and families. The design of Mitchell's apartment consisted of hardwood floors with tan colored walls, the living room and dining room were connected, and a ceiling fan hung to mark the perfect spot for a dining room table. The neighborhood was pretty quiet, only a few children playing in the nearby park and young married couples walking and showing public displays of affection, signifying that they are newlyweds. The detective sat up in the bed and rubbed his eyes, not really sure if he had heard knocking or not. The knocking came again, but a little harder this time.

"Ok, ok, give me a minute!" the detective shouted as he grabbed his bathrobe and put it on. He walked over to the front door and looked through the peephole. It was his partner, Detective Brown. "Oh shit, it's Michele," he said to himself, as he began brushing his hair with his hands and wiping the sleep from his eyes. He opened the door. The sight of the female detective caused his eyes to widen.

"Good morning Ray, did I wake you?" she asked, smiling at him. Detective Ray was still in awe over seeing his partner standing in the doorway. He looked her up and down with thoughts of how she tasted. The scent of her perfume caused a small erection under his bathrobe. "Ah Ray, you ok?" she asked.

"Yeah, I'm good, was sleeping that's all," he lied to cover the truth. "What are you doing here Michele and what time is it anyway?" he asked, as he opened the door wider for her to walk in.

"It is 7:30am and I couldn't wait to give you this information on the Cooper case," she began. "And besides, I brought breakfast." She held up two large bags with the word *IHOP* written across the front of them. "Got any plates?" she asked, sitting the bags on the counter.

"Sure, in the cabinet next to the fridge," he responded, pointing at the cabinet as to show her where they were. "Excuse me for a minute Michele," he said, as he walked towards the bathroom to wash his face and to calm down the full blown erection he now had as a result of seeing his beautiful partner. *Damn, that girl is too fine to look at this early in the morning without going deep inside her,* he thought to himself with a smile that was almost deviant. He used the bathroom then washed his face, brushed his teeth, then went into his bedroom to put on a pair of sweatpants and tank top, so he could show off his muscular physic. He walked back into the kitchen to find his partner had fixed two plates of pancakes, bacon, eggs, and hash browns.

"Sit down and dig in. I got a good lead to go over with you. Hey, you got any coffee?"

"Fresh out, sorry," Ray said, as he sat down and blessed his plate before eating.

"Oh, a praying man," Michele said while giggling and looking at Ray. "That's so sexy of you. I find it highly attractive that you pray, Ray," she said, giving him a look of approval.

He looked at her and smiled. "Thanks," was all he could say, but his thoughts were of other ways to thank her for the compliment. "You said you got some news on the Cooper case, right?" he asked.

"Oh yeah," she said, wiping her mouth. "Well, we got a tip from the streets that we should check out regarding Judge Grace Walker. There are some rumors floating around about her daughter. The rumor claims she had been treated a few times at the local hospital for bruises, black eyes, and broken bones. But it was never reported to Children's Services. It's also rumored that the judge's daughter has a drug problem and has been picked up a couple times, but never charged with anything, nor was there ever a report filed at any time. My sources told me they were with her a couple nights ago at *Club One*. They were there drinking and the Judge's daughter said her mother had beaten her for walking in on her and her boyfriend and a few of his friends with these two girls that looked to be about 12 or 13 years of age, having sexual relations with them," she explained.

"That's sick," Detective Mitchell replied. "But what does this have to do with the Cooper case?" he continued, while gulping down pancakes.

"Well, she was treated by Dr. Craig Cooper, get it, that's John David Cooper's brother. He never filed a report at the hospital or neither did he alert Children's Services," she said while sipping on the orange juice she picked up on the way to his apartment.

"Have someone go out to the hospital and question the good ole doctor. Let him know that we know about the missing reports, fish around a little, and see what we come up with," Detective Mitchell said and continued eating.

Detective Brown put down her fork and picked up her cell phone and made a call. She instructed the officer on the other end to go out to get the doctor and bring him into the station. She and Detective Mitchell both thought it would help them with the intimidation factor if the doctor thought he was under arrest and facing the possibility of jail time, not to mention losing his job and medical license. Maybe he would break, maybe not. "This is rather interesting," Detective Mitchell said, leaning back in his chair, obviously stuffed from breakfast. "Isn't part of Judge Walker's campaign about fighting child abuse?" he asked his partner.

"Yeah," Detective Brown replied. "Word is; she also has ties with this organized crime boss up in New York. Rumor has it that her campaign was secretly funded by him. No one knows for sure though because there's no paper trail."

Detective Mitchell thought for a moment and said, "It is known that she had let some guy from New York off the hook for soliciting prostitution. She just gave him a slap on the wrist and sent him packing two months before she was re-elected."

"Yeah, and the same creep donated 50,000 dollars to her campaign shortly after he was back in New York. It was so well covered, no one ever questioned where it came from," Michele answered. The two detectives sat in their chairs and sipped the remainder of their orange juice while going over facts. Detective Brown went over page after page of notes she had collected earlier that morning from her source and findings at the hospital. Detective Mitchell got up from the table and collected his and his partner's dishes and placed them in the sink, thinking he would clean them later. He came back to the table and stood to the left of Michele. While looking over her shoulders, he happened to notice the she had a piece of hash brown wedged in her cleavage. She was wearing a tank top and sweat pants herself, given she had just finished her 10 mile run she does daily. He leaned forward a little more where he was close to her face and looking directly at her breasts.

"Is there a problem detective?" Michele asked, looking up at her partner.

"Oh, it's just that you have a piece of food stuck in there," he said, looking down at her breasts and smiling. "Let me get that for you," he responded by sticking out his tongue in a licking motion.

Michele stood up from the table, stepping back from her partner. "Excuse me, I am a messy eater sometimes," she said, almost blushing. "I think I can get it, but thanks anyway. Listen, I'm going to go now. I need to go see the doctor and find out what he really knows about Judge Walker."

"No. Better yet, I want you to go talk to the judge's daughter. What's her name anyway?" Ray asked.

"Cassie Walker, she's only 16 years old, so I don't know how much questioning I'll be able to do without a parent present," Michele answered.

"Well, go talk to her anyway. Get what you can get out of her. And I'll go talk to the good ole doctor about what he's not saying," Ray said, trying to act more of a professional man now that his hormones were starting to stir up again. Sitting back down, he reached for his police notebook and pen and wrote something down. When he was finished, he handed the paper to his partner. "Call this number when you get to the station and ask for Ben Shaffer; he's a private detective and a good friend of mine. Ask him to meet us at the station about 2 o'clock today. We're going to need to get him involved on this. He knows a lot about organized crimes in big cities and how to take them down."

"Oh, so now I'm your partner and secretary?" Michele asked sarcastically, as she snatched the piece of paper from Detective Mitchell's hand and walked out of the kitchen and towards the living room with Ray following close behind.

"Well, I do need to take a shower and get dressed first, thought you wouldn't mind doing me a favor," he said, as they entered the living room. She stopped and turned around to face her partner with a look of major irritation.

"Did you ever stop to think that, by the time I travel back across town to my apartment, you would have already showered, dressed, and at the station to meet with Ben before I could ever get to the Walker kid," she said with anger obviously rising up in her at his statement.

He walked over to his partner and gave her a more seductive look. "Unless, you want to join me, my shower is big enough for two," he said, as he put his arms around her and pulled her close to him, feeling her body against his. She pulled away from him and walked towards the door. Her sexy swag made his nature rise even more visible now, even Michele noticed. As she moved closer to the door, his heart began to race from the scent of her perfume.

"Detective Raymond Mitchell," she began to speak in his ear softly, "I'm really feeling you and I'm wanting you just as much as much as you want me, but you know this can't happen with us working together, so unless one of us wants to quit the department, getting busy is out of the question. And let's just say, I think your *manhood* does look quite inviting." She blushed slightly as she looked down in the direction of his now full erection. "But now is not the time and I think I want more from you than just your body, but I'm not sure if we want the same things. And I don't want to be hurt by any man, for that matter. So, if all you looking for is a piece of ass, then I'm not the woman for you." She looked into his eyes deep, as if trying to see into his soul and began to speak again. "If sex is all there is to us, then I don't want I-"

Before she could finish her sentence, he kissed her fully on the lips, pulling her closer to his body and pressing her breasts against his chest. He could feel her kissing him back and embracing his touch. The throbbing in his pants caused his manhood to rise even higher than before. It rubbed against Michele's below the waist area, feeling her body for the entrance door. "Wait," Michele whispered almost breathless. "We should stop; this is not right. I mean, wrong timing." She pulled away from her partner, but slowly.

"What's wrong baby?" Ray asked, slightly dazed and confused.

"This is wrong," she replied. "We can't do this Ray, not now. I'm trying to tell you something man, and if you can't figure it out, then just forget it." She pulled away from him again but quickly this time and headed for the door. Without looking back, she sharply spoke, "I'll contact Mr. Shaffer and have him meet *you* at the station."

"What about you? Will you be there?" he asked quickly.

"Sooner or later, I need time to think about what just happened or almost just happened," she said, finally turning to look at him. "Listen Ray," she began," we could have something good here, but I need to know we both feel the same way about each other and right now, all I see from you is that you want my body and that's all." Ray's mouth opened at the statement she had just made. He was feeling both offended and embarrassed at the same time. "Don't say anything now, when we both know you're not thinking with your right head. And I really don't feel like being patronized by you, just to get me in bed. Try thinking of my feelings for a change and what I want. Maybe, you will figure out that I really want you and all of you. For better or worse and all that shit." And with that being said, Michele left, closing the behind her and leaving Ray standing alone.

"I am so in love with you, Michele Brown. I have never felt this way about anyone in my life. I want more than just your body, you crazy woman. I want to stand by you as your man. I'm just too stupid or chicken shit to tell you," he said to the door after Michele had left.

Standing alone in the hallway of his apartment, he thought back to the first time he ever laid eyes on her. It was her first day at the department; he remembered seeing her walking across the parking lot looking like an angel. He remembered how his heart started racing and how breathing didn't seem to happen at that moment. He knew it was love at first sight, even though he never believed in things like that but when it came to Michele Brown, he had sworn Cupid hit him with one of those arrows of his. Ray held himself with his right hand and headed for the shower. "She's already got my heart, but just too stubborn to realize it," he said to himself while closing the bathroom door, turning on the shower, and stepping in. He thought about what had just happened between he and Michele, smiled to himself, and began to relieve himself of all the sexual frustration he felt for his partner.

After getting dressed, he grabbed his things and left for the station with Michele still on his mind and smiling to himself. He arrived 20 minutes later, which gave him plenty of time to gather his thoughts of his partner and put them back in that small compartment in his heart. Locking his car and switching the alarm on, he walked to his office with little interruptions from rookie cops and their first year questions. Turning on the light, he walked into his office and shut the door, placed his jacket on the back of the chair that sat near the door, and sat down behind his desk when there was a knock on the door. Suddenly, the door opened. It was one of the rookie cops he was dreading running into back in the lobby.

"Excuse me Sir, but if you wouldn't mind, could I have just a moment of your time? I have a few questions I'd like to ask you," the rookie cop asked.

Not sure what this guy wanted, Detective Mitchell gestured for him to enter and watched him as he instantly closed the door. "What is this about?" the detective asked, looking the rookie directly in the eyes and giving him the most intimidating look without realizing it.

The rookie looked as if his nerves had just left him as he tried hard to swallow. "It's about your partner, Detective Brown," the rookie answered. A look of instant distaste for this rookie came across Mitchell's face as he stared at this young man who was asking about his partner. He just stared at him. "I was wondering if you know anything about her personal life. I mean, does she have a boyfriend or is she available? I'd like to ask her out, if possible," he innocently replied.

This information suddenly struck a nerve with Detective Mitchell, causing his emotions to begin to burn. He could feel the heat from his anger grow rapidly. "So, what do you want me to do?" he asked, trying hard to keep his cool and not let it show that he felt offended that this guy would have the nerve to come into his office asking questions about his chances with Michele.

"Well, if you could ask her the next time you're together if she's dating anyone that would be great. Thanks for your help dude," the rookie cop said, as he turned to walk out the door but not before handing the detective one of his business cards with his name and number on it. "Could you make sure she gets this? It has my personal number on it, thanks," the rookie said as he handed Mitchell his card and left the office, closing the door behind him.

"Sure, I'll make sure she gets this," he said sarcastically as he looked at the card, turning it from one side to the other then ripping it into small pieces and tossing it into the trash can that sat next to his desk. *What makes him think she would be interested in him? Plus, I'm gonna get her first.* He smiled at the thought then quickly frowned, thinking that he was acting like some high school teen with raging hormones that has his eyes locked on one of the popular cheerleaders and ready to pounce on any guy that even looks in her direction, as if to ask her out on a date or something. *She'll never go for that guy; he's too young for her anyway.* His inner voice spoke, which helped boost his confidence back to adult levels after that encounter with the rookie. Turning his attention back to the Cooper case was the best he could do to keep his mind from wandering and distracting him from the big picture, which is to catch the person or persons responsible for the murder of John David Cooper Sr.

CHAPTER 10

Evelyn sat at her desk drifting into thoughts of her best friend, as John Jr. rocked in his baby swing falling fast asleep. "Lord, please watch over my dear friend and protect her from harm," she prayed. She looked over at the baby boy in the swing and smiled. *I see both your mom and dad in you little man*, she thought. She heard the phone ring and a servant quickly answered.

"Hersher residence. May I ask whose calling? Yes ma'am, one moment please." Shortly after that, the servant was at the door of Evelyn's office. "For you, ma'am. It's Mrs. Cooper," she said and then walked away.

Evelyn quickly picked up the phone. "Marlie. Oh my word, are you alright? What have you found out?" She began asking what seemed to be a thousand questions, all in on big breath.

Marlie cut her off short. "Stop with of all the questions, Evelyn. I'm ok, stop all the questions and let me talk." There was a short pause as Marlie took a deep breath and began to update her friend about the events that had taken place. She started by telling her about the goons she met back at her house and how she almost met them face to face at the bank. She told her about the wedding photo with the case number on the back, regarding Judge Grace Walker.

"None of this makes any sense," Evelyn said in a shocked tone. "Are you going to turn this information over to the police?" she asked.

"I don't know yet, but I need to keep digging for more information before going to the cops, cause I need to know who did this to my husband and why," Marlie replied. She took a deep breath and exhaled before speaking again. "Sometimes, I feel like I can hear John's voice. I'm not crazy but I can hear him." Evelyn felt tears well in her eyes for her dear friend as she listened to her talk about the death of her husband. "How's my baby doing? I miss him so much," Marlie asked, as she wiped the tears from her eyes with the sleeve of the *Prada* jacket she wore.

"He's doing fine, having fun with the nanny and Charles. Charles has fallen for baby John so deep, he's talking about starting a family right after the wedding, go figure," Evelyn replied.

"And what's wrong with that?" Marlie asked.

"Nothing's wrong with it," Evelyn quickly answered. "It's just that I don't want any kids right now; maybe in two or three years after we are married. I want to enjoy being a wife first before I enjoy being a mother. Call me selfish, but that's how I feel. But anyway, John Jr. misses you. We show him your picture every day and he's learning to say mama, he's so cute."

"Well, listen Evelyn," Marlie began. "I'm headed to the bank now to see what's there and how it can help me figure out why this happened to John, so I'll call you after I leave from there. Oh, kiss my son for me and let him know mommy will be there soon and thanks again for your help."

"No problem Marlie," Evelyn said. "But keep me posted on what you find out because my uncle Phil is a private detective, and he's heard about what happened and he wants to help."

"That's great. I'll call you back in a couple days. I love you, Evelyn," she said and hung up the phone.

She quickly dialed the number on the back of the bankcard. After a few rings, a voice came on the line, "First Chatham Bank. How may I direct your call?" the operator began saying.

"May I speak with Evan Bradford, please?" Marlie asked.

"One moment please." The call was placed on hold then, music began to play. Some tune from an old 80's movie she remembered but could not put a name to place its soft rock style tune as she heard herself humming along to.

"Evan Bradford, how may I help you?" A deep southern accented voice came on.

"This is Marlie Cooper and I need to get access to my husband's safety deposit box to retrieve some things needed for his funeral," she began saying.

"Oh yes ma'am, my deepest condolences to you and your family. Mr. Cooper was a valued client to us and a well-respected man in the community. He will be missed dearly," Evan responded. There was a slight pause and then Evan spoke again. "There will be no problem Mrs. Cooper, when would you like to schedule an appointment?"

"Well, actually, I'll be there in about 20 minutes; there's some things I need from there today," she responded as she drove down *West Duffy St.* headed to the interstate that would take her into *Chatham County* and to the bank.

"Ok Mrs. Cooper," Evan responded with a smile so big on his face that it could almost be heard over the phone. "But I will not be in the office by the time you get here, but you can go to any one of the bank tellers and they can assist you with whatever you need until I arrive. Again, Mrs. Cooper, your husband was a valued client here at *First Chatham.*"

"Thank you," was all that Marlie said before ending the conversation. She placed the phone back in the holder that was attached to the dashboard and turned up the radio. *Dreaming* by Selena was playing. She smiled at the memories of the two of them, in happier times together. She thought about the birth of their son and how happy John was standing next to her, holding her hand through the entire labor and delivery. She thought about the time she and John sat in the backyard just holding each other and talking about whatever comes to mind or sometimes saying nothing at all; just being there together was enough for the both of them. Marlie smiled and then remembered her mission.

Suddenly, she felt that same cold chill she felt back in her husband's office at home. She then heard John's voice telling her, "You can't let them get away with this. Avenge me darling, avenge my death."

"I will baby," she softly said to herself as she turned the radio up just in time to hear a news report come on the radio: "We *interrupt this program to bring you this special report. We just received word that the daughter of Judge Grace Walker has been admitted into the hospital after an apparent accident where her car hit a tree in front of her home. Reports say that there was an argument between Judge Walker and her daughter prior to the accident. Reports also say that her daughter, Cassie Walker, had a blood alcohol level of .97, well over the legal limit in the state of Georgia. There is no word on her condition at this time. We will keep you informed on any new information as it comes in. for WCCP news radio. This is Milford Carter.*"

The song that was playing continued as Marlie turned the radio down. Something came to her mind as she continued to drive down the interstate. *There are more important things to report, like my husband's murder, than to waste air time with a report about ole Gracie's daughter getting trashed and wrecking her car.* She became angry at the thought, but little did she know, Cassie Walker would know more about her husband's murder than Marlie could ever imagine. Her thoughts of what Cassie could possibly know about her husband and who may have done this to him became random as she tried to focus on the road. She also thought about going to the hospital where Cassie was and making the little girl tell her what she knows by shaking her until she spilled the information, but common sense told her that it was not going to be that easy as to simply walk into the hospital and into her room like she's a relative, when in truth, she had never met this kid and surely there would be someone there to stop me from asking her any questions.

The voice of John came back to her head. "Cassie knows, she knows." Is what she heard him saying. She was not sure what it all meant, but she knew she needed to talk with the Judge's daughter, but how was she going to make that happen?

Shortly after the news report on the radio, Marlie pulled into the parking lot of *First Chatham Bank.* She put the car in park and turned off the engine. Checking her hair and face in the rearview mirror, she applied a touch of lip gloss. She also removed her jacket so that she looked more finely dressed and got out of the car, closed the door behind her, locked it, and turned to walk away. Every now and then, she would turn and look behind her, feeling as if she was being watched. "Lord, watch over me as I go in this bank. Help me to find answers to John's murder. Amen," she whispered the tiny prayer as she entered the bank.

Marlie looked around the bank and observed the people inside and her surroundings. The bank was not very big. It had five bank tellers with only three windows open for business, each having a glass shield on the counter for protection against any gunfire from bank robbers. To her left, she observed a long counter with about four people standing around writing out deposit slips, not really paying attention to each other. There was a woman in line with a young baby that was crying so loud that the sound drowned out the music playing softly on the intercom system. To her right, she saw three small cubicles that served as offices. Some of them had pictures of their children in them posing with big smiles on their faces. Some desks had wedding photos and framed diplomas of their accomplishments. Each office had a name plate with big bold letters above the door-less cubicles. Marlie noticed the one with the name Evan Bradford on it. *The man I need to see,* she thought to herself, as she waited patiently in line for her turn with one of the bank tellers.

"Good morning, how may I help you?" the teller asked with a smile.

"Hi, I'm here to see Evan Bradford. My name is Marlie Cooper, he's expecting me," she replied.

"Yes ma'am, I'll page him for you. Please have a seat in his office. He'll be right with you, Mrs. Cooper," the teller said and pointed in the direction of Evan's cubicle.

"Thank you," Marlie replied and headed towards the glass cubicle and sat down in the chair by the desk. The teller watched as Marlie took a seat. She then picked up the phone and dialed it as she kept her eyes on Marlie.

"Yes Mr. Bradford. She's here," the teller said in an almost whisper, then hung up the phone and walked over towards the office where Marlie had just entered and sat down. "Mr. Bradford says he'll be right in. Would you like something to drink?" she asked.

"No thank you, ma'am," Marlie politely replied. The bank teller turned and walked out of the small office, leaving Marlie alone to wait for Mr. Bradford, while listening to the soft sounds of *Billy Ocean* on the bank's intercom system.

"Tell her I'll be right there," Evan replied to the bank teller on the other end of the phone and hung up. He sat at the cafeteria table for a few minutes then picked up the phone again and punched in a number. The phone rang twice then a very deep voice was heard.

"Speak," the voice answered.

"Yeah, she's here. What do you want me to do?" Evan asked.

"Stall her. The boys are on the way. Don't let her leave, no matter what," the deep voice responded back to Evan. There was a click and the line went dead. Evan paused a moment before hanging up, not sure how long it would take for Rick and the boys to get there. He took a final sip of his Pepsi and walked to the trash to throw away the rest of his lunch. He brushed the crumbs from his tuna sandwich off his suit and headed back to his office to meet with Marlie. Stopping by the men's room before proceeding to meet *and* stall Mrs. Cooper, he pulled out a cigarette and lit it, taking a few drags on it before flicking it into the toilet and flushing. He washed his hands and dried them under the automatic hand dryer. His cell phone rang, startling him just a bit.

"Hello, Evan Bradford," he answered. There was a long pause. "Hello," Evan said again.

"This Mo. We'll be there in about 30 minutes. Is she still there?"

"Yeah. I'm headed up to see her now," Evan replied.

"Good. Keep her there. We on the way and don't give off any clues we coming, got it, or you'll have to deal with me personally. I don't like you much anyway," Mo stated to Evan, making a note to point out the fact that he doesn't like him.

"Sure Mo, just hurry because I don't know how long she'll stay," Evan responded sarcastically back, sounding clearly offended by the statement Mo had just made, then hung up the phone and placed it back into his pocket. He opened the door of the men's room and headed upstairs thinking to himself. *I'm going to be rich after this is over.* He smiled as he saw Marlie sitting in his cubicle office. He walked directly up to her, shook her hand, and began the process of stalling her.

Mo turned up the radio on the Lexus SUV they were riding in, headed to *First Chatham Bank*. Rick was driving and tapping his fingers on the steering wheel, as if getting impatient with the song that was playing. The sun was starting to shine brightly in the sky, causing the summer temperatures to rise quickly in this southern town and making Rick even more irritated.

"Can you turn that dumb ass song off, Mo.? It's giving me a headache!" Rick barked out.

"What's the matter with you, Rick?" Mo asked "Got a bug up your ass or something?" The two men in the back seat laughed at the comment Mo just made.

"This is not the time for joking around guys, this is some serious shit. We got a job to do and the Boss is expecting us to get it done fast," Rick snapped.

"So, what's the plan then?" one of the guys in the backseat asked while loading bullets in to the magazine clip of the revolver sitting in his lap.

"First things first," Rick answered in a commanding tone of voice. "We get to the bank. Evan is keeping the bitch busy till we get there. He's going to take her to the back of the bank and we'll grab her, throw her in the car, and take off. We'll kill her somewhere in the woods outside of town, ok. It's a simple in and out job." There was a quiet pause between the men as they all thought about the task ahead of them. "We got 48 hours to get this job done, so no screwing around," Rick finally said, breaking the quiet mode that had overcome on everyone in the car. The four men continued the rest of the drive loading guns and smoking cigarettes. A tune by *Cold Play* came on, causing Mo to start singing again. The air was becoming hotter as the morning sun moved higher in the sky.

"Anybody heard from ole Judge Grace yet?" Mo asked, breaking the concentration of the rest of the men.

"She supposed to call with info about the money." Rick laughed at the statement Mo had just made, then his thoughts seemed to take over his mouth as he heard the words come out before thinking. "She's in deep shit already if the Feds find out what she's been up to. Well, let's just say, we won't be seeing that money anytime soon if she gets busted. Plus, she got a big mouth daughter that keeps talking all over town about things she shouldn't know. Boss says if ole girl can't control her daughter, we might have to. She could bring us all down if she starts talking to the wrong people." Rick stopped talking and looked out the window. The rest of the men were confused by his words, but dared not asked Rick what he meant.

Shortly after their conversation, they pulled into the parking lot of *First Chatham Bank* and parked in the lot closer to the back door. Everyone became alert. Rick pulled out his cell phone and dialed a number. "We're here," he said then hung up quickly.

"What now Rick?" one of the guys in the backseat asked.

"We wait for the signal that she's alone and we can go in through that back door right there, grab her, and get the hell out of here," Rick replied as he leaned back in his seat and lit a cigarette.

CHAPTER 11

"Mrs. Cooper, I'm so sorry to keep you waiting," Evan said, extending a hand to shake Marlie's hand in a professional greeting style. Marlie stood up to meet his handshake and gave him a slight smile. "So, you want access to your husband's safety deposit box?" Evan asked.

"Yes, and if we can do this quickly, I'd really appreciate it, cause I need to get to the funeral home-"

Evan cut her off. "Sure thing Mrs. Cooper, I just need two forms of I.D. so that we can verify that you are who you say you are. Not that I don't know who you really are, but it is company policy," Evan stated, as he sat behind his big oak desk in his leather chair that was so oversized, it made him look like a small child who has been put in time out for doing something bad. Marlie took out her wallet and handed him her driver's license and one of her major credit cards, then sat back in the chair as she waited for Evan to respond. "Thank you, Mrs. Cooper. Now, if you don't mind, let me just step out for a few minutes. I'll be right back, this shouldn't take too long." Evan smiled that smooth, slick smile that showed he was a true southern gentleman then walked out of the office, leaving Marlie alone.

Five minutes later, he was back in his office. "Right this way Mrs. Cooper," Evan instructed Marlie to follow him as they walked towards the back of the bank to where there was a tall, solid steel door in front of them that led to a room where there were safety deposit boxes covering the walls, as if they were wallpaper. He opened the steel door and unlocked the barred gate to the room, looking to his left and down a few rows of locked boxes embedded in the walls that gave the illusion of metal wallpaper. He located the one marked *Cooper, J. D.* "I take it you have the second key, Mrs. Cooper?" Evan turned and asked to Marlie.

"Yes, right here," she answered, as she pulled the key out from around her neck.

"Great. I need for you to place it in the keyhole as I put this one in. We will need to do this at the same time," Evan replied. Both of them placed their key in the perspective hole of the safety deposit box, turning them in the same direction. Click, click. The sound came from the box and Evan slid it out of the wall. It had to be about a 3x5 size metal box that seemed to weight about 15 pounds and rectangular in shape and about 2 feet in depth. Evan placed the box on the table that was sitting in the middle of the room. He turned and looked at Marlie.

"Only your key will open it. So, you can do so whenever you are ready," he said with that winning smile he gives to all his clients. But there was something different about the look in his eyes. This caused Marlie to become a little uncomfortable.

"I'd like to be alone to go through my husband's things," she said, looking directly at Evan.

"But Mrs. Cooper, I think I should stay for, for support, you know. In case you need something," he said almost in a childlike tone, as he stepped towards her in his defense to stay in the room.

"No, I'll be fine, but thank you. If I need you, I'll call you. Ok," she replied in a sad tone and tears in her eyes. "I need to be alone to remember my husband." She turned to grab a tissue out of her purse and burst into tears.

"Oh Mrs. Cooper, please don't cry. I understand completely. I'll be right outside. Please, take your time. I am so sorry about this," he said as he hurried for the door, opened it, and quickly ran out. Instantly, Marlie's sobbing stopped. She ran over to the door and locked it, looking around the room to make sure no one else was there. She reached in her pocket and took out her cell phone and dialed a number. She began opening the box as she waited for the phone to start ringing on the other end.

"Savannah Police Department. How may I direct your call?" the operator asked.

"Detective Mitchell please," Marlie replied.

"One moment," the operator said and then put the call on hold. Soft rock played instantly in her ear. She began to remove the items out of the box. First, she took out a black velvet box that contains John's four carat diamond cufflinks Marlie had gotten for him on Christmas a few years back. She smiled as she remembered the look on his face when he opened the box. Next, she pulled out some stock papers and insurance policies. She also took out a rectangular shaped red velvet box containing a tennis bracelet John had bought for her on her birthday that she still thinks he paid too much for in the first place. She smiled to herself. "Oh John, you've always had great taste in jewelry," she said in a whispered tone.

"Detective Mitchell is not in his office at this time, but he did leave a message for you to call his cell if you needed him for any reason. I can give you his number if you like, Mrs. Cooper, "the operator said.

"Yes, that would be great," Marlie responded and began to write down the telephone number. "Thank you," she replied and hung up the phone.

Reaching inside the box again, she pulled out a small green book. On the front of the book was written in big bold black letters: **TOP SECERT AND PERSONAL**. "What's this?" Marlie said to herself, then opened the book and began to read it. "What the hell?" she spoke softly, then looked around the room again. Knowing that she was alone and the door was locked, she sat down at the table and turned on the lamp that was sitting on top. She found a yellow envelope inside the book that contained some pictures. She looked at the pictures and gasped at what she saw. They were pictures of young girls around the ages of 12 to 17 years old, posing in sexual and seductive positions. Touching each other's body parts in ways that no child should know at that age. Some of the pictures had young girls in sexual positions with men that looked old enough to be their fathers, if not their grandfathers. The men in the pictures Marlie came to realize that she recognized as being judges, congressmen, and the district attorney, fondling and having sexual relations with these young girls, using them as play toys while other men stood in the background jerking off to the sight of these young girls and the acts they were committing. She began to read the information in the book. She came across a section in the book, which was marked: **Case File 426193A Judge Grace Walker abuse case: (unreported)**

On the night of May 23, 1997 at 8:30pm, Judge Grace Walker brought her daughter Cassie Walker in to the emergency room of *Georgia Regional Hospital* claiming her daughter had fallen down the stairs after coming home drunk from a night of underage drinking. Judge Walker also stated that she and her daughter had gotten into an argument over her behavior, causing her to fall and may have broken her left arm. Upon further examination, the doctors also discovered many bruises and bite marks on the child. When asked about the marks, the child stated that her mother had broken her arm for walking in on her and hearing a conversation with her talking on the phone with a man by the name of *Big Sal*. The child also stated that she heard her mother order Big Sal to kill attorney Cooper at his home and to make it look like a robbery or a home invasion. The child was highly intoxicated upon arrival, shouting that her mom forced her to drink alcohol and do drugs by saying that if she didn't do it, then she would be beaten or possibly raped by one of her men clients. The child seemed to be very upset and frightened. She rejected to have her mom in the room and refused to see her, which was out of the ordinary for any child that was either injured or sick. Dr. Craig Cooper, the on-duty emergency supervisor, questioned Judge Walker about the allegations her daughter had made against her. Judge Walker denied these allegations and stated that her daughter had a drinking and drug problem and didn't know what she was saying. No Police were called, nor was a report ever filed at this time, due to Judge Walker's political involvement with running for the Supreme Court seat that recently became available after Judge Randolph died suddenly from a heart attack after taking *VIAGRA* and having a bad reaction. Furthermore, all hospital records have been sealed. The report was signed by Doctor Jarvis Keegan.

Marlie flipped through the pages of the file even more now, looking for anything that could connect this to John's murder. She came to some photos of a child with bruises all over her body. Many scratches and bite marks on parts of her body that no child should have. This was a severe case of child abuse at its fullest. As she flipped through photo after photo of this poor child, she couldn't help but think about her own son and how much she missed him and wondered how he was doing. "Ok ole girl, focus," she said to herself then closed the file. She reached in the box again and pulled out some more papers, not quite sure what they were as she flipped through them. She soon came to realize that they were threat letters that were sent to her husband, stating that if he didn't keep his mouth closed on what he knows about Judge Walker's operations, he would be killed. So far, all she could connect was that someone was threatening John about Judge Walker. *Maybe it was about this abuse case. Craig knew about this and he must have told John about it and John was going to report it to the authorities*, she thought to herself. She reached in the box one last time and pulled out an envelope. It was addressed to her. "What's this?" she questioned then started to open it. Suddenly there was a knock at the door.

"Are you ok in there, Mrs. Cooper?" Evan's voice echoed through the door of the private room.

"I'm fine, thank you. I'll be out in a few minutes!" Marlie yelled back.

"If you need anything, I'll be right out here. Do you need me to come in? I can be a great listener," Evan asked.

"No, that's alright. Please, I'll only be a few more minutes," Marlie replied back in a more of an irritated tone of voice. She listened to see if Evan was going to say anything else, but thankfully, he didn't respond.

Marlie returned to opening the envelope and pulled out the letter. It was John's handwriting. She looked around before reading it, then pulled her chair closer to the light and began to read the letter:

My Dearest Marlie,

My love, if you are reading this, I'm sad to say I am dead. It pains me so to know that you are hurting so and it is because of me that I have left you and John Jr. alone in this world forever. I love you so much. You and John Jr. are my life and for this, I am so sorry. You are my reason for living and that is why it pains me to tell you that I have been murdered for knowing too much information about Judge Grace Walker. What I am about to tell you it is very important and that you relay this to Detective Raymond Mitchell. He will know what to do. It all started when I got a call from my brother, Craig. He told me that Judge Walker's daughter was in the emergency room with severe injuries. He also said that they were ordered not to file a report about the matter. But the most curious thing was that Craig told me that the Judge's daughter spoke of something about a child sex trade her mother was involved in. Shortly after receiving this information from Craig, I began to investigate the accusations and found that some of the claim Cassie Walker stated about her mother was true. I manage to get a hold of a copy of the investment book Judge Walker keeps in her personal safe in her home. I got it from Cassie herself. Enclosed in this box you will find a book from Cassie Walker that provides information and should be enough to issue arrest warrants for most of the people listed. Get this book to Detective Mitchell as soon as you can and have him to talk to Cassie Walker for more information.

"Oh my God. This is serious. What the hell has John got involved in?" Marlie asked herself as she continued to read the letter in John's handwriting: *These are some of the names of some very high profile people, dates, and times of meetings (As it was called), Dollar amounts that were paid and meeting places for these escorts all under the age of 18 years old.* This information, Marlie came to realize, could destroy a lot of people's lives and certainly put these same people in prison for a very long time. The pages of names went on and on, hundreds of names. Many of which were people seen on the T.V and talk shows, promoting campaigns against child sex trafficking, abuse and prostitution.

I got to call detective Mitchell about this, she thought to herself as she pulled out her cell phone and began to dial the detective's number that the police operator had given her. Suddenly, she began to hear voices in the hallway outside the door. Marlie quietly closed her cell phone and placed the book and letter on the table and slowly walked towards the door. She placed her ear to the door and listened.

"What's taking so long Evan? Rick says he's tired of waiting. Is the bitch here or not?" Mo asked Evan in an almost impatient tone.

"Yeah, she's in there now, going through her husband's box of things. I let her have some alone time in there. She's not going anywhere. Soon as she comes out, you guys can have her. So, tell Rick to chill. I'll give him a signal when to come in. I'll open the door over there and you guys come in, and you can leave through there with her without being seen. Everything is still going according to plan." Evan continued to ensure Mo that everything was still on schedule and soon as Marlie stepped out of that door, they were going to get her.

Shit. This is not good, Marlie thought to herself. *You got to get out of here before they get you.* The voice of her husband came into her head again. Marlie looked around the room. There was only a door and two small windows that were placed on the far walls of the small room. One of the windows went into the front of the bank near the parking lot where her car was parked. The other window faced the back alley where the thugs were waiting for her. Evan knocked on the door once again.

"Mrs. Cooper, is everything alright in there?" he asked in that suave southern accent he has.

"Yes, I'm fine, just about done in here. I'm on the way out!" Marlie yelled back.

"Ok, well, my lunch break is almost over. I'll need to get back to work soon if that's ok, Mrs. Cooper," Evan answered.

"Alright. I'll be right there," she responded, trying to sound as if she was still emotional from going through her husband's belongings. She grabbed the letter, book, and the remaining items in the safety deposit box, including money John saved and stuffed them in her bag. She wrapped the bag over her shoulder and headed for the small window leading to the parking lot.

Moments later, Rick walked into the building from the back door that Mo had left slightly open just minutes before. "What the hell is taken so long? I don't have all day!" Rick almost yelled at Evan.

"Lower your voice man before someone hears you. She's in there," Evan replied.

"Well, we're going in now. This bitch is taking up too much of my time already and I'm ready to get back to New York." By this time, Rick was pissed off. He went to the back door and signaled for the rest of the men to come in. Then, he walked back towards Evan, reaching into his right jacket pocket, pulling out a 45 revolver and cocking it. The other men entered the back door, pulling out guns themselves.

"Open the door," Rick commanded Evan, looking him directly in the eyes, which caused a chill to run down Evan's spine. He knocked on the door one last time.

"Mrs. Cooper?" Evan called out and turned the knob on the door. "It's locked."

"What's up with that?" Mo asked.

"She wanted some alone time with her husband's things. Given he just died, well I thought-" Rick cut Evan off.

"Shut your mouth idiot and move out of the way. I'm tired of waiting. Mo, kick the damn thing down," he commanded.

"Wait. I have the key right here," Evan franticly replied, as he put the key in the lock. Rick pushed him out of the way and entered the room as the rest of the men followed, guns pointed in the direction of the table Marlie should had been sitting.

"Where is she?" Rick spoke. Everyone looked around the room, but no one spoke. They were obviously stunned by not finding Marlie in the room. "I thought you said she was in here, you little weasel. I ought to shoot you instead," Rick barked as he snatched Evan up by his suit jacket collar and pulled him close to his face.

Evan, on the other hand, looking as if he just unloaded a pound in his underpants, raised his hand in defense of Rick and pleaded for him not to hurt him. "She was here Rick, I swear. Look, she left her husband's box on the table. She's the only one who can access this, besides her husband. And we all know that he wasn't here," Evan explained to Rick as he stood on the tips of his toes, sweating out of fear.

"Look boss, the window is open. Maybe she climbed out!" Mo yelled from across the room, standing directly under the window Marlie climbed out of not 5 minutes ago. "You think-" Mo started to ask before Rick spoke up.

"She couldn't have gotten far. Boys, go check the parking lot," Rick said, obviously past pissed off by now.

"But I got to get back to work," Evan said, looking at his watch.

"Well, go then. I will deal with you later," Rick replied. "But, if we don't catch her, it's your ass I'm coming back for," Rick said in a threatening tone of voice as he released Evan's suit jacket. Evan wiped the sweat off his forehead that began to run down the bridge of his nose.

"I, I got to get back to work," was all Evan could say in response. The four thugs ran out of the back door holding their guns in their hands.

"She could not have gotten far," Mo said, as they all ran towards the front of the bank. Looking around, they saw no sign of Marlie anywhere.

"Look boss. She must have dropped this," one of the thugs said as he handed Rick a piece of paper. Rick opened the paper and began to read it. On it was the information for one of John's checking accounts from his law firm. Mo found another one, then one more. All with John Cooper's account information on them.

"She must be on foot, which means she didn't get very far," Mo said.

"Everyone back to the car!" Rick shouted the command as he and Mo turned and ran towards the SUV. The rest of the men ran to the SUV also, got in, and drove off fast in high pursuit of the direction Marlie could have headed.

Moments later, Marlie climbed from under one of the cars. She slowly got to her feet, watching the thugs speed off down the street. She let out the deep breath she had been holding ever since the men were standing in the parking lot in front of the car she was hiding under. She quickly made it to her car and got in. She pulled out of the parking lot of the bank and headed in the opposite direction of the thugs. She reached for her cell phone and began to dial the number for Detective Mitchell that the receptionist at the police station had given her. The phone rang twice before a recording came on prompting her to press 2 for Detective Mitchell. Detective Mitchell's cell phone rang twice before he answered.

"Detective Mitchell," he replied. A surprised look came across his face as he recognized the voice on the other end of the phone. It was Mrs. Cooper. He remembered that southern accent from their conversation they had the night her husband was murdered.

"Hello, Detective Mitchell? This is Marlie Cooper," she said, as soon as she heard his voice answer the phone.

"Yes Mrs. Cooper, I recognize your voice from our conversation at the hospital. How may I help you?" the detective responded politely. "I have been meaning to call you, but it's been really crazy around here. I don't have any new information for you at this time. I am sorry to say, but I do want to ensure you that we are on the case-"

Marlie cut his words off as she began to frantically speak up. "Please detective, I need to see you immediately. I was just at the bank. My husband has a safety deposit box at *First Chatham Bank* downtown and I have some information that I think may be important," she said.

"Where are you now?" Detective Mitchell asked.

"I'm headed towards the police station now to see you. Are you in your office?" she replied. "But I have to tell you. Some guys were at the bank when I was there. They were the same guys I saw at the hospital. I think they're after me. They are the same men I saw this morning trashing my house looking for something," she continued.

"Oh my God Mrs. Cooper. What did you say to them when you saw them in your house?" the detective asked with concern in his voice.

"Nothing. I hid in the basement behind our old grandfather clock we have stored down there. They didn't see me. I stayed there until I heard them leave," she answered.

"Don't say anymore over the phone Mrs. Cooper. I can meet you at the station. I'm not too far away from there, so I can be there in about ten minutes," Detective Mitchell said as he turned his car left on to Ogle Thorpe, headed toward the police station.

"I'll meet you there detective," she replied. Marlie hung up the phone and pressed the gas pedal harder as she headed towards the police station. All the while Marlie was headed in the direction of the police station, the four thugs chasing her were headed in the other direction. Not realizing that their victim had slipped through their fingers once again and was about to cause a political earthquake of scandal for quite a few people in the town of Savannah. But can she really trust anyone here anymore? *"Don't fret my love. It is time to put an end to this. You will be safe,"* *John's* voice came to her again as she drove. "I hope so baby. I really hope so," Marlie said out loud.

CHAPTER 12

It had been about four days since Detectives Mitchell and Brown had questioned Cassie Walker at the *Georgia Regional Hospital.* Word spread fast when the press got wind that she had been admitted. Getting back there for more questioning would be almost impossible with all the reporters parked in front of the hospital. Cameras pointed in every direction hoping to catch a glimpse of Judge Walker's daughter or better yet, get an interview with her. Detective Mitchell had decided to wait until she was released from the hospital before he would contact her. As he drove back to his office after just having talked to Mrs. Cooper, his mind raced in all different directions, trying to collect his thoughts before meeting with her again. "I wonder what important information she has. Hopefully, it's something we can use. Not just wishful thinking from a grieving widow," he said to himself. He turned on his car radio just in time to catch a special news report on Cassie Walker.

"We interrupt your regularly scheduled program to bring you a special news report. It is said that the daughter of prominent Judge Grace Walker is missing from Georgia Regional Hospital where she was admitted for reasons unknown at this time. It is believed that she was abducted from her hospital room sometime last night. Reports say that she was last seen in her room around 9 pm by the nurse on staff, then again at 11pm, when the nurses changed shifts and checked the patients on that floor. It was said that Cassie Walker was not thereafter a search of the hospital by the Savannah P.D., it is speculated that she may have taken by someone posing as a hospital staff member. No word on her whereabouts at this time but it is believed that some evidence was left behind that proves she may have been taken by force. Stay tuned for more detailed information as we receive information. From WCCP in Savannah, this is a special report. Now back to your regularly scheduled program.

Music continued playing the upbeat tune by the temptations. Normally, Detective Mitchell would sing along, (He had a hidden talent for singing that no one knew about. Not even his partner because he would never sing in front of anyone). But due to the information he just received via radio, his focus wasn't on entertainment at that moment. He pulled out his cell phone and dialed Detective Brown. Once she answered, he began to question her for any new information she may have. "Tell me what you know," he began.

Detective Brown took a deep breath and began to talk." Well detective, it doesn't look good," "she said. There were traces of blood on the bed sheets at the hospital and on the gown she was wearing. It was left behind. The officer first on the scene stated it was on the floor by the door. We think the blood could possibly belong to Cassie Walker. By the way things are overturned and the broken glass everywhere, along with the scratch marks by the door, looks like whatever happened in there, she was taken by force." Detective Brown stopped talking and waited for a response.

"Are you there, Ray?" she asked.

"Yeah, I'm listening and taking notes," he responded.

"Ok then," she continued. "This information has not been reported to the press and we're trying to keep it that way for now. Can you meet me at *Georgia Regional?* You have got to see this in person."

A puzzled look came across Detective Mitchell's face as he thought briefly about what she meant by that last statement then said, "I'll be there shortly. I have to meet with Marlie Cooper. She's headed to the police station now. But I'll try and make it quick. She says she has some information that might be important to her husband's case. I don't know how much she knows but I need to find out. In the meantime, stay on the scene at the hospital. Make sure no one comes in without showing identification first." He disconnected the call.

Detective Mitchell arrived at the police station about five minutes after his conversation with his partner. He entered the main lobby of the station. Looking around, he could obviously see that it was one of those days in here when you wish you didn't have a desk job. People coming in and out with complaints of a mugging by some drug addict or someone stole their car. An argument was taking place in the back of the station by a couple of drunken men that had been arrested for fighting in a local bar. They were handcuffed together and apparently not too pleased because of it.

"You got you some good company tonight, hey Frank?" Detective Mitchell joked with the officer sitting at the desk typing the report up for the drunk men who had arrested.

"Very funny Ray. I'm supposed to be off today, but Mack got the flu so they called me. Man, I'm supposed to be fishing right now. And you got jokes? Cute," Frank sarcastically replied, then grunted in disapproval of Ray's humor.

"It sucks to be you man, but sorry anyway," Detective Mitchell responded in a more sympathetic tone.

"What you doing here anyway?" Frank asked.

"I'm looking for Marlie Cooper. She's supposed to meet me here. Has she come in yet?" Detective Mitchell asked, looking around at all the commotion going on in the station.

"Oh yeah, you working the Cooper case right? Well, she's in your office. I let her wait for you in there. She said she didn't feel safe out here in the lobby. What she meant by that, I don't know, but she did seem to have a scared look on her face," Frank answered.

"Thanks Frank," Detective Mitchell said as he turned and walked up the stairs towards his office. He got to the top of the stairs and turned right. He walked past a few doors with name plates on them, indicating which part of the department it belonged to. He walked passed a door marked *Narcotics,* then one marked *Gang Units.* After passing all of the other departments, he finally makes it to the door marked *Homicide.* He opened the door and walked down the first aisle. After passing about the fourth cubicle to the left was his office and sitting there in plain view was Marlie Cooper, looking as if she knew someone was watching her.

"Mrs. Cooper, I'm sorry to keep have kept you waiting," Detective Mitchell said, as he extended his hand to shake hers in a professional greeting.

"That's alright. I haven't been waiting very long," she began to say.

"Please sit down Mrs. Cooper. May I get you something to drink?" the detective asked as he pulled out Marlie's chair, which was already out, but he was being polite.

"No thank you and please, call me Marlie," she said as she sat down and scooted her chair closer to his desk. "Detective, I have something I think that you need to see," she began as she reached into her purse and pulled out the letter from her husband, along with the book and files she found in the safety deposit box.

"What is all this Mrs., I mean, Marlie? You found all of this in your husband's safe deposit box? And please, call me Ray, it's only right; if we are going to be on a first name basis," Ray stated.

"Well, I went home after a long night at the hospital and found these guys in my house," she began, as she continued to put the paperwork in order. "They were looking for something that I guess they didn't find."

"Did they see you? What did they look like?" Ray asked, interrupting Marlie.

"Like I said on the phone, I hid until they left. But I did hear them talking and I heard two of the men's names, but as far as what they looked like, all I can say is that they were dressed in black suits. Kind of reminded me of some guys off that movie *Scarface* or something."

"What were the two names you heard?" Ray asked as he pulled out his pocket notebook and began to write as she talked.

"I remember one of them saying *Rick* and the other name was *Mo.* I remember that one cause I thought it was a little stupid for a grown man to be named *Mo,*" Marlie answered. She took a deep breath and began to speak again. "Anyway, after they left, I went into my husband's office to see what type of damage was done by the men. Needless to say, it was a mess, as well as the rest of the house. I was sitting at his desk when one of our wedding photos on his desk fell over. When I picked it up, I noticed it had some writing on the back of it." Marlie handed the wedding photo to the detective. He took the photo from Marlie and turned it over to view the back. *Case file 426193A- Judge Walker abuse case (unreported).* A surprised looked came onto the detective's face, as if he just somehow connected one dot to the next in this giant puzzle of a case.

"How did this get written on the back of your wedding photo?" the detective asked, as he stared at the photo.

"My husband wrote it. That's his handwriting," she replied. "But then I remembered he once told me that if anything should happen to him to get to his safety deposit box and it would explain who killed him and why. And this is what I found." She handed the detective the letter that her husband had written that explained what he knew.

"This explains why the judge's daughter was taken," he started to say.

"What do you mean *taken?*" Marlie asked.

"Something has happened to Cassie Walker at the hospital. She was just admitted for some kind of injury and now it's reported that she's missing," the detective answered.

"Do you think she knows something about my husband's death?" she asked in a worried but anxious tone of voice.

"I'm not quite sure. I need to get to the hospital to speak with my partner about this and she says that she has some information she needs me to personally see. Do you mind riding with me to the hospital? We can continue talking there," the detective asked Marlie, who shook her head and reached for her purse as she stood up to leave with the detective. They stopped by the front desk before leaving so that Ray could inform Frank of his whereabouts, just in case someone important comes looking for him. Then, he and Marlie left the building headed for his car that was parked in front of the police station. He made a U-turn out of the station parking lot in front of the station and headed down Handley Rd. towards the hospital.

Ten minutes later, he pulled his car up to the valet parking of the hospital, jumped out, walked to the passenger side and opened the door for Marlie, then tossed his key to the parking attendant and the both of them walked to the information desk located at the entrance of the hospital.

"May I help you?" one of the nurses at the front desk asked. The detective flashed his badge then asked for Cassie Walker's room. "Oh. Well, I'm Nurse Hanson. I was instructed to personally escort you to her room. I have something you should know. I've already spoken to Detective Brown, but she wanted me to tell you this in person."

For the second time today, Detective Mitchell looked puzzled, not really sure what to say. He just followed her to the elevator and up to the sixth floor. They exited the elevator and walked down the hallway to the last door on the right and walked in. There were police everywhere, doing fingerprint testing, taking samples for evidence, and snapping pictures of the items scattered all over the room. It looked as if some kind of struggle took place here. Detective Brown walked into the room and waved for Detective Mitchell to come in her direction. As he and Marlie approached her, he felt his heart jump a bit at the sight of his partner standing there.

"I'm going to marry that woman when this is all over," his heart told his mind, which made him smile slightly to himself. Introductions were made between Marlie and Detective Brown, which for some crazy reason made Detective Mitchell a little uncomfortable. "What do you have for me partner?" he asked because that's all he could think to say at that moment. She quickly briefed him on all of their findings then directed him in the direction of Nurse Hanson.

Nurse Hanson was a short, heavy-set woman with long black hair that was tied neatly in a big bun on top of her head. Her face looked stern but caring. She reminded Detective Mitchell of his eighth grade Spanish teacher, Mrs. Perez. She said that Cassie had given her an envelope and told her that if anything should happen to her, then to give this to Detective Mitchell personally. She handed the envelope to the detective. It was a 3x5 yellow envelope with the words *Detective Mitchell* written on the front in print letters. Detective Mitchell opened the envelope, pulled out a hand written letter, and began to read it:

Dear Detective Raymond Mitchell,

If you are reading this, it means that I am already dead or about to die. Finding my body will be difficult due to the fact, I was killed by someone in the executives' ward of New York. My mother, Judge Grace Walker, has strong ties to them. In fact, she is sleeping with Tony "The Boss." I don't quite remember his last name, but I do know he is an important figure on Wall Street. Yes, detective, this is some big shit.

He looked up at Detective Brown and said, "Listen to this." He began to read the rest of the letter out loud. *"Well anyway sir, my mother has been a part of some serious organized crimes, most of which she gotten away with. But this time, it's gone too far. Over the past six years, I have witnessed some horrific crimes against young girls in this town. Those cases of where a young girl comes up missing without a trace. Well, I know where they are or at least some of the bodies. My mom has been paying a few guys to kidnap girls. Snatching them off the streets, especially those who are hooking. Sometimes, they lure them into their cars by getting them drunk or telling them they know where to score some weed or pills. Most girls they pick up are party girls or young drug addicts, they're the easiest to get. Most of these girls disappear, never to be heard from again until you guys find their body in some ditch or shallow grave. Listen, I know that I was messed up on heroine and you probably think I'm crazy, but check it out for yourself. Go to 4665 W Broughton Street. At this location, you will find four young girls bound and gagged. I'm sure they are there because this is where they are taken right before they are moved to the Executives club for auction. These auctions take place every second Thursday of the month. That way, no one becomes aware. While they are at the Broughton house, they are repeatedly raped and beaten. I once heard one of the men say they were getting the girls prepared. They are given enough food and water to survive and are usually cleaned up before the auction. On every second Thursday of the month, my mom sells them to the highest bidder for them to do whatever they like with them. Some of the girls are virgins. They make the most money, momma says. But all of them are used for sexual pleasures. I know these things because I have seen it with my own two eyes. If you go to the Mayberry Construction site, about half way in where all the old junk cars rest, you will find the body of a young Asian girl, about 15 years of age. She was killed by Senator Herman Works almost 2 months ago. She was reported missing by her parents, who last saw her as she left home headed to her friend's house for a birthday party. The Senator has also had forcible sex with several of these young girls in my mother's house. She has a secret room that is behind the bookcase in her study. One night, I heard a strange noise coming from her study. When I entered the room no one was there, but I still kept hearing this strange noise. I traced the noise to behind the bookcase where I found that the bookcase was actually an entrance to some secret room. As I walked into the room, I saw Senator Herman Works having sex with a young girl that was bound and gagged. She was screaming and crying for help through the tape on her mouth. When I saw this, I yelled for him to stop. The next thing I know, I woke up in my bedroom with a hypodermic needle stuck in my arm and feeling as though I had been violated myself. I also overheard him tell my mother that he covered her face with a pillow because of all the screaming she was doing and he didn't realize he had killed her until it was too late. Mom's friends from New York had some men get rid of her body. I'm not sure of their names but they all had New York accents and one of them kept saying the name "Rick". Inside this envelope are copies of my mother's ledgers from her business she proudly calls, "The Little Lamb Operation." Every name and credit card information of all her clients are listed on these copies. I took them out of my mom's safe in her home office one day while she was in court and made copies of everything. The information I gave you should be enough to put my mother in prison for the rest of her life and finally give me some peace, even in death. This is also going to cause major problems for some very important people here from Wall Street to Congress. Please detective, be careful with who you trust, for my mom knows a lot of people in high places. But you must stop this. Stop her. Stop all of it. Look into some of your unsolved teenage abductions cases from the past. Some of these girls may still be alive. Not all of them were killed. Also, go to 6114 E. Hail Street here in Savannah. This is where my mother's main headquarters is located. You may find her there or maybe not. But you will see what type of operation she runs. I hope this helps you stop them all, but like I said, be careful. Some of your co-workers are involved.* **DON'T TRUST ANYONE."**

That was the end, except for her signature and date the letter was written. Detective Mitchell looked directly at Nurse Hanson and smiled politely. "Did you see anyone enter or leave her room at any time since you've been here?" he asked her as he tried to give her his warmest southern smile.

"No sir." she answered.

"When did she give you this?" he asked next.

"Two days ago when I came on shift. I went into her room to give her the prescribed medication and to make sure she was doing all right. She was sitting on her bed crying. I asked her what was wrong and she told me that she knew something about her mom and was afraid that it would destroy her family. She didn't say much after that, she just handed me that envelope and told me that if anything should happen to her that I should give this directly to you. I wasn't sure what she meant, but she made me promise not to say anything to anyone," Nurse Hanson replied.

Detective Brown was taking notes as the nurse talked with her and her partner. "Who discovered she was missing?" Detective Brown asked the nurse, who clearly was upset over this incident.

"I did. I came in to give her the medications as scheduled and I found the room like this. I thought maybe she was in the bathroom, but she wasn't. That's when I saw the blood on the bed and then that bloody gown over there. That's when I called the police," she responded through tears.

"Thank you Nurse Hanson. You've been very helpful," Detective Brown said as she escorted the nurse out of the room, then turned to her partner and said, "We need to check out these addresses. We also need to let the Chief know about all of this."

"Remember what the letter said. Not to trust anyone in the department. What if he's in on it too? Let me look at these copies and compare them with the information Mrs. Cooper has. Some of what is in Cassie Walker's letter is the same information that was in the safety deposit box of John Cooper. It's all corning together," Detective Mitchell said to his partner.

"Let's wrap up here and check out these addresses. We're going to need backup for this. If this letter is true and they have girls there, then you know someone has to be watching over them and I don't think that they will just let us walk in there and come out with the girls," Detective Brown said. "And I know just who to call." She pulled out her cell phone and began to dial a number. 'I'll be right back," she said, then turned and walked out of the room already talking to someone on the other end.

Detective Mitchell walked out into the hallway where Marlie was standing. She looked up at him with surprise as she overheard the detective say that Judge Grace Walker was involved in her husband's murder, and she is also involved in a lot child sex trafficking. "What's going on in there?" Marlie asked as the detective approached where she was standing, looking as if he just figured out something important and worried at the same time.

"We can't talk here," was all he said as he walked past, grabbing her by the arm to indicate that she needed to follow him as he headed in the direction of where his partner was standing, engulfed in her own phone conversation.

"Alright then, we'll meet you there, but if you get there first, wait for backup ok?" she said, then hung up the phone and turned to see her partner and Mrs. Cooper standing behind her. "You ready to go? I got backup headed to the location now. They'll be in position and ready to go by the time we get there," she said to him.

"That's great, but can you hold it down yourself? I think we need to split up on this one. That way we can check both places at the same time and try to save as many of those girls as possible. So, when you get there, try to minimize the collateral damage, ok?" Detective Mitchell said to his partner, then gently touched her cheek before he turned to walk away.

Detective Brown shook her head in agreement as he turned to walk away. She grabbed his arm and turned him to face her. "You better be careful, ok? And I'll meet you there as soon as I get a handle on things over on Broughton St," she said to him in a more loving tone, rather than a police detective. With a mutual look of love and concern for each other, they parted ways in two different directions. Detective Brown headed to Broughton St. and Detective Mitchell and Marlie headed towards E. Hail St., but not before dropping her off at the nearest Holiday Inn and instructing her to shower, eat, and try to rest and he would contact her in a few hours after this matter was cleared up.

Pulling into the parking lot of the motel, Detective Mitchell escorted Marlie to the front desk and waited for her to get her room before leaving. He checked his watch to make sure he was still on time when a thought came to his mind of tonight's events that was about to take place. He thought of his partner getting hurt in the raid she was about to engage in. "Lord, watch over Michele and her team as they go into battle. Amen," he said aloud, as he continued his drive to E. Hail St. for his own battle.

CHAPTER 13

Judge Grace Walker was sitting in her judge's chamber of the county court house fully engulfed in a phone conversation. On the other end, someone was obviously giving her some bad news. The look on her face showed that the situation was bigger than she thought. "Mo got hurt. Is he going to be alright?" she asked the person on the other end. A few minutes passed before she spoke again. At that moment, she received a call from the chamber intercom from her receptionist that was seated at her desk in the waiting area.

"Judge Walker, there's someone here to see you. He says he's your *cousin* and needs to speak to you about his *father,*" the receptionist said.

"Send him in," Judge Walker said, pressing the intercom button and then sitting back in her chair already knowing who the person was that was waiting to be shown in by the receptionist.

"Gracie, how's it hanging?" Rick said, as he entered the door of the judge's chambers. He walked towards her desk and took a seat in the chair to the left of her. "Boss sent me here to let you know we got your daughter. She's with us at the mansion, probably still sleeping off the drug I gave her to calm her down enough to get her out of the hospital. She's some fighter, very tough little chick," he said.

"What do you want Rick? You know that you not supposed to come here for any reason. You trying to get us caught up or something?" Judge Walker replied.

"Don't get your panties all in a bunch, Gracie. I wouldn't be here if it wasn't for your little girl," Rick answered.

"What do you mean by that? She won't tell; I already told you that. Plus, I keep her too high to talk to anyone and actually make sense. So, what's the problem?" she said with authority.

"Well, you see, Gracie. I guess you didn't keep her high enough because she managed to leak information to the cops. She told us herself when we brought her to the mansion. She said she snitched out the whole operation. Which Boss is not too happy about and that's why I'm here. You see, Boss got a call from the police chief. Gave him a heads up about the bust that they making at Hail and Broughton as we speak," Rick began telling the judge.

"What do you mean they're busting Hail and Broughton?" Judge Walker asked, almost shocked by the news. "Do you realize that all the information on the Little Lamb operation is at the Hail house? And all information leads back to the Boss and me. Shit, this is not good news at all. I just got off the phone with Boss and he never mentioned any of this to me. He just said you were coming with a gift for me from him. Why didn't he say anything to me?"

"I guess he wanted it to really surprise you and I *guess* it did. You see, I got some good news and some bad news for you. I already gave you part one of the bad news, so here's part two of the bad news," Rick said as he stood up and walked over to the window that was behind the judge's desk and looked out the window. "That's a pretty nice view you got out the Gracie. I never knew they had a garden in a courthouse, all pretty and shit," he said, as he viewed the landscape. Rick was really scanning the garden area for any people that may have been sitting out there at that moment, possibly having lunch or maybe going over court files with their clients. He saw no one. He turned and looked at the judge, who was still sitting in her chair facing the opposite direction, still in shock from the news she had just received.

Reaching in his jacket pocket, Rick pulled out a syringe with some kind of clear liquid in it then started to speak again. "Part two of the bad news is," he took a deep breath and began to speak again, "well Gracie, I need to let you know that the cops are on to you and will be here in about 30 minutes to arrest you for Operation Little Lamb and Boss says they plan to take you in and question the hell out of you for more information, which could lead to a lot of problems for a lot of people and we don't need that, now do we Gracie?" Rick asked, still looking out the window.

Judge Walker turned in her chair and looked up at Rick, who was looking out the window, watching the judge's reaction from the reflection. "What does he think; I'm gonna rat everyone out? Does he realize how much damage that would cause? I thought he trusted me. We have been seeing each other all this time and that bastard doesn't trust me? Who does he think I am?" she questioned.

Rick then turned back around to her desk and held her head down in disappointment and fear and anger and rolled up into one. At that moment, Rick turned and faced Judge Walker's back. "Well Gracie. There's still the good news," he said as he moved closer to the back of her chair.

"And what could that possibly be?" she responded, now holding her face in her hands and beginning to sob. Not from fear of the cops approaching, but from the fact that the man she called her boyfriend for four years. The one man she trusted with everything she had. The man whom she brought into her operation from the very start and the one she was in love with didn't *trust* her. Rick stepped forward and grabbed the judge by the head and mouth so that she could not scream. He pulled her head towards him and injected the syringe deep into her neck, releasing the clear fluid.

"The good news is, Gracie, that you won't have to worry about answering any questions because you won't be around to answer anything," Rick whispered in her ear as she struggled for a few minutes, trying to get out of his hold, then slowly began to relax until she stopped breathing. Judge Grace Walker was dead. "Boss sends his love," he said lastly and softly kissed her on the cheek and released his hold on her. She slumped over her desk, her eyes still open and a look of shock left forever on her face. Rick straightened his tie and ran his hands down the front of his suit jacket to remove any wrinkles that may have been there from the small struggle. He walked over to the bar and looked around.

Reaching over the wine glasses that were placed on top of the bar, he pushed a button that was hidden underneath the counter. Suddenly, the back wall of the bar area opened and Rick stepped through the secret door. It was actually a hidden elevator that led directly down to the parking garage. Stepping out of the elevator, he headed for his SUV. He casually pulled up to the gate and paid the attendant, slightly flirting with her, pulled out the garage and headed towards the downtown highway entrance ramp. He pulled out his cell phone and dialed a number; he said one word to the person on the other end, "Finished", and hung up the phone and continued to drive.

As Rick approached the entrance to the highway that would take him back to the mansion, he noticed a police check point. There were cop cars on all sides of the highway, stopping people and checking their trunks and back seats. Rick began to slow down the SUV a bit as he tried to think of way to get around the barricade of police ahead of him. He decided to exit the highway about 3 exits before the check point, hoping not to draw any attention in his direction. He made a right turn off the highway and headed down the first street he saw to avoid driving through as much traffic as possible. Not sure of where he was, Rick began to panic. "Calm down man and you can get through this," he told himself, as he continued to drive down the dark street. He came to a traffic light and made a stop. As he sat there waiting for the light to change, he looked around to see if there was anything that looked familiar to him and noticed a street sign that read: *County Courthouse straight ahead.* Damn. I guess I'm headed back to the courthouse," he said to himself. He reached in his jacket and pulled out his cell phone to make a call and noticed that he had no signal. "Great," he said and threw the phone on the passenger side of the SUV. He continued his drive in silence, trying to figure out his next move of how to safely and quickly get away.

He arrived back at the parking garage of the courthouse. He pushed the button to receive his parking ticket and watched the toll gate lift up slowly, allowing him to enter the parking garage. He drove up to the top of the deck and parked at the far end. He turned off the ignition just in time to see four police cars speed past him. He slumped down in the driver's seat so that he would not be noticed and could watch what was about to unfold. There were police running from all directions from the cars they had just pulled up in and rushed the door to the stairwell. Rick waited until all the police had run into the building before he got out of the SUV. He quietly ran over to the door of the stairwell and slowly opened the door. He peeked his head in first before fully entering the stairwell, as he heard the commotion from a few floors down. He decided to go up the stairs instead.

As he turned to walk up the stairs, he heard a voice that sounded all too familiar to him. "The Chief," he said to himself and smiled slightly as he took out his cell phone again, hoping to have a signal this time. "Yes," he said to himself and dialed a number. The phone began to ring as Rick heard a couple of police officers enter the stairwell. Rick pushed the end button on his phone and stepped back into the shadows of the fourth floor landing he was on and held his breath, in hopes that the police officers were not headed in his direction.

CHAPTER 14

On Tuesday, July 3rd 1997,two men walked into the lobby of the *Georgia Regional Hospital* dressed as federal agents. They walked straight to the information desk, flashing official looking identification badges as they approached the nurse that was sitting behind the desk." We're looking for Cassie Walker's Room," one of the men said to the nurse very direct, as if giving a military command. "We are here on official business." Surprised by their approach, the nurse quickly gave them the room number and informed them that she could have someone show them the way, but the men declined her offer, trying to sound as stern and official as possible, then turned and headed toward the elevator for Cassie Walker's room.

Lying in the fetal position on her bed, Cassie Walker cried silently in her pillows. Tears ran down her face like pools of running water. "Please God, if you're listening, help me help those girls and stop the bad people that are hurting them...Amen," she prayed. At that moment, the two federal officials walked into her room. At first, she had not noticed that someone had even opened the door. She stopped crying and looked up just in time to see a hand come straight down on her mouth so that when she tried to scream, nothing came out. Instinctively, Cassie bit the man's hand, which caused him to release his hold. Cassie jumped up out of her bed and tried to run for the door. The second man stepped directly in front of her and tried to grab her. Cassie managed to get out of his clutches and reached for the flower vase that was sitting on the table next to the phone. She hit the man over the head with the vase and the man dropped to the floor like a demolished building being imploded. She tried to scream, but the other had enough strength to grab onto her and hold on. She struggled back and forth in his arms as she tried to get away. The man held her head tight.

"Shut up, Bitch," was all he said as he injected something into her neck, which caused her to instantly black out, bringing nothing but silence to the room. As Cassie's body fell limp in the man's arms, he breathed a sigh of relief that no one heard any of the commotion.

"Mo, you ok man?" Rick said to Mo, as he watched his partner stumble to his feet and try to collect himself.

"Yeah, I'm cool," Mo replied. "Give me a minute though, the room is still spinning." Mo sat down on the hospital bed and shook his head a couple of times before standing up again. Rick placed Cassie's limp body on the floor and walked over to the door. Carefully and slowly, he opened the door and peeked out to make sure no one was at the nurse's station located directly to the left of the room they were in. Rick closed the door and turned to look at his partner. He noticed that Mo had blood running down the back of his head like a running faucet.

"You sure you ok? Rick asked Mo as he walked over to him and touched the back of his head. "You got blood pouring out your head man." A look of concern came on Rick's face for his cousin. Mo, on the other hand, didn't notice the blood due to he still was a little dizzy from the blow Cassie gave him. "Can you stand up?" Rick asked Mo.

"Yeah, I'm good. Still a little dizzy, but I'm good. Where's that little brat anyway? Did we get her?" Mo replied, still shaking his head and trying to get his sense of direction back.

"She's over there. We need to get out of here before somebody comes in here and catch us," Rick said. Mo stood up and shook his head one more time, took a step forward then stumbled backwards, falling back on the bed. He sat there for a few seconds before getting up again; this time, he stepped forward and headed to the bathroom. He grabbed a towel from off the counter and pressed it against the back of his head then walked back into the room where Rick was standing over Cassie.

"Ok, I'm ready," Mo said, as he looked down at Cassie. "You Bitch," he said, as he kicked her in the stomach out of anger for her hitting him in the head.

"Chill out man, we don't have time for that now and besides she's just a kid," Rick said, grabbing Mo by the arm to get his attention. "We really need to go. Help me pick her up and I'll put her coat on. If anybody asks any questions, let me do the talking ok?"

"Sure Rick. I don't think I feel like talking anyway. I don't feel too good. My vision is getting blurry and my head feels like it's going to explode," Mo answered, sounding almost childlike and his words a little slurred.

"Hang in there cousin, we'll be back at the SUV real soon. Just keep it together for now and we'll get you checked out when we get back to the mansion," Rick said, growing more concerned for his cousin. The two men picked up Cassie's still limp body and Rick wrapped a blanket around her legs and half of her arms as they placed her in a wheelchair. He slowly opened the door and peeked out again. The nurses at the desk were busy with phone calls, filing, and handling other situations that they didn't notice the two men walk out the room with Cassie. They walked down the hall and towards the elevator. They reached the elevator and Mo reached out to push the button when Rick reached for his hand.

"Let's take the stairs ok, it's safer," he said, as he directed Mo towards the exit door the led to the stairs. Opening the door, Rick looked around to make sure there were no cameras on the walls of the staircase. There were no cameras anywhere. Mo and Rick headed down the stairs to the lower parking deck where they had parked their SUV. Cassie began to moan slightly, indicating that she may be coming around. The two men quickly placed her in the back of SUV and Rick placed a piece of duct tape over her mouth, in case she became fully conscience and began to scream. Mo climbed into the passenger side and collapsed back into the seat, feeling even dizzier than before. Rick jumped into the driver's side, started the car, and drove off quickly, but not too fast as to attract attention. Exiting the parking garage, he made a right turn and headed south on Taylor St., passing the front of the hospital where there were still TV news trucks parked everywhere, still trying to get the scoop on Judge Walker's daughter.

"Stupid idiots, you want to interview Cassie Walker? Well, here she is assholes," Rick mocked the camera crews standing at their trucks operating equipment and TV monitors and news reporters prepping for their on-camera shoots, updating the public on the latest news of this situation. Rick drove passed all of them and headed for the highway. He took his cell phone out of his pocket and dialed a number. The phone rang a couple of times before someone answered. "I got her," Rick said to the person on the other end. "Ok," was the last word he said, then hung up the phone and placed it on the dashboard as he looked over at his cousin, who had become very quiet and was beginning to breathe hard. "Hey man, you don't look so good. Is your head still bleeding?" Rick asked, reaching over and touching Mo on the shoulder.

Mo responded in a slur of words that were not comprehensible to Rick as his head rolled from side to side. Rick noticed that the white towel Mo had taken from Cassie's hospital room was now as red as the brightest ruby. "Shit, I got to get you some help fast man. Hang in there, we almost there." Rick pressed the gas pedal harder as he headed to the location he was instructed to bring Cassie. He picked up his cell phone and hit the redial button and placed the phone to his ear. "Listen, Mo has been hurt and I think he may need a doctor fast. He's losing blood like crazy and he not speaking right. I can't understand a thing he's saying. We'll be there in 5 minutes. Just have someone ready to treat him ok?" he said, and then hung up the phone and focused on the road to make sure he didn't catch the attention of the highway patrol that usually are on the roads this time in the evening.

He reached his location, which was in the Victorian district of Savannah. He pulled up to the gate and pushed the button to be let in. The huge gate opened and Rick drove up the long driveway that had willow trees along the side of the road that sort of masked the big mansion located at the end of the driveway. He stopped directly in front of the main doors where he saw a man in a white coat standing with his arms folded and waiting for Rick to stop the SUV. Rick turned off the SUV and jumped out of the driver's side and ran quickly to the passenger side where Mo was sitting with his eyes closed. He opened the door and helped Mo get out. Mo fell into Rick's arms, causing Rick to stumble back slightly. "I got you cousin; it's going to be alright," he said to his cousin with a shaky voice. Mo didn't respond. The man in the white coat helped Rick carry Mo into the mansion. The man directed Rick to a room that was down the hall just a few doors from the main entrance.

"Let's put him on the bed," the man said to Rick. "I'm Dr. Cooper by the way," he began to speak.

"Wait a minute. You related to the snitch that was going to rat out this whole operation?" Rick asked the doctor.

"Yes, he was my brother. And I know exactly who you two are, so let's just get this over with because my feelings for you right now aren't too good and if it was left up to me, you both would be dead also," the doctor said in an angry tone of voice.

"Is that a threat Doc? You want to go there with me? Try something and they will be burying you right next to that snitching brother of yours. He should have kept his mouth closed and his nose out of places it didn't belong. You want to try something with me, then go ahead fucker and watch your wife become a widow in about 2 seconds," Rick threatened.

"Screw you, punk," was all the doctor could say, knowing that he was already in danger of being killed if he didn't treat Mo. He rolled his eyes at Rick as he removed the blood soaked towel from the head of his unwanted patient. "This looks bad. I'm going to need you to get my bag over there on the table."

Rick walked over to the small cherry wood table that sat on the other side of the room. He grabbed it quickly, causing the items inside the bag to jiggle around and making sounds to indicate that some kind of glass bottles were in there. He walked back to where the doctor was starting to clean the wound in the back of Mo's head. "Here you go Doc," Rick said, as he handed him the bag. The doctor snatched the bag from Rick's hand, opened it, and began to dig around in it for something. He pulled out a bottle of saline water and began to pour it on the open wound in the back of his unwanted patient's head. Mo didn't say a word at this time due, to he passed put about ten minutes after he got in the passenger seat of the SUV and the doctor began to cut the hair off from around the wound, which made Rick feel a little sick at the site of the wound in his cousin's head.

"That shit looks gross," Rick said to the doctor as he backed up from Mo and the doctor.

"Look man, if you gone bitch up at the site of blood and shit, then I need you to leave the room. I can't take care of both of you at the same time," the doctor barked at Rick. Without saying a word, Rick headed for the door. He reached for the knob then stopped and walked back towards the doctor. He took out his gun and pointed it directly at the doctor's head and cocked the trigger.

"He better not die or that's your ass Doc," Rick threatened. The doctor froze from what he was doing, turned, and looked at Rick in the eyes as he directed the nose of the gun to his forehead.

"Go ahead, make my day," he replied, trying to do his best Clint Eastwood impression. "Cause if you do that, you will be doing me a favor. I got nothing to lose, right?" he said smugly with a crazed look in his eyes that caused Rick to lower his gun and back away from him slowly, but still had the gun pointed in his direction.

Rick reached for the door and opened it. Walking out, he yelled back to the doctor, "Don't let Mo die or you *will* answer to me!"

Rick closed the door behind him as the doctor watched him leave. "Go fuck yourself," he replied once the door was shut, then turned and looked at Mo. "I really don't give a shit if you live or die pal, but here we go anyway." The doctor pulled his rubber gloves on one at a time and began to try and remove the glass fragments from the head of Mo who was totally out, so there was no need for any anesthesia.

CHAPTER 15

Detective Brown radioed into dispatch to make sure backup was in position for the sting on Broughton St., instructing all officers on the scene to hold their position until she arrived. She also asked if her uncle was there yet. He was a decorated police detective who has served for more than twenty years on the Savannah Police Force working strictly for the homicide department. He was a strong man for the age of forty-five years old and well built. His name is Michael Eli Brown, which most people just called him 'pops'.

The detective arrived on the scene in time to see all the police officers in position and holding steady. She turned off the ignition and got out of the car. Pops walked over to her, greeted her in his professional manner, and then filled her in on the events up to now. "There's been no activity in there within the past fifteen minutes. But there has been movement from inside the house. There have been at least two shadows that walked past the downstairs window several times, which we believe is to be the living room area. Also, shadows in the upstairs window to the right that would seem to be a bedroom. Our radar signals are picking up someone from inside screaming as if in pain. We need to move fast to save these girls. Lord knows what they are doing to them in there," Pops advised Detective Brown. "It's your call detective," he said to her, as he watched her check her weapon.

"Is every unit ready and in position?" she asked over the portable radio attached to her shoulder.

"All units in position and ready for entry," a response came back over the radio.

"Let's move in," Detective Brown instructed. And with those instructions, the whole team slowly moved closer and closer to the house on Broughton St. using quick steps and hand signals. The music blasting from the house was some hard rock song that sounded more like devil worshipping chants than a rock song. Just below the loud music you could hear the screams of girls begging men to stop hurting them as the men continued to beat and rape their young victims. Detective Brown could feel her stomach drop as she heard the screams of these young girls and the laughter of the men inside that were hurting them. Detective Brown signaled for some of the men to cover the backdoor of the house and for some of them to cover the side door, just in case there were more people in the house than initially expected.

With everyone in position, Detective Brown made one more hand signal and three of the officers tossed smoke bombs through lower levels of the house, including the basement, as the rest of the team stormed all entrances of the house. Gunfire rang out in every direction, as well as breaking doors and windows in every direction of the house. Walls being blown open and police rushing anyone in the house that dared to run or retaliate in any way.

The entire sting took about thirty minutes from start to finish, with many arrest and some unfortunate deaths, including some innocent victims. Survivors were transported to Georgia Regional Hospital for treatment, some to the Savannah county police station, and the others to the county coroner's office for their body to be identified. In the aftermath of the raid, chaos was everywhere. Pop walked out of the house from what was left of the front door with his gun still in his hand. He stood on the porch looking like the hero of any action movie, surveying the view while wiping sweat from his forehead. He searched the crowd until he saw Michele standing by one of the ambulance trucks parked in front of the house on Broughton St.

"Good job Detective," Pops said to Detective Brown, as he approached her talking on her cell phone, not quite noticing Pops at all. "Michele, are you alright?" he asked her.

"Yeah, it's just that I've been trying to reach Ray and he's not answering his phone," she said with a worried tone.

"Didn't you say he's at the Hail St. sting?" Pops asked.

"Yeah, but he told me he would keep in touch and I haven't heard from him yet. That sting should be over by now. His men were already there in position also," she said, sounding more scared now than worried.

"Relax, he's fine. Probably took longer than expected. You know how these things can go," Pops replied, this time putting his hand on her shoulder in a comforting motion. He knew his niece was in love with her partner, even though she never told him, but he could see it in her eyes every time they were together or even at the mention of his name.

"You're probably right Pops. He'll call me," Detective Brown said to her uncle.

"So, when ya'll gonna hook up and get married? Time for you to settle down and he's a good man too. Plus, I think ya'll make a nice couple and would make some really cute babies," Pops asked his niece, sounding almost like her father rather than her uncle.

"Oh Pops, you silly old man," Detective Brown said, momentarily blushing at his statement. I'm headed back to the station. You need a lift?" she asked her uncle.

"Sure do," he said. "Do you know how hard it is to ride the bus in this get up?" Detective Brown laughed out loud.

"Let's go. I think they can handle the rest from here," she said, as they walked back to her car, got in, and drove back to the station.

CHAPTER 16

Detective Mitchell arrived on the scene of the Hail St. house where part of Operation Little Lamb operates. He turned off the car and looked in the direction of Marlie. "Wait here," he said to her in a polite but direct manner. She nodded her head in response to his command. Making sure he had enough rounds in his gun, he got out of the car, careful not to be seen by anyone passing by on the street. He walked up to the back of a white laundry delivery service truck and knocked on the door three times. The door flung open quickly and closed quickly as he made his way inside.

"What you got?" he asked to the guy sitting at the table in the back of the van.

"We got major activity happening; there's been many cars and trucks hauling boxes of things out of that house for the past forty-five minutes. There has been no sign of any young females as of yet. Oh and we got a bonus for you. Guess who arrived just five minutes before you did?"

Detective Mitchell gave the officer a look of disappointment that he would play guessing games at this time, when he should stay focused on the task at hand. "Senator Herman," the officer said. "He looked as if he was afraid of something, or he just passed gas and everyone heard it," he joked. Growing tired of this young officer's not so funny jokes, Detective Mitchell turned the laptop towards him and looked at the computer screen. It was a view of the living room's front windows. You could clearly see men and women moving around in a hurried fashion.

"We need to move in now while the senator is still in there. We can catch him with his hands in the cookie jar," Detective Mitchell said, trying to make a joke himself, but the young officer just stared at him as if he just spoke something in a foreign language. The detective grabbed one of the portable radios off the table, pressed the button, and began to speak into it. "Is everyone in position?" he spoke out.

"North side ready," a response came back.

"South side in position," came another reply. And soon came the responses from the east and west sides of the house.

They had the entire house covered so that no one would be able to exit without running directly into the police.

"Ok then, on my call, move in. Over and out," Detective Mitchell replied to all stations. He then placed the radio back on the table and reached for a bulletproof vest and put it on. He opened a cabinet that was mounted behind the front passenger seat of the van and grabbed a twelve-gauge shotgun, loaded it, and cocked it ready for action. He exited the van, careful not to be seen.

Marlie watched all the action from the front seat of Detective Mitchell's car that was parked safely out of sight. She watched in disbelief that this was actually happening and she had a front row seat to the whole thing. She felt as if she was at a movie premier that had been highly advertised as being the greatest movie of the year. Detective Mitchell met up with his old buddy Ben Shaffer, who happened to be on the scene as well. Wondering what he was doing here, he approached his friend who was posted in position on the north end of the house that faced the side door. "Hey Ben. What are you doing here? I didn't expect to see you, but thanks for coming anyway," Detective Mitchell said to his dear friend.

"I was headed to see you anyway when I heard the call," Ben said. "I found some information that you need to know about the lawyer's murder case you got me working on," he continued. "The lawyer's brother is involved in the Judge Walker case. Did you know he treated the judge's daughter and never made a report of it? But we can discuss it after all this is over."

Detective Mitchell agreed that they would discuss it later, making a mental note to make sure to get an arrest warrant for the good doctor, as well as Grace Walker. He no longer considered her to be a judge and had lost all respect for her due to knowing what she was doing with these little girls. He had also made a call to the station to have the desk clerk pull missing person's files from the past eight years for him to see if what Cassie Walker told him in her letter is true or if there really is a connection there. He brought his focus back to the task at hand and instructed everyone to move in. All at once, the entire task force moved in with almost the same outcome as the raid on

Broughton St. with guns shooting off round after round and people running in all directions with chaos everywhere. The entire incident took place in the course of thirty minutes flat, with several arrests and many injured. Among the injured was Ben Shaffer. He was shot in the shoulder. Senator Herman was arrested and taken to the station along with numerous people that were in the house when the raid first happened. Among the many arrested, six of them were judges, four attorneys, and one other senator that first lied about who he was to keep his name off of the 10 o'clock evening news. Detective Mitchell made sure his old friend was not badly injured before he called his partner, who he knew would be upset with him for not calling her sooner.

He dialed her number and heard the phone ring two times before he heard her voice. "Are you alright? I was so worried about you, "she said immediately.

"I'm fine baby," he heard himself say before he could even think about what to say.

"How did everything go? Were there any injuries to any of your men?" she asked, then began speaking before he could say anything.

"Ben was shot. He's ok though. He was shot in the shoulder. The paramedics said it went straight through, so it looks like he'll be fine. How did yours go?" he asked her in return, with just as much concern for her as she had for him.

"Everything went according to plan. There were a few casualties and life threatening injuries to some of the people involved. A couple of people got cut up from all the broken glass. But we got the girls safely out of there and a unit is headed to the Mayberry Construction Site to recover the body of the young girl there and look for any more bodies. When will I see you?" she asked.

"I'm headed to the station as soon as I wrap up things here. Looks like I'll be out here for a while," he answered.

"Then I'm coming to you. I'm done here. I was just waiting for your call. I'll meet you there whether you want me to or not," she barked at him as if she were talking to her husband instead of her partner.

"Ok. I know I can't change your mind, so I won't even try. I'll see you here. I'm parked at the end of Hail St. You will see my car parked under the larger oak tree," he said, almost laughing at the tone in her voice.

"I'll see you in ten minutes," she said then hung up the phone. She grabbed her purse and headed for the front door. Something in her stomach stirred as she thought about seeing her partner. She knew in her heart that she was in love with Ray Mitchell and somehow, she knew that he was in love with her or at least had feelings for her. "All the times he's flirted with me and I rejected him. I could have been in his bed a long time ago. How could I ever deny myself the chance to be with a man like that?" she asked herself. She made her way to her car that was parked on the second level of the parking deck, unlocked the car door, and got in. She started the engine and put on her seat belt. She reached for the rearview mirror to check her makeup and make sure she looked good for her future husband. As she turned the mirror to face her, she noticed someone sitting in the back seat of her car. "What the?" was all that came out of her mouth before the stranger in the back seat grabbed her so she couldn't move and injected something into her neck, causing her to black out completely.

CHAPTER 17

Back in Savannah, Evelyn sat at her desk with a worried look on her face. She hadn't heard from Marlie in three days and she was worried about her best friend. John Jr. sat in his swing next to a window in Evelyn's office where she could keep an eye on him. She turned and looked in his direction and smiled. *Wow,* she thought to herself. *This precious little child has no idea what is happening around him. How his life will never be the same and he will never have the chance to grow up knowing how truly wonderful his father was.* Then a strong wave of anger and courage began to fill her body from her toes to her head in a fast rush, as if something inside of her just burst into a ball of colorful flares shooting out of a roman candle. She turned back to her desk and reached for her Rolodex to find the listing for Charles' office. She scrolled through it until she came across his number. A small flash of guilt came across her face as she had the quick thought of how awful it was that she could not keep his number memorized in her head after being with the same man for all these years now. She dialed the number and listened. She tapped her perfectly manicured nails on her desktop as she waited for someone to answer.

"Good morning Sunshine Pediatrics, how may I help you?" the receptionist said.

"Hi Terry," Evelyn said to the receptionist. "Is Charles with a patient now or is he available to talk?" she continued.

"He's finishing with a patient now. I'll connect you to his private line. One moment please," the receptionist replied, then placed the line on hold. The smooth sounds of Kenny G played in Evelyn's ear as she waited for Charles to answer. As she held the phone to her ear, she began to think about the last time she had spoken to Marlie. She remembered her saying that if anything should happen to her, she wanted her to keep John Jr. and raise him. It bothered her of the thought of her best friend being in danger or worse, possibly dead. At that moment, Evelyn made the conscience decision to fly to Savannah and find her friend.

"Hi honey, I'm glad you called. I was thinking of having Chinese for lunch and I know it's one of your favorites, so why don't you and John Jr. join me downtown?" Charles said, as soon as he got on the phone.

"I'm sorry, but I can't. I need for you to do me a favor if you can," she replied. I need to go to Georgia for a few days; I was wondering if you could ask your mom to watch John Jr. until I get back?" Evelyn asked.

"What are you talking about?" he asked, obviously surprised by her statement. "I thought you were calling to maybe ask me out to lunch or something. Now, you are asking me to have my mom watch John Jr.? Oh, I get it. You want a little alone time for a few days; that's where my mom comes into the picture, right? That sounds great. You know we haven't had sex since the baby came to stay with us and I really would appreciate it if you could find some time for your husband. I'm kind of loaded and ready to shoot, if you know what I mean," he said jokingly.

"No Charles, that's not it, even though that sounds lovely," she began to speak slowly as she explained to Charles about the dreams she's been having about all the things that Marlie had told her, and how she has a feeling that something bad was going to happen to her friend, and how she needed to get to Savannah as soon as possible. She went on for about ten minutes before Charles cut her off.

"What!" Charles responded. "Are you serious?" He sounded upset that she was planning to leave town without consulting him before she made plans.

"Yes Charles. She's my best friend and I'm also responsible for her son. That's enough for me and please don't try and stop me because I'm going anyway," she almost demanded. "I've already purchased my airline ticket and I'm leaving tonight, so I really need to know if your mom can take him for me or not?" she demanded.

"Okay, let me get off the phone and call my mom to make the arrangements. Can you get me a ticket on the same flight you're on?" he asked.

"No Charles. I need for you to stay and hold things down here, in case Marlie comes back or calls. I need for you to find out where she is and what's going on down there. You can be a great help doing that," she replied with a direct command, as if she were a general in the military ordering her troops to attack the enemy. Charles didn't know what to say after that. He had never heard Evelyn sound so worried and in control at the same time. Sweat began to run down the back of his neck as he listened to his fiancée continue to explain her decision and why she felt it was necessary to go alone. He reached for his address book while continuing to listen to Evelyn and flipped through the pages until he came to the number he was searching for, then stopped on that page. He listened to Evelyn for a few minutes longer before he stopped her by saying.

"I have to go now. I have patients waiting for me, but keep me informed of your whereabouts and if you find Marlie," he said before saying goodbye. He noticed the time. It was 9:45 in the morning and he knew that the person he was about to call was awake by now. He tapped his pen on his desk as he waited for an answer from the other end. The phone rang three times before someone answered.

"Hey Chuck, why are you calling me so early for?" the person on the other end was *The Boss.*

"Boss, we got a serious problem man," Charles said, trying not to sound worried, but failing at it. "Evelyn is planning to go to Savannah to find Marlie and if she finds her, we could be screwed," Charles said in a frantic tone.

"Don't worry man," Boss said in a calmer tone than his partner. "I sent Rick and the boys to handle that matter. They'll stop her and by the time your woman gets there, Mrs. Cooper will be dead."

"Evelyn is headed down there tonight; I don't know how to stop her without telling her of my involvement in all this. She's Marlie's best friend and if Marlie get her hands on that safety deposit box, who knows what's in it but remember that John found about our operation through his big mouth brother," Charles replied.

"How much digging did he actually do?" Boss asked.

"I'm not sure. Marlie was supposed to contact Evelyn when she got to Savannah and went to the bank to get the box, but that was three days ago, and now Evelyn thinks something happened to her and is headed there tonight," Charles answered.

"First off, relax man and take a deep breath," Boss commanded. "Next, you have to stop your woman from getting on that plane tonight," Boss paused in the middle of his sentence. "Better yet, I *want* you to go with her. Find out as much as you can without drawing suspicion to yourself. Can you do that?" Boss asked sarcastically. "But most of all, contact me if you find Marlie. Stick with your woman; she'll lead you right to her. When you find her, I want you to kill them both."

"But that's my fiancée and her best friend. Have you forgotten that?" Charles asked, almost yelling into the receiver of the phone. "I can't kill her or her friend. I happen to love her and plan to marry her, in case you forgot. So, don't ask me to do something like that."

"I knew that before I said anything. I still can't understand how such a beautiful and intelligent woman like that could ever be interested in a wimp like you. I bet if another man were to flirt with her, you would just stand there and watch," Boss said as he began laughing.

"Whatever man, but what are we going to do? She said that she wanted me to stay here and wait for Marlie to call," Charles replied, obviously irritated by the comment Boss had just made.

"Insist on going and pretend to be a man and put your foot down about the issue. She'll change her mind and be turned on at the same time. Women love when a man takes charge," Boss responded, then hung up the phone without saying goodbye. Charles hung up the phone and sat back in his chair. His thoughts raced in every direction. He took a deep breath (as Boss instructed him to do); then picked up the phone again and called Evelyn. After several minutes of insisting that he go with her, Evelyn gave in and made flight arrangements for him to join her. He also insisted that they fly first class, which is the only way he flies.

CHAPTER 18

Arriving at the courthouse about forty-five minutes after receiving the call that Judge Walker was dead, Detective Mitchell radioed ahead to the first officer on the scene to make sure that the area was properly sealed off, so that the press would not have access to anything. He parked his car behind the police black and white car, then exited the car with his jacket in his hand. He met up with his partner, who had drove her own car due to she was not sure if Marlie was going to be allowed to tag along with them or not and not too happy about the fact that she was even around Detective Mitchell in the first place.

"No news cameras or trucks yet that I can see," she said, as her partner approached. She then asked, "Where's *Mrs. Cooper?"* With obvious jealousy in her voice.

"She's back at my office. I left her in good hands. Why you ask? Did you want me to bring her here with me? "He asked, knowing that it would get to Michele.

"Yeah right. I guess she'll be your next partner then," she replied, sounding even more annoyed as she rolled her eyes at her partner and walked away. Not really sure how to respond to her last statement, Detective Mitchell decided not to say anything. She looked more beautiful to the detective when she allowed her feelings to slightly show. He knew in his heart of hearts that he was going to marry her and finally become the traditional family man his parents always wanted.

Putting his focus back on the situation at hand, Detective Mitchell took a deep breath and followed his partner into the courthouse to view the body of their prime suspect, who was now dead. Inside the judge's chambers, Detective Mitchell was surprised to see that nothing was out of place or even knocked over. His first instinct was that the judge knew who her killer was. She had to allow this person to enter into her chambers without even her receptionist giving it a second thought. "Who discovered the body?" Detective Mitchell asked the officer that was first on the scene.

"Actually sir, I did," the officer said. "We had come to serve the arrest warrant. Her receptionist buzzed for her on the intercom to let her know we were here, but there was no response."

"What did you do after she did not respond? And did any of you touch anything?" Detective Mitchell asked, as he scanned the office to make sure nothing was out of place or if there were any visible evidence of a struggle.

"No sir. I only touched the judge, just to check for a pulse though and when I found she didn't have one, I radioed into the station to send EMT and transport," the officer replied.

"What is your name, by the way?" Detective Mitchell asked, feeling almost embarrassed that he forgot to ask in the first place.

"Officer Carlos Perez, Sir. First year with the Savannah P.D.," the officer answered. Knowing now that he was dealing with a rookie, Detective Mitchell took his time asking the next few questions to make sure that this rookie didn't mess anything up. He made sure to ask all the right questions so that he could get the whole story of what they saw when they first arrived. Question after question, the rookie officer answered each one with great detail and exact times of what he saw. This impressed Detective Mitchell and slightly reminded him of his days as a rookie cop and how he used to be a hot headed, cocky, and a little arrogant kid, thinking he could stop crime all by himself until he was shown the truth about what it really meant to serve and protect.

Officer Perez was a tall, very muscular gentleman with dark hair that seemed to lay back on its own, as if trained to do so. His deep accent gave way that he was of a Latino decent. Which made Detective Mitchell laugh inside, thinking to himself, *how did this guy end up in the south when clearly he should be in Florida with the rest of his people?* Knowing that was a racist thought he just had, guilt came from his heart to his mind in a matter of two seconds. He turned to look for his partner, who was talking to the coroner who had just arrived a few minutes ago. He wondered how she would feel if she knew he could even think of any kind of racist thought. He shook that question out of his mind quickly, knowing in his heart that he had no racist blood in his body. Officer Perez continued to answer the questions given to him in a matter-of-fact kind of manner, showing all the confidence that most rookie cops have in the beginning of their careers. And when finished, he looked the detective square in the eyes and asked to be excused. Detective Mitchell excused the young officer and walked towards his partner who was still talking with the coroner.

"So, what do you know so far?" Detective Mitchell asked the coroner.

"Well, detective, seems she's been dead for only an hour, but there is something strange here though," he continued, as he lifted the judge's head and turned it to the left side, showing her profile, and then he pointed to the left ear where they all notice that her earring had been ripped out of her ear, and then he turned her over and the same thing on the other side. She also had a puncture wound on the right side of her neck, which means that someone injected her with something. Killed her quickly and from the expression on her face, she never saw it coming," the coroner answered.

"What's that all about?" Detective Brown asked surprisingly. Looks like whoever killed her took the time to rip her earrings out of *both* ears. It must have been something that would lead us to them. What the hell was she involved in?" Just as Detective Brown was asking her questions, one of the other officers that was collecting evidence yelled out detective Mitchell's name and waved in his direction, as to say come to him.

"Detective, I think I may have found something," the officer said, as he pointed to the vase that was sitting on the third shelf of the bookcase. Detective Mitchell walked over to the bookcase to get a closer look at the vase. He noticed at the bottom of the vase that there was a small hole with a glass covering on it. "A video camera," the officer said.

"Ok, let's find the monitor for this. Everyone look for a T.V. monitor somewhere in this office, it's connected to this camera," Detective Mitchell called out to everyone in the room. "Where's the chief?" he looked at his partner and asked.

"I don't know. He was just standing right here five minutes ago. I saw him talking on his cell phone," she replied.

"That's strange. Why would he leave when he knew Judge Walker was our main suspect? He even said that he wanted to arrest her personally for what she had done," Detective Mitchell said, as he reached in his pocket and pulled out his cell phone and began to dial the chief s phone number.

CHAPTER 19

Chief Robert Berry pulled up to the courthouse in his black unmarked police car with the siren flashing in the front window. He parked his car and got out. He greeted the detectives that were in their cars, following closely behind him as they got out. He gave them brief instructions and then proceeded to go into the courthouse to view the body of Judge Grace Walker. As the chief and his fellow officers approached the judge's chambers, they all dispersed into different directions to begin to gather information on the crime scene. He began asking questions to the officer first on the scene, along with Detectives Mitchell and Brown, just as his cell phone rang. He reached into his pocket and pulled it out, looked at the number on the caller I.D., then turned and walked quickly out of the room without saying a word to anyone.

"Who is this?" the chief asked the caller on the other end.

"Come to the stairway now, and don't let anyone see you," the caller said and then hung up the phone. The chief looked at his phone and then placed it back into his pocket. He looked around to see if anyone was watching him, then turned and walked down the hall towards the stairway. He looked around one more time, then pushed the door open to the stairway and entered.

"Where are you?" the chief yelled out into the dimly lit stairway.

"Up here," a voice whispered. Walk up two floors to the landing," the voice spoke again. The chief began walking up the stairway two floors above where the crime scene was. It was much darker on this floor, making it harder to see then on the other floors below.

"Ok, where are you?" the chief spoke out again into the dark.

"I'm here," the voice said and then began to walk towards the chief. The chief turned and saw that it was Rick, walking out of the shadows. He exhaled and began to whisper to him in a direct tone of voice.

"What the hell are you doing here?" he asked Rick.

"Handling some business with the judge, if you know what I mean," Rick answered.

"You did this? What the hell were you thinking?" the Chief replied in an angered tone.

"I'm just following orders," Rick said directly.

"Orders. What orders? We were about to arrest her for involvement in the operation, but I was supposed to make sure she got off so that no one else would get in trouble, if you know what I mean. I didn't get the chance to do my part. You do know Boss will be pissed about this. She was his main lady," the chief said.

"Never mind all that," Rick interrupted the chief. "You got to get me out of here."

"How the hell am I supposed to do that when in about ten minutes, this place is going to be surrounded with police and reporters. What do you think I am, some kind of magician or something?" the Chief replied, very angry by now.

"Listen, I really don't care if you pull a rabbit out of your ass, but all I know is that you better get me out of here or Boss will pull *your* ass out of a hat. Figure out a way to get me out of here *now* or I'll make a call and let him know you turned over on him and the whole organization. Now, I know you don't want that, do you, Chief?" Rick demanded.

And with that, the Chief looked Rick up and down then grunted loudly, then instructed Rick to go to the 5th floor and go to room 525 and wait in there. "That's Judge Wilson's chamber and he's on vacation for two weeks, so they have no reason to check his chambers. You'll be safe in there until this all dies down," the Chief instructed Rick as he handed him the key to Judge Wilson's chamber. They were best friends, close like brothers, so having a key to his office was nothing unusual. Rick took the key and quietly ran up the stairs to the 5th floor. The chief waited there until he heard the door open and then close. He fixed his tie and walked down the stairs two floors down. He opened the door slowly and peeked around before opening it enough to get out and wouldn't take too long to close behind him to indicate that he had just entered from the stairway.

"Hey Chief, where were you?" Detective Brown asked, as she walked up toward him.

"I was in the john, if that's ok with you detective," the Chief snapped back at Detective Brown.

"No problem Chief, it's just that we found something odd on the victim's body that we thought you need to see. I thought you were standing right behind me, but when I turned around, you were gone. And you said nothing to anyone that you were leaving. I just wondered where you had gone," Detective Brown answered in the most respectful tone of voice she could find, when she really felt like checking him for coming at her in such a disrespectful manner. Instead, she just looked at him, turned her nose up, and walked away. The Chief followed her back into Judge Walker's chamber room to see what the rest of the officers had found that may be a clue to the murder. Standing in the doorway of the chamber room, he wiped sweat from his brow as he tried to gain his composure, knowing that he knew more about this than anyone could ever imagine.

CHAPTER 20

Back at the Savannah Police Station, Marlie paced the floors of Detective Mitchell's office wondering what was going on, knowing that the detective had just got a call that Judge Walker was dead and he left her here without fully knowing what information she had gotten from her husband's safety deposit box. It sort of pissed her off that she even had to stay there in the first place. She walked over to the water cooler that was in the office and poured herself a cup of water. She looked at her watch to see that the time was now 7:30pm and it was Thursday. She thought of Evelyn and wondered how she has promised to contact her a few days after she arrived in Savannah and how she had not kept that promise. Then, she thought about her son and how she longed to hold him in her arms and rock him to sleep like she used to do just three months ago.

Not wanting to wait for the detective to return any longer, Marlie walked up to the front desk and demanded to know when Detective Mitchell would return, but in the gentlest tone. "Excuse me," she said with no response from anyone working behind the desk. "Excuse me, please," she said a little louder, to get no reply. By this time, she became upset for not getting the attention of the desk officer. Knowing that if she lost her cool then that would not get her anywhere, except for maybe a jail cell, she took a deep breath and repeated herself. Looking at her watch, she noticed that it was 9:30pm. She thought about calling Evelyn while she waited for Detective Mitchell and his partner to return. This would actually give her something to do while she was stuck in this police station with all these officers that are deaf and dumb, sitting around pretending to be busy. She chuckled at the thought she had just had as the officer at the front desk was calling her name.

"Mrs. Cooper, why are you out here? You are supposed to wait in Detective Mitchell's office for your own safety," the officer said, almost sounding as if he was demanding a child to go to bed.

"I wanted to know when Detective Mitchell was coming back. He said he would only be about an hour and I have been waiting for about two hours now. I am hungry, tired, and would like to get a shower, so I can't wait for him any longer. Will you leave him a message for me that he can reach me at this number?" she asked, as she went to reach in her purse to get a pen and paper to write on.

"I'm sorry Mrs. Cooper, but we have strict instructions to keep you here," the officer replied. "It's for your own safety. Someone out there is after you, in case you forgot, and I refuse to let something happen to you on my watch, if I'm not being too forward. So, if you don't mind little lady, *please* go back into Detective Mitchell's office and have a seat. I can have someone get you something to eat if you want, but as far as a bed and shower, we only have the ones down in the jail cells," the officer said to her, trying to show respect and kindness in his face, even though he felt annoyed at the fact that he had to babysit and not even a baby.

She looked the officer up and down, as she clearly took offense to the officer's statement, but declined to say anything further in response. Instead, she gave him that polite, upper class southern smile that made her feel above him and stated, "Yes, I would love something to eat, given I'll be here for God knows how long."

"I'll find someone who can get you a menu for some take-out. Burgers are the only thing around here, if that's okay with you, unless your taste buds are too *rich* for ground chuck," the officer sarcastically replied."

"That would be fine," she answered, clearly just as annoyed with this officer as he was with her. She walked back into Detective Mitchell's office and sat down in the chair across from the detective's desk that had papers scattered everywhere. Her cell phone rang, playing a catchy, country tune by Garth Brooks. "Hello," she said.

"Hello, Marlie, is this really you?" the voice on the other end said. "Oh my God, I have been trying to reach you for two days now. Where are you? Are you ok? How can I find you? I'm here in Savannah. I was worried about you, so Charles and I flew down here to check on you," Evelyn said, almost running out of breath.

Marlie laughed as she felt some relief, knowing that her best friend was now in Savannah. "I found all these books and papers in John's safety deposit box that says that Judge Grace Walker was running some kind of child prostitution ring here in Savannah and some other cities too. It's really serious and a lot of people are involved, but I can't really talk about it over the phone and I'm waiting to see Detective Mitchell and his partner, so I can show them what I have found. I really need you here. Do you know how to get here?" she asked when she finished explaining.

"I'm sure the driver knows how to get there. He's from here," Evelyn answered.

"Great, I'll see you soon then. Oh, by the way, they won't let me leave because some guys are after me, so tell them you are my sister and demand to see me if you have to. Detective Mitchell told them to keep a close eye on me and not to let me leave. For my own safety, they keep saying," Marlie said, finishing her conversation and hanging up the phone. She walked back to the detective's office and straight up to the front desk to see that the same officer she just had a conversation with was still there. She looked him straight in the eyes as she instructed him to allow her *sister* to come where she was when she arrives without giving her any hassles. And with that notice, she turned and walked back into the detective's office, took a seat and crossed her legs at the ankles, like a proper southern lady, and waited for Evelyn to arrive.

CHAPTER 21

At the mansion, Mo laid in a comatose state, half alive and half dead with a strong possibility that the Grim Ripper would be paying him a visit before the sunrise. All kinds of tubes and plugs were hooked up to Mo, who had no idea of what was going on. He just laid there cold, stiff, and quite, half breathing on his own and machines doing the rest. Dr. Cooper read the monitors that beeped every two minutes as it kept the blood pressure, heart rate, and pulse readings of Mo as he barely hung on to life.

"Why don't you hurry up and just die, you bastard?" Dr. Cooper whispered to Mo, as if he could actually hear him, still grieving for the death of his brother by the hands of this man. He watched the heart monitor beep and then beep again. With each beep, the doctor became more and more angry at himself for telling John what he knew. Had he not done that, his brother would be alive today. "I wish," the doctor began to say and then stopped mid-sentence.

He suddenly felt the room become very cold, almost bone chilling. The doctor rubbed his arms as to help warm himself. He noticed that he could see his breath in the air as the air became heavier. A tense feeling came upon him, as if crawling up his back like a spider coming in for the kill. Anger rose up in the doctor like a volcano erupting full steam. He looked up towards the door to notice that the guard was sitting there, asleep. A voice spoke into the doctor's ear that repeated the same thing over and over again. *Kill him. Pull the plug while the guard is sleeping. Look at that stupid bastard over there. He is a dumb monkey that does whatever you pay him to do and look at the kind of job he is doing. You know you could get away with this. Avenge your brother. That is the least you can do for him,"* the voice whispered to him. The doctor paced back and forth, still watching the guard very closely. Rage grew so intense inside his gut that it felt as if razor blades were trying to cut him from the inside out. He looked at his watch, not really seeing the time, then walked over to the bar located in the corner of the room and poured himself a double shot of whiskey and took a big drink. That now familiar, cold, chill filled the room again, causing the doctor to quiver slightly. He turned around and looked directly at the door where the guard was still sleeping. "Idiot," the doctor said, softly hoping not to wake the guard at the door, who was still sleeping soundly like a baby.

"Craig," a voice from behind him whispered. The doctor turned around quickly to see no one standing there. He took another sip of the whiskey he held in his hand as he continued to watch the monitors beep non-stop. *"Craig,"* he heard again, but this time, it sounded as if it was coming from the other side of the room. The doctor turned quickly. He shook his head then walked over to the high back chair and sat down. The plush velvet embraced his slightly muscular body like the soft comforter that lay on his own bed back at his apartment. He placed his face in his hands and began to sob quietly as he thought of his brother. As he sat there with his face in his hands, he began to get the feeling as if someone had just walked up and sat down in the chair directly across from him. *"Don't look at me, just listen to my voice,"* the voice began to say. This time, the doctor recognized the voice. It was his brother, John David. He started to lift his head when he heard his brother speak again. *"Craig Dean Cooper. I said don't look at me!"* the voice spoke again. The Doctor kept his hand over his face as his big brother commanded him to do. He was both afraid and confused at the same time. He didn't know what to do at this point and was almost more afraid than confused.

"Why won't you let me see you, John? I need to see you. I want to see you," the Doctor asked his big brother.

"I don't look like you remember me and I want you to keep that memory of me as a whole man, strong and whole," John David replied.

"Why are you here?" the Doctor asked.

"Revenge," his brother answered. *"Pull the plug while the guard is sleeping. Pull the plug and then walk out the room. I'll do the rest."*

"But the guard, he will surely know I did something. He'll run tell Boss and then they'll kill me," the doctor said, as he sat still in his chair listening to his brother. By this time, the doctor started to wonder how that guard could sleep through the noise of their conversation. There was no whispering going on and the chill in the room alone should have caused the guard to at least shiver in his chair, but no movement came from the guard. He sat motionless in his chair with his head down, arms folded, breathing heavy and loud.

"Don't worry about that stupid idiot over there. He won't wake up because I won't allow him too. He will stay sleep for as long as I want him to. Pay attention and listen well. Craig, I want you to finish your drink, walk over to that monkey's bed, and pull the damn plug. Then, I want you to walk right out the door. Don't worry about the guard. Close the door behind you and make sure you tell the other guard sitting out in the hall that you going to the bathroom and walk away. Head directly for the side door that is at the end of the hall, walk out the door, and head to your car. No one will see you, I promise. Go home Craig. Just go home. I'll do the rest."

The ghost of John David Cooper vanished after he spoke those words. But first, he reached in his little brother's direction and touched his shoulder. Dr. Craig Cooper felt a cold chill brush against his shoulder as he sat in his chair, still holding his face in his hands. He began to weep when he felt the chill then anger rose just as fast in him. He looked up to see the guard still sleeping by the door. He wiped the tears on his face, took two more sips of his whiskey, then got up from his chair. He paced the floors for a few minutes, snapping his fingers to some catchy tune only he could hear, almost testing to see if the guard would wake up. This caused the doctor to laugh slightly to himself as he continued to pace back and forth across the room.

Finding himself at the side of the bed of both his enemy and patient, he couldn't help but allow his thoughts to go back to the night his brother was killed. He remembered walking into the hospital room seeing his brother laying on the bed. Blood stains covered the center and the head of the sheet, indicating where the bullet had hit him. The doctor remembered crying as he held his wife in one arm and his sister-in-law in the other, not really hearing the police officer that was talking at that moment. These memories caused his anger to grow stronger and the hate for Mo became easy for the Doctor. He walked up to the heart monitor, looked at the readings it was giving, then turned his head slightly to the left to make sure the guard was still sleeping and then for some odd reason, the doctor took some pleasure knowing he was doing this. He reached down and rubbed his manhood lightly, causing it to rise and slightly move down his right leg. Turning his focus back to Mo, he leaned forward just above his patient's head and spoke softly in to his left ear, "God will punish you for your crime. Justice to you, sir, has been served."

And with those final words, the doctor pull the life support system on Mo, smiled one last time, then turned and walked out the door without the guard waking up, as his brother had just told him. There was another guard sitting in a chair directly outside the door, as his brother had also told him there would be. The guard was a younger guy with a physic of a bodybuilder. The doctor could obviously see that this young guy was hired as muscle only; he didn't look too bright, easy to pull a fast one on this kid. "Hey man, where you think you going?" the young guard spoke aloud as he jumped up from the chair he was sitting in, reading some fast car magazine.

"I'm going to the bathroom, want to come with me? Maybe give me a hand or two?" the doctor replied very sarcastically, closing the door and trying to distract the guard from what was going on in the room behind him.

"Don't get smart old man. I don't want to have to smoke you right here in the hallway for being a smart ass," the young guard said, as he reached for the handle of the pistol he had tucked in his back.

"Well, when you ask a *dumb ass question,* sometimes you get a *smart ass answer,*" the doctor replied in the same manner as before. "Where else would I be going? I have a patient in there to take care of, in case you forgot. I *am* a doctor, remember. But, sometimes our human side has to use to bathroom. So, if you would excuse me, I don't want to do my business here in the hall, so I'm going to go the bathroom, ok?" The young guard grunted a few times at the doctor, looking him up and down, then allowed him to pass as he sat back down in his chair and continued to read his magazine. The doctor walked down the hall towards the door marked men's room. Before turning to enter, he glanced back down the hall in the direction of where the young guard was sitting. He noticed immediately that the young guard had his face buried in that car magazine and had stopped paying attention to him. The doctor pushed open the door of the men's room, causing the door to squeak loudly. The guard never looked up in the doctor's direction. The doctor turned and walked down the steps towards the kitchen. Once there, he headed to the back of the kitchen where the side door was located. Pausing long enough to make sure he wasn't being followed, he opened the side door and looked out, scanning the driveway for any other guards, before walking out and closing the door behind him. He stood behind one of the tall pine trees that was a part of the walkway decor and removed his white doctor's coat and tossed it behind the trees. He then straightened his tie, rubbed his hand over his shirt to smooth out the wrinkles, and walked quietly to his car, hoping not to be seen by anyone.

Once inside his car, he started the ignition and slowly drove away. Thinking of what was about to happen to *his* patient, Mo, made the doctor laugh slightly to himself. He imagined the life support monitor ringing hysterically as Mo began to slowly stop breathing. He imagined the heart monitor going off, indicating that his heart had stopped. He also imagined the look of surprise on Rick's face and the others, for that matter. "You threatened to kill me if Mo dies, remember?" the doctor said aloud to no one in particular. "Well, now you have to find me first and that will *never* happen. May you all rot in hell for your crimes. Now, I begin to avenge my brother's murder and I'm not done yet. Not until every one of you that are involved, pay," the doctor said as he began to laugh louder and louder, then he screamed and then silence, never to speak again. The doctor had transformed from a well-respected, upscale doctor into a revenge seeking silent maniac. Still having thoughts of what was going on in the room of his now victim, he felt his manhood rise up. He needed to pleasure himself out of appreciation for what he had done and the welcoming euphoric feeling of getting away with murder. He held himself in his right hand and slowly began to stroke up and down as he drove towards the highway never to be seen again, at least for a while.

CHAPTER 22

New York City is one of the most famous cities in America. With all the bright lights and Broadway shows, it's a major celebrity attraction. Actors, actresses, singers, producers, and more come to New York for whatever party for whatever reason. Fashion shows are a seasonal thing there in the city that never sleeps, which always bring celebrities to this great city. Success didn't come easy in this city, but once you've achieved success, this opens doors to connections that you could only imagine. Even connections to the underworld of drugs, gambling, prostitution, and just about anything a person could want to fulfill any fantasy. Down in Harlem on 121st Street, there's a house at the end on the block. This house looked small in size. A quaint little cottage that looked as if some old widow had lived there for many years. There was a white marble graveled driveway that was lined with beautiful tulips in all different sizes and colors that made you feel welcome from the first step on to the well- manicured lawn. Green shutters covered every window in the house that complimented the all white house with red trim. This house almost stood out compared to any of the other houses on the street. One could probably say it looks like this would be a vacation house for Santa Clause. But this house is like no other house.

This is known as 'The Operation Little Lamb House.' Welcome to the place where your deepest fantasy can be fulfilled. Many have come and plenty come back. This house is where all the young girls end up after being taken from different states, cities, small town, and communities. If they make it to this house, they will never be seen or heard from again in their hometowns. Although, only a few of the girls that are taken actually make it to this house; if they do, then they are considered prizes to the Boss. Inside this house, sitting at a long oak wood dining table, sat 'Boss'. No one would ever imagine that he would be sitting in this house or even in the neighborhood for that matter. Boss was a very high-class older man, well into his mid-50's and had the look of a 32-year-old. He was tall, well built, and had the stamina of a young boy. He had a scar that ran from the left temple to the lower right jaw line, which he wore with pride. For many years, his private plastic surgeon had practically begged him to have it removed, but every time Boss would decline, saying that "It will always remind me of the struggle I had to endure to make it this far. And with what I've been through, I am lucky that this scar is the only wound I have."

He was a strong, proud, and powerful man that had more control over the city than the mayor himself. He had white hair that had one patch of solid black that ran from his forehead to the back, which gave the appearance of a skunk with its colors turned backwards. Boss sat at the table going over ledgers of finances lost due to the double raids the police had done on his two working houses, as they were called. He was trying to figure out how to recover some of his losses without getting too *dirty* in the mist of all that is going on. He knew the police had connected Grace to his operation, thanks to her big mouth daughter, who he said he would handle her the way a *father should*.

No one knew Cassie Walker was the Boss's daughter, until now that is. Everyone knew that Judge Walker was the Boss' lady and had been for many years and saw little Cassie playing all over the house, whether it was here in the big apple, at the Hampton, or when they were in Savannah, but no one ever thought Cassie Walker was the Boss' daughter. The telephone rang from the other room and Boss could hear one of his servants pick up and began talking. "Hello," the servant answered. "May I ask who this is? Oh yes Chief, one moment please."

Boss could hear the footsteps of his servant as he walked down the hall and into the dining room and without saying a word, he handed the phone to Boss. "Who is it?" Boss asked calmly, as he looked over his right shoulder as his servant was entering the room.

"It's the Chief Sir," the servant replied, as he continued to hold the phone out towards Boss. Boss took the phone and then paused and took a deep breath, preparing himself for more bad news he knew was coming. He put the phone to his ear and listened for a few seconds to make sure he didn't hear anyone else on the other end or some type of recording click as the Chief pushed the play button. Boss trusted no one in this business, not even Judge Walker whom he claimed to love and have a child with.

"Hello?" Boss said.

"Hey Boss, sorry to bother you like this, but we got a situation on our hands that I think you need to know about. I'm sure you know by now that Grace is dead, "the Chief said.

"Old news Chief. Who do you think put the hit out on her? Is that all you wanted cause I'm pretty busy right now. It's been a hell of a night for your little toy soldiers at the station. They started dipping their noses in my business, now I have two houses to recover losses, thanks to your punk ass lead detective Ray Mitchell. What did he think would happen? He thinks he's smart, but he can't think past his partner's tits.

How could this happen? You supposed to work for me and that little cop job is just a cover to keep my people safe, but instead, you let that Detective Mitchell bust my houses and take my profit. What are you going to do about him? That detective owes me big for my loss!" Boss yelled into the phone at the Chief.

"Calm down sir. I think we got a slightly bigger problem on our hand right now," the Chief replied.

"What are you talking about, bigger problem?" Boss asked, trying to calm down.

"Well, your little hit man that you sent to off the Judge, well sir, I got him," the Chief answered.

"What?" Boss questioned.

"Boss, just listen, I don't have much time. It's Rick, you sent him to do a job and the little shit got caught up. He couldn't get out of the building in time before my men got there. They were on the way to arrest her and bring her in for questioning in regards to some murders down here. He hid in the stairwell and then called me. I hid him in another judge's office and told him to stay there until I came back for him," the Chief began saying.

Boss sat straight up in his chair when he heard what the Chief was saying. He stood and started to pace the floor. Back and forth, he began to walk faster and faster with each step pausing briefly to light his cigarette, then started pacing again. "Hello, Boss? Are you still there?" the Chief asked.

"I'm here, keep talking," he replied, as he took a puff of his cigarette.

"Well, the problem is how am I going to get him out of there without getting caught?" the Chief continued. "I'm going to need some help Boss. With all these crime scene investigators and detectives hanging around, I can't get back upstairs to get him without someone noticing I'm gone. Hell, that nosey ass Detective Brown noticed I had disappeared when Rick first called me, so I know it's going to be hard for me now. This is what I need from you, that is, if you're interested in helping your son. I mean, I know you grieving over the judge and all that but this is your son we are talking about here," the Chief finished in a more sarcastic manner that Boss had picked up on and interpreted it to be frustration over the situation at the courthouse.

"No need to be a smart ass about the situation. You know how I felt about Grace but business is business and pleasure should never be mixed," Boss replied and said nothing else.

"I need for you to send a couple of your men down here dressed like our rookie cops. Send them down here and sign in at the front desk. Tell them to use the names Franklin and Smith when they sign the book, then have them take the elevator to the 5th floor to room 525. The name *Judge Wilson* will be on the door. Rick is waiting there. Tell them to use the service elevator down to the basement; I have a gray sedan parked four cars down on the left. Tell them the keys will be under the back driver's side tire, on the ground. They can get out to the street from there and disappear. Let them know that if anyone stops them to let them know they were ordered to take the prisoner to the county jail and because of the prisoner's threatening behavior, they had to sedate him and transport him from the basement," the Chief finished, almost out of breath.

"Great plan genius, but where we supposed to find cop uniforms here in New York and how the *hell* am I supposed to get them down there tonight?" Boss yelled through the phone. "I know one thing, you had better not let anything happen to my son or your wife will soon be a widow, I promise you that."

"Calm down Boss. Just fly them down in your private jet. I'll have someone meet them at the airport to take them where they need to go. If they follow instructions correctly, I'll have your son home by breakfast," the Chief replied, trying to sound upbeat about the situation but knowing he was scared shitless.

"Ok, I'll send two of my men. One of them will be A.J.. I think you remember him and the other is Bret. He's a new kid and kind of got the look of a cop. I'll call my pilot and tell him to gas up the jet and they'll be on the way within the hour," Boss replied more calmly this time. "Just don't let my boy get hurt, understand?" He now sounded more like a dad than a mob boss.

"That sounds good Boss. Have A.J. contact me as soon as they touch down and I will tell him where to meet my guy. Don't worry Boss, I'm going to make sure that your *boy* gets out of Savannah," the Chief said with that same sarcastic tone that he had earlier.

"You had better make sure of that or I'll kill you myself and take great pleasure in doing so." When Boss finished that last statement, he slammed the phone on the receiver and tried to take a hit from his cigarette that was now completely burned out. The Chief listened to the other end for a few seconds before he hung up his phone.

"That bratty kid of yours, who thinks he so Billy Bad Ass got himself in deep shit and can't get out. Now, my ass is on the line for this punk kid I don't even really like," he said after making sure Boss was not on the phone, then placed his cell phone back into the breast pocket of his Men's wear house discount suit, straighten his tie, and walked back into the judge's chamber where the crime scene investigators were still busy collecting evidence. He wiped the sweat from his forehead, then put on a fake smile and started asking questions.

CHAPTER 23

As she splashed water on her face, she felt the strength in her legs come back. She took a few gulps of the cold water by cupping her hands together and swallowed. The cold water felt refreshing to her throat, which was raw from screaming for help that never came back at the hospital. Feeling more of her senses coming back, she turned off the water and dried her face on the towel that hung from her shower. She stood there for a few more minutes, feeling more in control of herself. She walked out of her bathroom and went to the closet for a change of clothes. When she finished, she headed for the telephone to call Detective Mitchell, then soon realized that the line was dead. "Shit," she said, slamming the receiver down. She looked around the room for her purse, not sure if it was here in her bedroom or back at the hospital. She knew that she had to find it, that would be the only way to contact Detective Mitchell to tell him what had happened to her and that she was now at her own home. After realizing that her purse was not there, she sat back on her bed and took a deep breath, lying back on her pillow closing her eyes.

Beginning to drift off into a sleep again, she was startled by the sound of men's voices coming from downstairs. She slowly sat up, not wanting to create that dizzy feeling again, and just listened. She heard two men talking. They were yelling at each about something she couldn't quite make out, but she did hear one of them say to the other, "It's blood all over the place." Someone's in here and they're bleeding? What the hell?" she said to herself, then reached for the doorknob to open it. But it did not open. She was locked in her own bedroom. Who would have done this? She thought for a second and then tried the knob again. Accepting it would not open, Cassie placed her ear to the door and tried to listen harder.

"Sit here A.J., that wound looks bad man and I need to find something to stop the bleeding," Rick said to A.J. as he helped him to sit in one of the chairs at the kitchen table.

"Thanks man. This really hurts, but I think I'll be alright," A.J. said to Rick. "Besides, I got to get you back to New York. Your pops paid me a lot of money to get you home safely and that's what I'm going to do. You hit too, kid?" he asked, looking up at Rick.

"I'm cool. Took one in the shoulder, but it went straight though the muscle. It's not even bleeding anymore. How about you man. Are *you* going to make it back home?" Rick asked.

"That's the plan kid. Besides, I got to take that kid upstairs with us," A.J. answered.

Rick paused for a moment then turned and looked at A.J. with a puzzled look on his face. "What kid upstairs?" he asked.

"Cassie," A.J. replied with a grunt from the pain in his side.

"She's here? I thought she was at the mansion? We took her there ourselves. That's how Mo got hurt, remember?" Rick said with slight anger in his voice.

"So, you don't know then?" A.J. asked Rick.

"Know what?" Rick replied, now facing A.J..

"The brat escaped from the mansion; she just walked out and no one paid her any attention because all of the focus was on Mo," A.J. said. Rick really looked confused now and it showed all over his face. He didn't know what to say next, but A.J. clearly understood his expression. "Obviously, you don't know about that either. Well, sit down son, this is going to be a hard one for you to swallow." A.J. extended out to Rick as to motion him to the chair next to him at the kitchen table. Between coughs, A.J. explained to Rick that Mo was dead and how they thought the guard had killed him, as John's ghost had told the doctor it would be. And that Cassie Walker was actually his half-sister and how she had managed to get away while no one was looking, but was caught and brought here. "She's upstairs, probably sleeping from the drugs we had to give her to calm her down. She's one tough little chick. She got that from your pops, no doubt," A.J. continued as Rick sat there stunned at the information he had just received.

"I want to see her," Rick demanded.

"I don't think that would be such a good idea, given the fact that she doesn't know you're her brother and that Boss is her father." Rick got up from the table and began to pace the kitchen floor. "I remember that brat coming to the house with her mom on the weekends, but no one could tell me she was my sister?"

"Maybe they thought you were too young to understand and wanted to wait till you got older before they told you the truth. You know how parents can be sometimes? They think that they are protecting you from getting hurt when they always end up hurting you in the long run," A.J. answered. Rick looked at A.J., then smiled.

"Thanks man, for telling me at least. I guess I'll deal with that when the time comes, but for now, we gotta get you cleaned up so we can get out of this God forsaken country town." Rick checked the downstairs bathroom for a first aid kit, grabbed the antiseptic spray and antibacterial cream, along with a couple of bandages and tape, and went to attend to A.J.'s wound. He applied the spray to help stop the bleeding and then the cream to help fight infection and carefully bandaged his partner as if he were trained in the Boy Scouts. Once done, he gave A.J. a couple of pain killers to help control the pain till they were back in New York, where he could get some proper help.

"Can you walk man?" Rick asked A.J., as he placed the last strip on tape on the bandage.

"Yeah, I think I'll make it. Besides, I don't plan on dying in this Hicksville town. Let's get out of here; the plane is ready and waiting for us. All we have to do is get your sister upstairs and get to the Chatham County Airport before someone catches us. I don't think they caught up to us yet, but they definitely know we're here. Those two cops we had that shoot out with have surely by now called for backup. They saw the license plate of the SUV, so it's just a matter of time till they trace it back to here. It is ole Gracie's car anyway, right?" A.J. replied.

Rick didn't bother to answer. He was already headed up the stairs to see the kid who has always been in his life, but never knew she was his sister. His heart raced slightly with every step he took. He stopped at the top of the stairs, where Cassie's room was. He took a deep breath before unlocking the door, having his guard up in case she decides to attack; Rick opened the door to find Cassie sitting on the edge of her bed. She looked up at him and began to speak. "I guess you've come to kill me. I heard you talking downstairs, so let's just get this over with," she said, as she started to lie back on her bed and close her eyes. "I'm ready. Take my life now so that I can be in heaven with God."

Rick stood there in disbelief for a moment, and then smiled slightly. "Boy, you are messed up from all those drugs you been taking," he said out loud.

"I'm no addict. My mom kept me drugged all these years cause I know her secret and she doesn't want me to tell," she said to Rick.

"Well, we don't have time for you to tell it to me right now. We gotta get out of here before the cops come. We need to get back to New York, back to pops; he's waiting for us," Rick explained.

"What do you mean *pops is waiting?* Whose pop? My father died when I was a baby," Cassie said to Rick.

"I'll explain everything to you later on the plane, I promise, but now we gotta get out of here, so let's go." Rick helped his sister to her feet and made sure she was ok to walk out of there on her own. They both went downstairs to where SJ was standing in the kitchen drinking from the Vodka bottle he took from the Judge's personal stash he found. He looked up at them as they came down the stairs and began to laugh out loud.

"You two even look alike," he said, as they both approached him.

"Never mind that man, let's get out of here," Rick said. The three of them left out of the side door that led to the garage. Rick helped Cassie into the back seat and sighed as he watched her lay her head on the seat, still drugged, but holding up pretty good. He felt bad for drugging her at the hospital and felt even worse for slapping her around in the fight they had when they kidnapped her. A.J. climbed into the passenger side of the SUV, making small grunting noises from the pain he was in. Rick quickly climbed into the driver's side, raised the garage door, then started the SUV and slowly pulled out, hoping not to draw anyone's attention as he pulled out of the driveway and headed to where *their* dad's private jet was waiting to take them all back to New York.

CHAPTER 24

Evelyn and Charles arrived at the police station about 45 minutes after her phone conversation with Marlie. She looked around the police station and frowned at the sight of all the criminals and prostitutes she suddenly felt surrounded by. She grabbed Charles' hand and gave a tight squeeze. He looked at her and gave her hand a reassuring squeeze that everything would be alright. As they approached the front desk, Evelyn gagged at the smell of the man standing in front of them. He seemed to be homeless and by the wretched smell of urine, alcohol, and obviously not having a bath in about 6 months; Evelyn knew that it was not her place to judge anyone. She was raised to be a true southern Christian that did not judge people by their circumstances or situation. She was raised to always help those in need.

"Excuse me," Evelyn said in the direction of the police officer sitting at the front desk.

"Yes ma'am, how may I help you?" the office said plainly, without looking up from his desk.

"I'm looking for Marlie Cooper. She supposed to be-" Evelyn was cut off by the officer.

"Please fill out these forms and have a seat over there. Someone will be with you as soon as possible," the officer said, extending what looked like a notebook of paperwork to Evelyn, still not looking in her direction. Without fully thinking of what she was doing, Evelyn reached forward and she snatched the officer by the arm, which forced him to lean forward and look her square in the eyes.

"I think it is such a disrespect to a person when you address them as a number instead of a person. Now, if you would kindly tell me where I can find Marlie Cooper, it would be greatly appreciated on my part and such a gentleman on your part. My name is Evelyn Hersher. Attorney Evelyn Hersher, that is. And if you value your job, which I know you do, then you will point me in the direction of my sister," she said politely and with a smile. Stunned by her actions, the office pointed in the direction of Detective Mitchell's office, where Marlie was waiting, without saying one word to her. He knew who she was, as did everyone in the station. Her name carried weight in the city of Savannah as being one of the most fearless and dominating females in the southern judicial system. She was most known for the infamous case of a serial killer that went on a 3-year non-stop killing spree back in 1991, where she was seeking the death penalty and won her case hands down. She was also known for going after corrupt police officials and corrupt politicians that were always in the public eye, trying to buy votes and pretending to care for the community. Those were her personal favorites and she kept that to herself.

Evelyn and Charles walked down the small hallway, until they came to Detective Mitchell's office. But, before they could walk in the room, Marlie had already spotted them and was running towards Evelyn. "I've never been so happy to see you," Marlie expressed, as she hugged her friend tight. "I've got so such to tell you."

"About what you found at the bank, right?" Charles cut in."

"Yeah, I found out a lot of people in this town have been up to some very naughty things, if you know what I mean," Marlie replied in a whispered tone, so that only the two of them heard her. She looked around the hallway to make sure no one was paying attention to them, and then she quickly instructed them to come into the office. Knowing that it would draw attention in her direction eventually, she decided not to close the door, but instead walked to the far end of the room, where she was out of sight, and began to tell Evelyn and Charles what she had found. She showed them some of the documents that John had kept and the book that had all of the *clients* Judge Walker had and the amounts of money they so-called contributed to Operation Little Lamb. There seemed to be hundreds of names, dates, and amounts of money that was paid out. Charles was secretly in shock over all the information that Marlie had just shown them and was thankful that his names was not amongst the list of names. There were very high profile people on this list. Most of them were married, with children and grandchildren for that matter. Many of them would have their careers ended instantly and *all* will lose everything.

"Where's the bathroom? It was a long flight and I really need to go," Charles said, sounding almost childlike and fearful at the same time.

"It's down the hall to the left, next to the water fountain. You can't miss it," Marlie said, pointing the directions out to him without looking up from the paperwork she and Evelyn were going over.

"I'm gonna nail them bastards to the wall," Evelyn spoke, sounding both hurt and angry over what she was reading. "How could someone use a child for their own sexual pleasures? Those poor innocent babies. Marlie, I want in on this and we have to take this to the Attorney General's office as soon as we get out of here. I'll make a couple of phones calls and have a car pick us up and take us back to Atlanta. We gotta get this information out there as soon as possible," Evelyn commanded in her Attorney/Army General tone of voice.

Hearing Evelyn say that made Charles began to sweat. He said no words, instead, turned and walked down the hall towards the sign marked *MEN'S ROOM*. He pulled open the door and walked in and before the door could close completely, he pulled out his cell phone and called Boss to fill him in on the information he had just found out. "She knows more than I thought Boss. I mean, her hubby had a log of information in his safety deposit box. How he got that information, I don't know, but from what she just showed us, it's enough to destroy a lot of people overnight, including Senator Herman, who we all are praying continues to keep his mouth closed about the operation. He already screwed himself and is going down, but Boss, he could take a lot of people with him. Including *me,*" Charles frantically spoke into his phone, staring at himself in the mirror.

"Calm down Charles. If you panic now, then this could mess up a whole lot of things. We need to think of a plan and quick," Boss said, trying not to sound scared himself. "Listen Charles, this is what you are going to do. You are going to get both yourself and your woman and the widow out of the police station. However you do that is up to you. Take them to the Chatham County airport. My private jet is there waiting for Rick, A.J. and Cassie to fly back here. Meet them there. I'll call Rick and let him know you're coming. Bring both of them here and we'll

figure out the rest then. But for now, don't call me, I'll call you."
And just like that, the buzz from the dial tone was all Charles
heard in his ear

CHAPTER 25

Detective Brown opened her eyes to find that she was both bound and gagged. She tried to wiggle her hands free but only to find that the duct tape that was wrapped around her hands was too tight to budge. Her head pounded like a Conga drum as she blinked a few times to help clear her vision. She had been abducted. Looking around, she noticed that she was in the back of a utility van. Not much was in this van, except some rope, a couple of shovels, more duct tape, and plastic bags. From her training and her many years of experience on the Savannah Police Force, she instantly knew that her abductor had planned on her coming out of this alive. Detective Brown began to sit up, just enough to not be noticed by the person driving, and looked out the window in the back of the van. She noticed a few places that looked very familiar, which let her know that she was actually in downtown Savannah. She could hear the radio playing in the front of the van and she could also hear someone singing from up front as well, which she figured that whoever this person was thinks she's still passed out and not paying attention to her or her movements.

Going into survival mode, the detective began to look for something to help free her hands. If she could get them free, she had a fighting chance. The van made a sharp right turn, which caused the detective to roll to the left, which actually helped her. To her left, there were a few tools hanging on the wall of the van. One of the tools looked to be some sort of extra-large screwdriver that seemed to be sharp enough to cut away the tape on her hands. Having her hands tied in front of her made it easy to reach for the screwdriver, but using it would be a whole new challenge. After about five minutes or so, the detective managed to free herself from the duct tape and also untie the loosely tie rope around her legs. Once free, she sat up and looked out the window again. This time, she noticed that they were on the expressway and from the signs she could see, it looks as if they were headed to the Chatham County Airport. *Why is he headed to the airport?* She thought to herself as she watched a few minutes longer at the landmarks to get an exact location of her whereabouts.

The van began to slow down as the driver made another right turn, which led to a dirt road. Signs saying *Airport Officials Only* were to the left of the back window Detective Brown was looking out of and she knew that the driver had taken some back road. She knew she would have to do something and soon, if she was to survive this. She grabbed the extra-large screwdriver and held it tight, preparing herself for battle. The driver of the van made one more right turn and then stopped and turned off the ignition. The detective could see him sitting in the front seat, staring off into space. She laid back in the position she was originally in, just in time as the driver turned and looked at her.

"Still out," was all the driver said before he turned back around and exited the van. He walked to the back of the van and paused for a couple seconds before reaching for the door handle. The detective sat up and crawled to the far end of the van so that when the driver opened the door, he would not expect to see her attack. She could hear the driver insert the key into the keyhole of the back door, just as his cell phone rang. He paused and reached into his jacket to answer the call. The detective could hear the driver began to argue with someone on the phone. Her heart raced as she could hear that the driver was getting more and more angry with every word that he spoke.

His voice sounds familiar, the detective thought to herself, as she listened to the conversation that was going on five feet away from where she sat crouched like a hidden tiger, ready to attack at any moment. She listened closer to the voice as she realized that she *did* recognize that voice. "Chief Berry!" Detective Brown whispered to herself. "He did this to me? What the hell is he up to?" The detective crawled to the window and looked out again. She noticed that the driver had moved away from the van and was now standing in front of what looked like a tool shed. He was facing the door, but the detective could tell by the silhouette of the driver and the sound of his voice that it was for sure Chief Berry. She checked the door handle to see if he had succeeded in unlocking it before his phone rang. "Yes," she said, as the door began to open. She quickly and quietly climbed out the back of the van without causing a noise. She closed the back door of the van as quietly as she could and while in a squatting position, she made it to the driver's side door, checked to see it the Chief was still on the phone, and then opened the driver's side door. She did not get in the van for fear that the Chief would come back and catch her, so she scanned the front seat for anything that would help save her life.

The first thing she noticed was a two-way radio lying on the front seat. She could hear that the Chief had it set on a channel that was connected to every officer at the scene at the courthouse. She picked up the radio and stuffed it the front pocket of her uniform. Then, she noticed that there was a 45caliber handgun lying next to where the radio was. She grabbed the gun and checked it to see how many rounds were in it, then placed that in her pocket.

As she was closing the front door, she heard the Chief's voice coming towards the van again. Crouching even lower to almost a crawl, Detective Brown ran into the woods in the direction of the airport. Her vision was still slightly blurred from whatever drug he had injected into her earlier. She staggered and stumbled her way through the woods until she came to an open field. She slowed down her running to catch her breath and began to become dizzy to the point that she dropped to her knees and blacked out. She awoke a few minutes later to the sound of Chief Berry's voice yelling out to her, saying that she won't get too far before he catches her and kills her. The detective rose to her feet and tried to run again, but all she could do at that moment was just walk. She remembered the radio in the breast pocket of her uniform shirt and pulled it out. The darkness of the night made it hard to see the radio in her hand but she managed to find the talk button.

"Mayday, mayday. This is Detective Michele Brown of the Savannah Police Department. I have been kidnapped. Can anyone hear me? Over." There was no response from the other end.

"I can hear you. Get back here now and *that's* an order officer!" Chief Berry yelled out from only a few feet away from the detective. Detective Brown began to run again, to make more distance between her and the Chief before she would use the two-way again. She ran as far and as fast as her drug induced eyes could take her before she fell to the ground and laid there gasping for air. She tried the two-way once again and this time, she received a response from dispatch. She gave the dispatcher as much information as she could of her whereabouts before she blacked out again and this time, she didn't move.

The Chief arrived shortly after Detective Brown passed out at the edge of the field that led to the landing strip of the Chatham County airport. He looked around in the darkness, hoping to spot the detective running up the landing strip trying to reach the terminal to safety or still out here in the fields of high grass and blackness still trying to make it this far. *Had he run so fast that he ran ahead of her?* The Chief thought to himself, as he stood listening for any noise that sounded like a person running or breathing hard for that matter. Not sure how far she might have gotten, the Chief pulled out his cell phone and pressed the one button that automatically dialed a number. He listened to the phone ring three times before someone answered.

"She got away," he said to the person on the other end. "You said this would be a simple. No one would get caught, you said. Now that bitch is out there and sooner or later, she's gonna make it back to her partner, then we're all screwed," he continued, but yelling now.

"You idiot, how could you let her get away like that? You better find her and quick, or you're a dead man," the person on the other end said and then hung the phone up in the Chief's ear.

At this point, the Chief became frantic. "Hello?" he said to the phone, even though all he heard was a dial tone. The Chief cursed and without thinking, he threw his cell phone into the middle of the field of what looked like an ocean of total darkness. The Chief yelled out loud again and without warning, took out a .22 caliber pistol, held it to his head, and pulled the trigger. The noise from the gunshot caused Detective Brown to open her eyes. She still felt a little drugged, but slightly better than before. She sat up from where she laid and rubbed her eyes to help regain proper vision and looked around at her surroundings. There was total darkness all around her; she couldn't see her own hand. Instantly, she remembered her mini flashlight that she kept in the lower left side of her police belt. She reached for it and turned it on. She scanned the area for any signs of the police chief. She saw no one. Feeling even more conscious, she rose to her feet and scanned her surroundings once more. This time, she noticed something on the ground about ten feet from where she had once laid. She slowly pulled out the 45 and cocked it and proceeded to walk toward the thing lying in the grass straight ahead. As she came closer to the object in the grass, she noticed it was Chief Berry. She moved in closer to him at a more rapid pace, but had the 45 aimed directly at him.

"Chief, is that you?" she yelled in his direction and there was no reply from the Chief. Just a few feet ahead of her, lying in the tall grass, was the Chief. He was bleeding from the head and making some kind of gurgling noises. Michele ran to his assistance and began to talk to him, not sure if he could hear her or not. She looked up to see the lights of the ambulance coming closer. As the ambulance came to a stop, the paramedics ran from the truck to the assistance of Michele and the Chief. The detective blacked out again, but this time from relief from being rescued.

CHAPTER 26

The Savannah Police station seemed to quiet down a bit shortly after Charles had come back from the men's room. He continued to think of the conversation that he had with Boss just a few minutes ago. He had to come up with a plan to get both of the women out of the station, but couldn't think of nothing at this short of a notice. He was not the type of man that could make such snap decisions, given his profession as a doctor; he was trained to study the situation before making any diagnosis. He said nothing as he walked into the room and tried to pretend that everything was alright for now. Marlie and Evelyn were still sorting through the books and files that was in John David's safety deposit box and whispering so that no one would hear them. They both looked up towards the door as Charles approached them.

"So, what else have you found?" Charles asked, addressing the both of them. Evelyn rose to her feet and walked towards Charles. She looked him in the eyes and then slapped him across the face so hard that his nose started bleeding. He reached instinctively for his face and nose. The slap dazed his vision to a blur for a few seconds. He looked up at Evelyn with a look of confusion and shock. "Eve, what the hell" was all he could get out of his mouth before she slapped him again.

"You're involved in this too, Charles? You're a part of why my husband is dead?" Marlie asked with tears in her eyes and her voice sounding as if she had already been crying.

"Let me explain," Charles said as he began to close the door of the detective's office, but looked around the waiting area before doing so, to make sure no one was watching. He walked toward Evelyn and reached for her hand. Instantly, she resisted him and walked to the other side of the room. He sat down in the chair that was close to the door, took a deep breath, and began to speak. "Before you write me off and run to the front desk and tell them what you think you know. Let me, at least, plead my case, counselor," he said, looking at Evelyn and then at Marlie.

"This is bigger than me. I swear when I first was told about this, I had no idea that it was this deep," he continued.

"What are you talking about, you idiot? There was a child prostitution ring going on and from these records of clients, your name is at the top of the list. Not only are you a client, but you're a partner in this organization," Marlie said.

"If we can just get out of here, I can better explain this to you. Please believe me, I had no idea how deep this went. Can we please go somewhere and talk about this? Let's go to your hotel room Marlie, can we do that? I just don't want to talk here. I swear, I will tell you both everything," Charles pleaded.

"Oh, I don't think so buddy. We are going to stay right here until Detective Mitchell comes back and then you can explain how you're involved in John David's murder," Marlie almost screamed at him. "We trusted you Charles; you were like family to us. We vacationed together plenty of times. You were like another brother to John." Charles said nothing and just stared at Marlie as if she were a stranger to him and then turned his gaze onto Evelyn and smiled at her, still not speaking. He reached into the side pocket of his suit jacket and pulled out a gun. It was small, but big enough to frighten the women. He looked at his watch to check the time as he stood up from the desk and walked over to where the women were standing with surprise on both their faces.

"Charles. What-" Evelyn began to say before she was cut off by Charles placing his finger gently on her lips.

"This is what we *will* be doing. First, we are going to walk out of this police station nice and quietly. If any one of you try and do anything to cause attention, I don't have a problem shooting you. Now that you know some of the truth, I have nothing else to lose. Then we are going to the airport. We got a plane to catch. Once we are out of here, I can explain to you the truth. Marlie, I'm sorry John David was killed, but he was about to open the biggest can of worms Savannah has never seen. So, enough with the questions and let's just get out of here," Charles demanded, as he pointed the gun in their direction and instructed them out the door. The station had calmed down quite a bit, given that over half of the station was now at the airport responding to the call dispatch sent about the Chief and Detective Brown. No one notice Marlie, Evelyn, or Charles leave the station.

The three of them calmly walked out of the front doors and into the parking lot where the rental car was parked. Charles instructed them into the car and had Evelyn drive while Marlie sat on the passenger side. Charles sat in the backseat so that he could keep his gun pointed on the women at all times. He gave Evelyn the directions to the airport as she backed out of the parking spot and slowly drove out of the police station and headed for the expressway. "I will never forgive you for this Charles Malone," Marlie said, as she turned her head towards the backseat.

"When we get back to Atlanta, I don't want you to come back to the house. Let my assistant know where you will be staying and I'll have your things sent to you. I can't live with a pedophile," Evelyn said, as they drove towards the airport.

"Who says you'll make it back to Atlanta?" Charles asked in more of a sinister tone and said nothing more.

CHAPTER 27

Detective Mitchell arrived at the airport fifteen minutes after all the other units had gotten there. He jumped out of his car and walked up to the officer that was standing by the first car he saw. He asked the officer where he could find his partner and the young officer pointed in the direction of the two ambulance trucks parked side by side on the runway. He walked up to the first truck and knocked on the window, flashing his badge so that the paramedic would open the door. As the door opened, he noticed it was Chief Berry. Detective Mitchell asked the paramedic how his condition was as he looked at the Chief and saw that he was bleeding from the right side of his head. He wondered if the Chief could hear him as he spoke words of encouragement to his boss. He asked if his partner was in the other truck and what type of condition she was in. The paramedic told him that he would have to ask the others of her status and that they were more focused on saving the Chief at this moment, then asked the detective to leave the truck so that they could get the Chief to the hospital as soon as possible, if he was to have even the smallest chance of living.

Detective Mitchell climbed out of the ambulance truck and walked to the other truck, knocked on the window, and flashed his badge as he had previously done. They opened the door for him to climb in. He got the information about his partner's condition and left the truck. They told him she was injected with some kind of drug, but would have to get her to the hospital so the doctors can run tests to find out what she was given. They also told him that her vital signs were all normal, which was a good thing and that they believe she would be okay once the drugs wear off.

Feeling relieved for his partner, the detective left the second truck and headed back to his car, which he just realized was still running. He pulled out his cell phone and called the station to check on Marlie Cooper. To his surprise, she was no longer there. He asked if anyone knew where she was or if she left some kind of message saying where she could be reached, but received a negative reply to all questions. Detective Mitchell hung up the phone and sat there for a moment, trying to figure out why Marlie would leave the station, if she had information that was important to her husband's case. Why didn't she leave a phone number or some kind of way to be reached? *Could something have happened to her?* He thought to himself, then quickly brushed that thought out of his head. He knew that she was last seen at the police station, so how could anyone harm her there. She was safe there so she must have gotten tired of waiting and just left. "If what she has is *that* important, then she'll contact me," he said aloud to himself.

Just as he was about to drive off heading for the hospital, his cell phone rang. "Detective Mitchell," he said, but no one responded. Suddenly, he began to hear voices in the background of whoever had just called him. He listened for a few minutes and then recognized that it was the voice of Marlie Cooper. He could hear another female voice as well and as a male voice saying that he would kill them both if they didn't do what he said. The detective also recognized the sound of airplane motors and knew instantly that it was coming from an airport, but which one, he was not too sure. He listened closely for a few minutes, hearing a conversation between Marlie and the male voice

"Why are we at the Chatham airport?" Marlie asked Charles, making sure she said the name of the airport. She was trying to set Charles up by having the detective on the phone and talking loud.

"Well, since you asked, we're headed to New York dear friend. Got some people there that have been waiting to meet you," Charles answered.

"Who?" she asked, still trying to get as much information out of him as she could.

"Don't worry about that now. In time, all of your questions will be answered. Now, shut up and walk," he demanded.

"You'll never get past airport security with that gun, you know. So, how are you supposed to handle that, *Mr. Big?*" Evelyn shouted.

"If you two don't shut up, I'll put a bullet into the both of you and get on that plane alone. Besides, we won't be going through security. Boss has a private plane out on runway 13,so there will be no need to deal with all that mess in there. Now, can we get to the damn plane before they leave us?" Charles demanded again and pushed Marlie in the back with the palm of his hand, causing her to stumble and fall.

Overhearing the entire conversation, Detective Mitchell radioed into dispatch to have all units go out to runway number 13 for a possible kidnapping in progress. He gave dispatch a description of Marlie and informed them that she may have been abducted right out of the police station. He continued to listen to the phone conversation and heard one of the ladies say the name Charles Malone and he relayed this information to dispatch and had them run a background check on Charles Malone, the possible abductor. He drove his car in the direction of runway 13 as he began to see the lights of other officers moving in behind him. He received a call on his car radio from dispatch, asking which airline were they to report.

Looking around, the detective noticed all types of airplanes. Some of them had logos of major airlines and some of them were marked with indicators that they were private planes and some marked with shipping companies on them. The detective reported that he overheard the abductor say that a private plane was waiting for them on runway number 13, and from what he could see, there's about three of them out here. He was already at the runway with backup closely behind. He instructed them to spread out and check all three planes for Marlie Cooper and her abductor, Charles Malone. Lights from the police cars began to fill the night sky as if the sun was beginning to rise, welcoming the morning, as they pulled closer to the private planes and surrounding them so that none could move or try to take off. Detective Mitchell was already out of his car and giving hand signals to the approaching backup team. Each officer parked their car in position and exited with guns drawn and ready to shoot.

Rushing each of the planes simultaneously brought on the element of surprise to the pilots and passengers of two of the planes. The third plane was not as easy for the police to access. Gunfire rang out from the cockpit windows instead. Officers retreated to their cars and began to return fire. Shots rang out in every direction. Detective Mitchell radioed to the officers that were aboard the two planes to escort the passengers and pilots off quickly and get them to safety.

Inside the remaining private plane, Rick and A.J. were at each of the cockpit windows, shooting off round after round at the police officers that were firing back at them with the same intention to shoot to kill. Charles continued to hold both Marlie and Evelyn at gunpoint, pretending to keep them from trying to escape, but in reality, he was just as afraid as the women on the plane. Rick looked over at Charles and instructed him to help them keep the police at bay, while the pilot takes off. "Get over and help keep these bastards back," Rick demanded at Charles.

"But, I have to keep the women under control over here. Remember, we're supposed to get them back unharmed; your dad said so," Charles said, speaking in a cowardly tone of voice.

"You little punk. If you don't get up off your ass and get over here now, I'll shoot you myself and throw your stinking body off this plane!" Rick screamed, pointing his gun in Charles' direction. Fear began to show clearly on Charles' face and Marlie began to pick up on it. She looked over at Evelyn and noticed that she was working the tie that was wrapped around her hands. She soon was free from the bindings and began to remove Marlie's bound hands as well.

"What now Marlie?" Evelyn whispered to Marlie, who was looking around for some kind of weapon to defend herself. Marlie found what looked to be a metal pipe that was lying on the floor under one of the plush seats of the plane. She crouched low as she reached for the pipe, and with one swift blow, she hit Charles over the back of the head, causing him to fall flat on his face and out cold. Marlie quickly jumped to her feet and pulled Charles out of sight, while Rick and A.J. continued shooting at the police.

"Find a weapon," Marlie said to Evelyn, as they hid Charles' body in the back of the plane and covered him with blankets. The two women searched Charles' pockets until they found the gun he had once pointed at the both of them. Evelyn checked the chamber of the gun to see how many bullets were actually in it and found that it was fully loaded.

"What now?" Evelyn asked.

"We gotta get off this plane before it can take off," Marlie began to say as she watched the two men at the windows shoot round after round at the police. She noticed that they were pretty distracted with all the gunfire going back and forth and knew that they had not noticed anything that was going on in the back of the plane. She closed the screen of the private galley halfway so that they would not be seen, then turned to Evelyn and told her to help get the small window open. The two women began to pry open the small window with the pipe that Marlie had just used to knock Charles out. The window opened slightly, but just enough for them to push it up the rest of the way.

"Ok Evelyn, you go first. Climb out onto the tail wing and jump; it's not a far drop and once you hit the ground, run for your life," Marlie said to her friend and gave her a hug. Evelyn looked worriedly at Marlie as she began to speak.

"You *will* be behind me right?" she asked.

"Sure, right behind you, now go Eve," Marlie replied. Evelyn turned and climbed out of the small window and jumped down onto the tail wing. She turned to help Marlie climb out as gunfire still rang into the night air. Suddenly, she heard Marlie scream as her body fell out of the window and onto the tail wing. Blood began to flow down the tail wing from Marlie's back. Evelyn crawled over to her friend and began to pull her in the direction of the end of the tail wing so that they could jump off. She saw that Marlie was unconscious and knew that she had been shot, but was not sure if she was dead or alive at the time. Gunshots rang out in their direction and Evelyn knew she had to do something quick or they both would be dead. She reached into Marlie's pocket and pulled out the gun that they took off Charles and began shooting towards the window they had just jumped out of. She noticed that the shooter was one of the men that were shooting at the police a few moments earlier. He must have figured out that they were escaping when Charles never came up front to help them. The man in the window shooting at them was A.J.. He had come to the back galley and found Charles on the floor and saw Marlie climbing out the window, and shot her in the back, but did not expect to be shot at when he looked out to see if she was dead. One of the bullets landed into his left shoulder, causing him to fall back onto the floor. Evelyn grabbed Marlie by the arm and slid down the tail wing, landing hard on the ground. Now hurt herself, she began to pull Marlie out of the way of all the shooting and into the tall grass that was on each side of the runway. She began checking Marlie to see if she was still alive and was relieved to find that her friend was still breathing. Marlie was badly hurt and Evelyn knew that she had to get help and fast, if she was to save her friend's life.

"I'll get help, just don't die on me. Keep breathing ole girl, help will be here soon," Evelyn said, breathing heavy herself. She looked around and saw the lights of the police cars and began limping in their direction. She stumbled a few times before reaching one of the police officers that was standing by his car. "Help," was all Evelyn could get out before she collapsed into the arms of the officer. The officer carefully helped Evelyn into the backseat of the police car as she gathered the strength to explain what had happened and that Marlie was still out in the fields, unconscious from the gunshot wound in her back.

Gunshots crashed through the cockpit windows of the private jet as A.J. laid on the floor reloading his gun. Looking around, he noticed that the pilot of the plane was crouched under the pilot's seat with his head tucked so far under his body that he reminded A.J. of a turtle with his head in his shell, afraid of the animal that is trying to have him for dinner. Once reloaded, A.J. instructed the pilot to get back in the pilot's chair and fly them out of there as fast as he could, but the pilot insisted that the plane would never be able to take off as long as all the police cars were parked in front of it. The pilot knew that if he tried to fly this plane that it would cause major damage to both the plane and to the officers and their cars as well.

"Listen asshole, you have one second to get in that chair and start this plane and get it in the air, or your wife will soon be a widow!" A.J. yelled at the pilot and pointed his gun in his direction. The pilot gasped deep and then put his hands up in air in an attempt to protect himself from being shot in the head.

"Alright, I'm going!" he screamed out and climbed into the chair and began to flip all the switches needed to start the engines. The plane made a loud sound that indicated the engines were beginning to run as the pilot began flipping switches and preparing for takeoff. Rick stumbled from the back of the plane and fell next to A.J., holding his shoulder. "Are you alright, man?" A.J. asked Rick, as he watched him fall to the floor, bleeding from his left shoulder. He pulled Rick to where he could get a better look at where the blood was coming from.

"It's not as bad as it looks. I think the bullet went straight though," Rick answered, breathing hard and groaning from the massive pain he was feeling. The two men exchanged a few more words and then decided that they needed to get out of there. Crawling on their knees, the two men headed towards the cockpit, keeping their heads low so that none of the flying bullets would not hit them. A.J. crawled to the window and began firing at the police officers that were hiding behind the doors of their car, trying not to be hit themselves. He yelled at the pilot to start moving the plane at once.

The plane began to move forward, inching closer and closer to the police cars that had formed a barricade in front of it and smashed through them as if they were toy matchbox cars, causing a few of them to burst into flames as the wheels of the plane crushed them. Detective Mitchell ducked behind the door of his car as the explosions began to erupt from the cars that were being smashed under the wheels of the jet that was trying to move down the runway to take off. He radioed into the airport tower to notify them to clear the runway and divert any planes heading in their direction or preparing to land. He also radioed into dispatch to alert them to send for more backup and to stop all incoming and outgoing planes so that they don't get caught in the chaos. He instructed them to send the fire department, which was already in route. All hell seemed to be breaking loose as the plane moved down the runway and began to turn right, the gear was up and ready for takeoff.

"Why aren't we in the air by now?" Rick asked, as he stumbled to his feet to reach where A.J. was standing. He felt a little light-headed and fell to the floor of the plane, then tried to stand again. He looked down at his shoulder and saw that his left sleeve was now soaked with his own blood, which caused him to realize that maybe he was injured worse than he initially thought. Rick began to panic from the thought of actually dying or at least he thought he was, as he tried to stand one more time, but this time, the room began to spin fast as he gazed in A.J.'s direction before blacking out. He collapsed with a hard thump on the floor of the plane.

The pilot began to beg A.J. to let him stop the plane before the police shot them all as gunfire continued to fly in every direction from the police cars that were in hot pursuit of the moving aircraft trying to stop it. A.J. glanced back into the airplane and saw that Rick was passed out and he knew it was from the bullet wound in his left shoulder. A.J. began to panic himself, then controlled that fear quickly. His main mission was to get them out of there or die trying. He ordered the pilot to speed up as he pointed the gun into his right temple to enforce his order. The pilot stepped on the gas pedals of the plane and felt the aircraft accelerate to a faster speed.

"There's another barricade of cars and trucks straight ahead of us. I need to stop the plane before we hit them!" the pilot yelled out to A.J., who happened to be looking out of the window and all the oncoming traffic headed their way.

"Keep going, smash through them if you have to, but get this damn plane in the air now!" A.J. yelled back at the pilot, pushing the barrel of his gun harder into his temple. He glanced back in Rick's direction again and saw that he was no longer out cold on the floor. He assumed that he had come to and was in back of the plane with Charles keeping the women bound and gagged. He never realized what had happened in back of the plane about ten minutes ago, and he had no idea that Marlie and Evelyn had escaped. Rick never had the chance to tell him and Charles was still unconscious in the back galley.

The plane edged closer to the barricade as Detective Mitchell prepared his men to fire on his command. Everyone was in position and ready to shoot as they watched the plane move closer to where they stood. "Everyone aim for the tires when I say go!" Detective yelled and then commanded his troops to fire at will, as he began to pull the trigger of his 9mm handgun in the direction of the approaching aircraft. Shots rang loud into the night as if a war had begun in the middle of runway 13, forming a battle ground of exploding cars that were being crushed underneath a giant tank armed with military ammunition big enough to cause instant disaster to half of the airport.

Inside the plane, A.J. continued to command the pilot to get going and get the aircraft in the air faster. He yelled for Rick to come up front but received no response. He looked out the door of the cockpit to see if Rick was on his way up to the cockpit, but saw no one coming. "Don't stop this bird for nothing. Run over everything and everybody that gets in the way. I'll be right back, and don't try anything funny or I will shoot you. I don't want to kill you just yet cause you need to fly this plane, but I will if you pull anything funny. Got it Captain?" A.J. said to the pilot before he turned and walked out of the cockpit and back towards the galley. "Rick, you back there?" he yelled, as he moved closer toward the back of the plane. He tripped over something big and long that was lying on the floor of the galley and landed flat on his face. "Shit," he said aloud and began to stand. It was dark in the galley and A.J. had no idea of where the light switch was located. Pulling out his butane lighter, he struck it to spark a fire to give him some light to help see what he had just stumbled over. A.J. noticed that it was a blanket he had stumbled over. It looked as if someone had balled it up and placed it against the wall to move it out of the way, but for some reason, the blanket felt hard.

A.J. reached down with the lighter in his left hand and used his right hand to pull the blanket aside to see what was underneath and realized he was looking at Charles. He was bleeding from the back of the head and out cold. "Charles, hey man, can you hear me?" A.J. asked, as he reached down to check for Charles' pulse. A.J. breathed a sigh of relief when his two fingers felt the beating of a pulse coming from Charles' neck. He shook him a couple of times until Charles came to. He helped Charles to his feet and asked him what happened. Charles explained how Marlie and Evelyn escaped bondage and hit him over the head with something, and the next thing he remembered was being helped to his feet. "Well, where are they now?" A.J. asked Charles, who was still trying to get his senses back together and control the bleeding that was coming from his head.

"I...I don't know; they came up from behind and the next thing I know, you were pulling me up off the floor," Charles replied. A.J. rushed over to the galley and grabbed the towel that was located on the small sink. He gave the towel to Charles and instructed him back to the front of the plane where all the action was happening. He handed his, now, partner an AK-47 Rifle and told him to start shooting. Charles did as he was told. He knew that they needed to get this plane off the ground and that they could not afford to get caught; bad enough Evelyn now knew the truth and was now out of his life for good. Charles pointed the rifle out the window of the cockpit and began to fire off round after round of shots. He was more afraid of getting caught, rather than of dying. He couldn't bear the thought of being in prison, not even for one day, let alone twenty plus years. Charles glanced to his right to see A.J. shooting out the other window as he continued to yell at the pilot to keep the plane in motion.

Outside the plane, Charles saw what seemed to be hundreds of police cars surrounding the moving aircraft. Stopping was not an option. He heard A.J. yell at the pilot to move faster and start getting off the ground now. Suddenly, the pilot did something unexpected. Instead of putting the plane in the air, he made a sudden left turn and headed towards the airport hangar, driving full speed. The sudden shift in the airplane caused Charles and A.J., as well as the pilot, to fall hard to the right and on the floor. The pilot quickly jumped back in his chair. He shifted the throttle down, which caused the plane to move in an upward motion while heading straight for the airport hangar.

"What are you doing, you idiot?" A.J. screamed, as he knew already what the pilot had planned. He pointed his gun at the pilot's head and fired one shot into his right temple, causing him to slump over in his chair like a twenty-pound bag of cement. A.J. turned to Charles just in time to yell out "Get Down!" Charles looked up just in time to see the nose of the private plane crash into the side of the airport hangar. He instantly dropped to the floor and the aircraft moved deeper into the hangar, tearing apart the metal walls as if they were paper. Glass was breaking and flying in every direction from both the hangar and the plane itself. The plane exploded like fireworks on the Fourth of July, causing everyone on the ground to duck and run for cover. The plane continued to roll deeper into the hangar like a rolling fireball. Fire trucks immediately began to get in position to extinguish the plane and the hangar at the same time.

Detective Mitchell rose from behind his car to see flames shooting high in the air. He walked from the back of the car and looked around to see if anyone was badly hurt. There were officers scattered about, some of them were hurt from either a gunshot wound or from the big explosion that just happened. He reached for his radio and began to send a call in for more help from the neighboring counties when he noticed a police car heading straight for him. The car stopped just a few feet in front of him, and the officer driving got out and greeted the detective. He opened the back door of the car and Evelyn jumped out and walked towards him. "Are you Detective Ray Mitchell?" she asked him.

"Yes, and who are you?" he replied, as he extended his hand to shake hers, like the southern gentleman he was.

"My name is Evelyn Hersher, Attorney Evelyn Hersher," she said, as she met the detective's hand and began to shake it in a greeting fashion. "I'm friends with Marley Cooper. She told me to find you. We know who's behind John David's murder. She said to tell you to meet her at the hospital; this is really big and I think you need to see this in person. A lot of people are going to go down for this." There was another loud explosion that came from the hangar and everyone dropped to the ground. Evelyn stood up and looked towards the hangar. She made a loud gasp as she realized that was the plane that she and Marlie had escaped from just a little while ago. She turned to the detective and told him how she and Marlie jumped out of the back of the plane and how Marlie was shot and now on the way to the hospital. She also told him that her ex was on the plane and that he was involved in all of this, just as much as a lot of people in this town. The detective told Evelyn that he would try to get there as soon as he could get a handle on the situation there, but informed her not to speak to anyone until he got there and keep him updated on Marlie's status. He called over one of the officers that was standing by his car watching the unscheduled fireworks display and instructed him to drive Ms. Hersher to the hospital and stay with them until further notice. The officer escorted Evelyn to his cruiser and back into the backseat. A few words were exchanged once more between the officer and the detective before the officer got back into the front seat and then drove off.

The detective turned his attention to the situation at hand and began to move towards the action to get information on how much damage was done.

CHAPTER 28

Deep in the fields of the landing strip, Cassie Walker helped her brother move farther into the woods that were at the end of the strip. As they moved deeper into the woods, Cassie could see the lights of the highway up ahead of them and she knew that if they could reach the highway, then they would be safe. They stopped briefly to catch their breath. Rick seemed to grow tired fast and having a bullet lodged deep in his shoulder didn't help much either. "Can you keep moving or do you need more rest? I think we are far enough out of sight that no one can see us. We can rest here awhile if you need," Cassie said to Rick, who was bent down with his one hand on his knee and the other holding his shoulder.

"Just for a few minutes," Rick answered. He looked over in the direction of the hangar and saw the huge fire that was going on there. "What happened? The last thing I remember, I was on that plane trying to stop those two ladies from getting off. One of those bitches shot me and I blacked out," he continued.

"Yeah, you did get shot. I watched the whole thing. You went up front and passed out. I knew I had to get off that plane and when I saw my chance, I just grabbed you and took it. I pushed you out the same window those ladies jumped out of and I got out too. Sorry if you got hurt, but I didn't know what else to do," she finished explaining to her newfound brother. Rick rubbed his side and felt the pain in his hip and upper thigh. It happened in the fall, but he was fine there. He was more concerned for his shoulder that was still bleeding pretty badly. He sat low and leaned his back against one of the many tall oak trees and closed his eyes briefly. He listened to the sirens of the fire and rescue trucks as they battled the fire that was now a full blaze.

"So, you're my sister? All these years you've been running around the house, driving me crazy, I just thought that you were just the judge's daughter. Did my dad, I mean *our* dad, know this?" Rick asked, looking in Cassie's direction.

"Yeah, I guess, but look, I just found out myself and I'm just as shocked as you are, so stop looking at me as if I was a part of keeping some big secret from you," she snapped back.

"All my life I remember you and *your* dad, and he has always treated me kindly until I found out what they were up to. Then, he and my mom started treating me like crap. They beat me and drugged me as if I were some of those girls they kept." She held her head down and wiped the tears that were starting to form in her eyes. Rick couldn't help but to feel guilty as she continued to talk about what she found out, and what her mom and their dad did to her to keep her from going to the police from the very beginning. "Do you remember the time we came to New York for Christmas and my mom told you that me and your dad had went to do a little personal Christmas shopping and we were gone till the next morning?" she asked Rick. "Well, truth is that we never went Christmas shopping. *Your* dad actually took me to this nightclub in uptown Manhattan. I don't remember the name of the nightclub or where it is cause he had given me something to drink, said it was a Sprite or something, but he didn't tell me he had put something in it. Had me feeling dizzy and shit, but I remember what I saw that night and what happened."

She stood up and walked towards another tall oak tree and looked in the direction of the highway. She took a deep breath and then turned to face her brother. A look of distaste and anger came into her face that Rick could clearly see, even in the dark of the night. "Listen girly, I had nothing to do with that. I was only 15 myself and I believed your mom when she told me that you guys went shopping," Rick replied in his own defense.

"I know, but you never questioned why he always took me places with him and he never took you. That's because you were so busy hanging with your friend and too busy to even care what was going on, but that's ok. I guess if you had known I was your sister, maybe you would have helped me back then and even when I got older," Cassie said in an almost forgiving tone of voice. "Maybe we can start over as brother and sister if we get out of this."

"Yeah, but you gotta get clean first," Rick replied.

"I never wanted to be like this. You think I asked to be constantly drugged up like some addict? I was never into drugs. I wanted to be a lawyer. I wanted to help fight the crime in this city. All the thieves and drug dealer and even the child traffickers and pedophiles. It disgusts me to see those men sexually abusing those little girls as if they were grown women. And most of those men, I remember being at my mom's house for many of her parties she gave and there are other judges and lawyers and their assistants. I know them all," Cassie said coldly, turning her face, as if she was about to vomit.

They both turned in the direction of the landing strip as they heard policemen voices headed in their direction. They were searching the area for any injured people and also fragments from the plane that would give them some kind of clue as to who was really on it. "We gotta get out of here now," Cassie said, reaching down and helping Rick to his feet. "If we can reach the road, we can catch a ride with one of the passing cars to get away from here and get you some help for your shoulder. It's still bleeding and I really don't need you passing out again; you're kinda heavy."

Rick chuckled a little as he placed his arm around his little sister's shoulders and they began to quickly head for the highway. Rick thought to himself about what it would have been like had he known back then that this was his sister. Flashbacks of her playing with her dolls in the front parlor of his home in New York; he also remembered how he hated for her and her mom to visit because it always seemed that his dad favored her more than him, so he decided to ignore them all and do whatever he wanted. He thought they didn't care what he did as long as he stayed out of their way, while precious little Cassie got all the attention. Had he really known what they were doing to her and she was his sister, maybe he would have taken the time to get to know her and love her as a little sister, and maybe then he could have protected her from all the bad things they did to her. Maybe he would have begged to go with them when they would take Cassie on all those so called shopping trips. Guilt flooded in him like a river dam that had just broken. Tears formed in his eyes as he looked down at his little sister helping to carry him.

"I'm sorry for everything Cassie," Rick said in a soft tone. For the first time in his life, he was apologizing to someone. Part of it was from all that she had been through, but for the most part, it was for murdering her mom. How would he be able to tell her this now that he knows she's his blood?

"None of this is your fault. I mean, you didn't know what they were doing to me and to all those little girls, or did you?" she asked, looking up into his eyes.

"Let's talk about that when we get somewhere safe, ok. I promise I'll tell you what I know, but it seems that you may know a little more than me, but we will talk," Rick answered. They reached the highway shortly after getting up from where they rested. Cassie had no trouble hitching a ride from a passing truck driver. Rick pulled his jacket tighter to cover the bullet wound in his shoulder as they climbed into the cab with Cassie going in first so that Rick could sit by the door to help shield his injury, so that the driver didn't get suspicious.

"Where you two headed?" the truck driver asked.

"The nearest gas station would be just fine, thank you," Rick answered, trying not to sound like he was in any pain, even though his shoulder was throbbing and burning from the wound.

"My brother's car ran out of gas a few miles back and we've been walking a long time before you picked us up and we're both tired from the walk, so if you could please drop us off at the nearest gas station, we can call our dad to pick us up," Cassie continued for her brother. Rick was impressed at the quick thinking she had just displayed. He knew they had that in common, only he was in so much pain at that time that he couldn't even think straight if he took a long time to think about it. He nudged his sister's arm and gave her a quick smile in approval of the lie she had just made up.

"Sure thing little lady, I'm sure your parents are worried about you two. You both look so young, almost too young to be out here alone. How old are you two anyway?" the truck driver asked them, now looking at them suspiciously.

"I'm 22 and she's 17," Rick replied sharply. The truck driver glanced over at Rick, then back at the road and continued the drive in silence. He reached over Cassie, who was in between the driver and her brother, and turned on the radio to some country station that was playing some upbeat song, which made him start to sing. The off key sound of his voice began to bother Rick as he tried to concentrate on their next move on getting out of town without getting noticed. He turned and glared at the driver as if he was ready to shoot him at any minute and began to open his mouth to tell him to shut up when the driver reached and turned the radio up a little louder, so that the song would drown out his voice. Rick closed his eyes and tried to focus on their escape plan and Cassie just laid her head on his good shoulder, closed her eyes, and tried to rest herself as the three of them drove down the highway and away from all the drama at the airport

CHAPTER 29

Back at the hospital, Marlie laid in the recovery room after the doctors removed the bullet from her back. Evelyn was there waiting to hear from the doctors as to how her friend was doing and when she could see her. The doctor informed Evelyn that they managed to retrieve the bullet and that she had lost a lot of blood, but she would be alright in about a week or two. He also told her that she could have visitors as soon as she wakes up, but because he thought Evelyn was her sister, he told her that only she could see her for now. Evelyn thanked the doctor and asked him to point her in the direction of which room she was in. The doctor signaled for the nurse, who was sitting behind the desk of the nurse's station, and instructed her to escort Evelyn to Mrs. Cooper's room.

Evelyn walked into the recovery room to see Marlie laying in the bed unconscious. She rushed over to her side and gently took her hand and placed it on her face. She was thankful that her best friend was going to be alright and bowed her head to give thanks to the man above. As she prayed quietly, she felt Marlie squeeze her hand. "Marlie, can you hear me? Can you open your eyes?" she asked aloud. "Please, open your eyes. Come on, you can do it."

"Will you stop talking to me as if I'm running some kind of race?" Marlie whispered, still in a groggy state, but coming too quickly.

"Good to know you still have that old southern wit," Evelyn joked.

"What, what happened?" Marlie asked.

"It's a long story, you just rest up and get better, ok? There's plenty of time to talk about what happened, but for now, I've contacted the State Prosecutor's Office and already got the ball rolling on all the arrest warrants we're going to need. Do you realize that this will be the biggest bust in the history of southern justice? So many people are about to go down for this operation they called 'Little Lamb', even that bastard Charles," Evelyn answered her friend.

"Charles was on the plane; I hit him over the head. Did I kill him?" she whispered.

"Well, if you didn't, the explosion sure did," Evelyn replied in an almost satisfying tone at the comment she had just made.

"What explosion? Was he still on the plane? What happened Evelyn?" Marlie tried to speak a little louder before she began to cough uncontrollably. Evenly poured her friend a glass of the ice water that was sitting on the table in Marlie's hospital room. She helped Marlie take a few sips to moisten her throat and help her stop the coughing. She told her that they would talk later, once she recovered enough. She told her how she was going to need her to be strong and healthy if she was to help take down all those clients from that operation she discovered.

"What about the girl, she was on the plane when we jumped? Did she get off too or was she on the plane when it exploded?" Marlie asked.

"I saw her once when we first entered the plane, but I never saw her after that," Evelyn answered. Moments later, Detective Mitchell entered the room as the two women sat talking to each other. He reintroduced himself as a police official and began to ask them questions. Evelyn did most of the talking for Marlie, who was still coughing off and on from the dryness in her throat. Evelyn began by informing the detective that she was too an officer of the law, (legal division to be exact) and that she was here on behalf of Marlie Cooper and wanted in on all the action of what was about to happen here in the town of Savannah Georgia.

Evelyn pulled out the files that Marlie retrieved from her husband's safety deposit box with all the information on Operation Little Lamb and more than enough evidence to put a lot of the officers of the court in prison for a very long time. She showed the information to the detective for him to review. The detective almost fell to the floor as he read all the names of the different judges, attorneys, bailiffs, and even some court reporters, all of which he knew and some of them he knew personally. Detective Mitchell sat down in the chair next to Marlie's hospital bed and placed one hand over his forehead and began to gently rub, indicating that he had a headache, and with all these names and all the illegal games these people have been playing, the detective felt as if his head was about to explode.

"Detective," Marlie whispered through her sore throat. "The men that followed me at the hospital, when my husband was murdered, were the same men that were in my house. One was named *Rick;* I remember hearing one of them call his name. These men were the ones I saw the night my husband was killed, I'm sure of it. They followed me to the bank as well; the bank manager has something to do with this also. His name is Evan Bradford. He tried to keep me occupied while these goons were on their way. I heard them in the hallway of the bank and I had to climb out of the window and hide till they left. They were sent to kill me, I know this because of the information John David had, which means he was going to go to the authorities with this information and someone had him killed to keep him quiet," she said before going into an uncontrollable coughing spell once more. Evelyn reached for the glass of water and helped Marlie drink some more. Once the coughing episode stopped, Marlie asked Evelyn to help her sit up so that she could be more comfortable. She took a few more sips of the water, which felt refreshing to her sore throat and began to review all the evidence with Evelyn and the detective.

"Ms. Hersher, it's my understanding that you knew one of the passengers on that plane back at the airport?" the detective asked Evelyn.

"Yes, but what do you mean *knew?*" she replied.

"I also understand that he was your fiancé?" the detective asked, without answering Evelyn's question. "Did you know about his involvement in this operation?"

"Yes he was, with *was* being the operative word, given that we are no longer together and no, I had no idea of any of this until Marlie showed me all this information. I confronted him about this in your office back at the police station and that's when he kidnapped Marlie and me and took us to the airport and put us on that plane. I told him that I was going to nail him to the wall for this. I told him how disgusted I was at him knowing that he was a part of some sick child sex trafficking ring and right under my nose, and who knows how long he's been involved in all this, but I promise you I will get answers from him," she snapped out angrily.

"I don't think you'll be getting anything out of him any time soon ma'am," the detective replied. "I take it that you don't know, but Charles Malone and the rest of the passengers died when the plane crashed into the hangar. It exploded, and no one survived. I'm sorry," Detective Mitchell said, trying to be as sensitive as possible while telling Evelyn what happened as Marlie sat listening.

"What about the girl?" Marlie asked the detective.

"When the firemen searched the plane, they only found three bodies. No other signs of anyone else were found," the detective answered and then turned to look at Evelyn and began questioning her again. It was just easier to talk to her because Marlie could barely speak and she needed to rest her voice as much as possible. "You said Charles put you two on the plane? How did you get off without being seen?" the detective asked.

"Once Marlie knocked Charles out with a metal pipe, we found a small window in the back of the plane, broke it, and climbed out. That's when one of the other men that were already on the plane shot Marlie in the back as she was climbing out. I shot back at him, but I don't know if I hit him. He did fall back into the plane after that. I think he may be one of the bodies they recovered," Evelyn replied.

"I see, it's a good thing you were able to escape and I'm glad that you two are all right because we have some heavy work ahead of us. This is really big stuff and I want to make all the right moves if we are going to take down all these people involved *and their* so called clients. We have already retrieved a lot of information on Operation Little Lamb from the two raids but none of it really had any names that would link this to the head person involved, but with that and now this information you have and the letter from Cassie Walker, it all make sense and now our entire judicial system right here in Savannah is about to crumble. The news reporters are going to have a field day with this if they find out anything and we don't need that," Detective Mitchell said. "This is a matter for higher authority."

"I've got friends in Atlanta that can help us in this matter. I've got a lot of connections back home. I'm a household name, you know," Evelyn said with a smile of confidence and cockiness, then grabbed her cell phone and began to dial a number. She asked for Pat Hardon, one of Atlanta's most powerful prosecutors with connections to the State Attorney General's office and a dear friend of hers. She began speaking to someone on the other end and then walked out of the room to have more privacy conversation.

The detective asked Marlie how she was doing and if there was anything that he could get for her. She just replied, "Catch the bastards that killed my husband," then reached for the glass of water again. The detective promised that it was just a matter of time before the people responsible for her husband's death would be arrested and sent to prison for a very long time. He also explained to her that this was going to get deeper than just her husband's murderer because from all the evidence they had collected, someone had him killed to keep him quiet. They were going to find out who by arresting all those people in those books and files. Someone was bound to talk if they put enough pressure on them. Detective Mitchell asked if he could take this information with him and wished Marlie a speedy recovery, then turned to leave the room.

Marlie stopped the detective before he could reach the door and asked him about Cassie Walker. She wanted to know if they had ever found her when she was abducted from this very same hospital she was in. The detective turned and walked back towards Marlie. He told her that it was confidential, but confided in her by telling her the truth. They had not found her as of yet, but was still searching the area for her whereabouts. "Do you have a picture of her by any chance?" Marlie asked.

"Yes, I do, but why-"the detective wanted to ask before Marlie cut him off. She cleared her throat and took another sip of water before her attempted to speak.

"I think she may have been on the plane with us. I remember seeing a young girl sitting in one of the chairs when we first got there. She looked as if she had done drugs her whole life, but she was so young. She looked me in the eyes and gave an expression as if she knew me. That's why I need to see a picture of her, please."

The detective took out his wallet and pulled a photo of Cassie Walker out and handed it to Marlie, who looked at it and confirmed that this was the same young girl on the plane with them. The detective immediately radioed into dispatch to have them contact the fire chief and to let him know that he was on the way to speak to him. That's all the information he wanted to put on the radio, remembering Cassie's letter to him saying not to trust anyone, especially on the police force. He told dispatch to let him know he would be there in about an hour then disconnected. "I'll find out if she was on that plane and I hope your right about her possibly getting off in time before the crash. But first, I need to check on my partner and the Chief, since ya'll in the same place. Call it a one stop shop," he said jokingly, then turned and walked out, heading to his partner's room first He couldn't wait to see her, even though he already knew she would be fine.

Distracted by the thought of his partner, he bumped right into the back of Evelyn, who happened to be standing right outside the door as the detective walked out. Awkward looks and apologies were given by them both as Evelyn told him that she would contact him later to let him know what she set up, then continued her phone conversation as if he never bumped into her at all. "Well, excuse me ma'am," the detective mumbled under his breath, then turned and walked down the hall towards his partner's room to see how she was feeling and also check on the Chief, who was involved up to his neck in this as well as other people he knew.

CHAPTER 30

Detective Mitchell spoke briefly to his partner, updating her on what they discovered and all the people involved. She had recovered from the drugs the Chief had given to her earlier that night when he kidnapped her. She told her partner that she was feeling fine now and wanted to help, but the detective insisted that she take time off to get better. He promised her that he would keep her posted on what happened when the arrest warrants were served, kissed her on the forehead, and gave her a small momentary embrace of passion then let her go. Detective Brown reached up and placed her hand on her partner's face and looked him in the eyes. No words were said at that moment, but Detective Mitchell knew exactly what his partner was trying to say. "I'll be alright and this will be all over soon. It will be like solving one big riddle that has a tragic punch line for a lot of people," he said and smiled at his partner. He leaned forward and kissed her long and passionately on the lips and then gave her another hug. He told her he would see her in the morning to make sure she gets home after they release her, then turned and walked out of the room before she could say anything.

A few doors down from his partner's room laid police Chief Berry, fighting for his life. How ironic it was for him to be here. His mission was to take Detective Brown out to the woods and kill her and leave her body in the shed that was in the middle of the woods. No one would find her body for weeks and by then, all tracks would be covered and business as usual, but he failed at his mission and now his punishment is life or death now.

Detective Mitchell opened the door of the Chief's room and quietly walked in. He looked around at all the tubes and machines that were hooked up to him, helping him to breathe and monitoring his heart rate with every beep. Pain medication being pumped into him through I.V. tubes to help manage pain, even as he laid there in a comatose state. He wondered how the Chief, of all people, could be involved in such a crime like this. The detective watched the monitors as they lit up with almost all the colors of the rainbow as the Chief laid there motionlessly. His chest moving up and down with every beep of the machines that were helping him to breathe. A sadness came over the detective for the police Chief and then that sadness turned to anger as he remembered how he got here in the first place. He leaned down and whispered in the Chief's ear, as if what he had to say was only meant for the Chief to hear and as if the chief could actually hear him. "Sorry Chief, but if death don't get you, *I* sure will," he said before he turned and walked out the room and headed to the fire station to talk with the fire Chief to see if they had possibly discovered the body of Cassie Walker in the rubble of the airplane.

CHAPTER 31

The truck driver pulled up to the gas pump of a gas station that was just off the fourth exit, five miles up from where the plane crash had taken place. Cassie and Rick both thanked the driver for the ride before getting out, as the driver wished them a safe journey home. They headed for the phone booth that was located outside of the convenience store of the gas station while the truck driver stayed behind and pumped gas into his truck, having no clue who these two kids were he had just given a ride. Rick searched his pockets for change to make a call, but could find none. He looked at Cassie, who quickly handed him a quarter to make a call. He smiled at her and gave her a little nudge, as if in approval of her knowing he needed change. They both gave a small giggle while Rick placed a few of the quarters into the phone and began to dial a number, long distance of course.

"Hello, Pop is that you?" Rick asked after a few seconds while waiting for someone to answer the line.

"Son, it's me. Where are you and are you alright?" Boss replied.

"Yeah, we're fine. I was shot in the shoulder, but I'll live. We just need a way out of this town, dad. A.J. is dead. He was on the plane when it crashed," Rick said.

"Who's we?" Boss asked. "Is Charles with you? What, A.J. is dead? What's going on down there, son?"

"We can talk soon as we get back, but for now, we need to get out of this town before they catch us. There are cops all over the place down here," Rick answered. Boss paused in his words and thought about the *we* Rick kept saying in his conversation and asked him one last question which was who he was talking about. Boss had just heard his son tell him that A.J. was dead and now he was telling his father that Charles was dead as well and that the person with him was Cassie. He promised his father that they would talk about all that had happened there and about how he'd just found out the truth. Rick didn't quite say what that truth was over the phone; he wanted to talk to his dad face to face on this one, with Cassie there also. They exchanged a few more words before Rick hung up the phone. He paused with his head down for a few minutes before he turned and looked at Cassie.

"Well, what did he say?" she asked her brother.

"He says he needs to make a few calls first to have one of his many connections pick us up and get us home. He said for us to find a room somewhere and call him when we get it, and he's gonna send someone to get us. They'll call us when they get here, so we need to find somewhere to lay low until then," Rick said. Cassie said nothing else and began to look around in all directions for any sign of a motel. There were all kinds of businesses around. Many diners, gas stations, as well as K-Mart, all within a five-mile radius with a string of motels lined in two rows on both sides of the street at the end of the road.

"We need to head in that direction. It doesn't look too far to walk if you can make it, "Cassie said, looking at Rick. "But we need to get you some bandages and antiseptic to clean that wound before it starts to get infected."

"I don't have any money on me right now, Cassie. I think I may have lost it back on the plane when we got off, so how are we supposed to get a room, let alone, any kind of medicine and bandages?" Rick began to say before dizziness overcame him and he stumbled back against the phone booth.

"Don't worry about that; right now, we need to get you taken care of. I have money to get what we need. Right now, we just need to focus on getting up the road and leave everything." Rick said nothing more and just trusted that his little sister knew what she was doing. He stood up and wiped the sweat from his forehead and looked around to make sure no one was watching them. He looked up the road in the direction of the motels that were at least a half a mile up the road, which seemed to feel like twenty miles to Rick, who was in pain and still losing blood from his wound. The two of them began to walk in the direction of the motels being careful to stay in the shadows of the dimly lit road so not to be noticed by any passing cars that may stop and begin asking questions, which neither one of them wanted. They both just wanted to find a room and rest.

When they reached the first motel, Cassie told Rick that she would go and get them a room. Rick stopped her and reminded her that she was too young to just walk up to a motel counter and get a room. He told her that he would go get it while she waited for him out there. Cassie agreed with her brother and gave him a hundred-dollar bill to pay for the room. Rick reached for the money and wondered how she could have this much money on her, but the pain in his shoulder quickly took that thought out of his mind. He walked into the entrance door of the motel. There was not much in there except for a small table that had what seemed to be old newspapers and magazines from six months ago. There was an old man sitting behind the counter of this cheap motel. He seemed to be watching some news report about the plane crash at the airport. Rick rang the bell that was on the counter, which startled the old man, causing him to jump out of the rocking chair he was sitting in.

"Can I help you there, boy?" the old man asked in an annoyed tone, as if offended by the interruption.

"Need a room," Rick replied.

"You by yourself I see. How long you planning on being here in town, boy?" the old man asked, this time looking Rick up and down.

"Just overnight. My dad's picking me up in the morning," Rick paused with his words and looked the old man up and down. "What's with all the questions, you got a room available or what?" Rick demanded.

"Sure boy, no need getting pissy about it," the old man said, as he reached for the room key marked 23 on the ring. He walked back to the counter and told Rick the room cost 40 bucks a night. Rick gave the old man the hundred-dollar bill and waited for his change. The old man took the bill and held it up to the light, verifying that it was real and not counterfeit. He handed Rick his change, as well as the key, and asked him to sign in. Rick signed the register book under some name he had just made up and took the key, thanked the old man, and walked out. "Check out is at noon, no later!" the old man yelled out to Rick as he walked back to his rocking chair to finish watching the news report.

Cassie watched her brother come out of the main office of the motel and back in her direction. He told her their room number as he approached her. They both walked over to the room marked 23 on the front of the door. Rick put the key in the hole and turned it. The lock clicked once and the door opened. Cassie walked in first with Rick following, shutting the door behind him. Cassie found the lamp on the table and turned it on. Rick collapsed on the bed and made a grunting sound, indicating that he was still in a lot of pain. He rolled over onto his back and took a deep breath, before sitting back up and trying to remove the jacket he was wearing.

"I need to dress that wound and get the bleeding to stop," Cassie told Rick, as she began putting the medical supplies she purchased on the table and opening things to get started. Rick removed his shirt to see that the white T-shirt he was wearing was now blood red. Nausea overcame Rick like an ocean wave crashing into the side of cliff. He held his head down and placed his hand over his mouth to hold down the stomach acid. "Let me help you with that, "Cassie said, as she began to remove his blood soaked shirt. Rick leaned back against the pillows on the bed and took a deep breath. Cassie walked back over to the table and grabbed the antiseptic and bandages. She took the antiseptic and poured some of it on the bandages. She told her brother to take a deep breath and that it would burn, but it would help to stop the bleeding. Rick readied himself the best way he could by biting on one of the pillows as she poured the antiseptic over his gunshot wound and placed the bandages over the top. He gave out a low scream from the burning sensation that almost felt worse than the gunshot wound itself, then calmed down and opened his eyes. He looked at his sister, who was busy patching up his wound, and began to feel that guilty feeling he had felt earlier that night for not protecting her when she was younger. Rick's guilt began to speak loudly to him.

How ironic is it for her to be helping you now, being kind to you when you never gave a shit about her? All the abuse she's been through and who knows for how long and what did you do? Turn your back on her and hated her for spending so much time with your dad, when all along dear old dad was abusing her in ways that are unspeakable. You never helped her or protected her like she's doing for you right now. Some kinda brother you are. His inner thoughts got the best of him at that moment and Rick did something he hadn't done since he was a little baby. He began to cry. Tears poured down his eyes like a river flowing downstream, during the rainy season. He took his sister's hand and just stared at her in the eyes.

She rubbed his hand and said," I know Rick, it's ok, just rest up so that you can be strong enough to call your dad so you can get back to your home."

"You're going with me. I want to confront dear old dad about what he did to you and I need you there with me. After that, I'm heading to Miami and I'm taking you with me. There's no way I'm leaving you behind. I will never leave you behind again as long as I live. I promise," Rick said.

"Wow, I didn't see that coming," Cassie said with a smile on her face, trying to change the mood. "But listen, I need to stay here and find Detective Mitchell. I need to let him know that I'm alright. The last he heard from me was in that letter I left him, when you and that other guy grabbed me from my room."

"That other guy that you hit over the head, you mean. Well, he was our cousin. He didn't know you were my sister either," Rick explained.

"Oh," Cassie said and then asked how he was doing and did she hurt him bad. Rick told her that his name was Mo and that he had died, but not from the injury she caused, but from that crazy bodyguard that was supposed to be watching over him. He pulled the oxygen plug and let Mo suffocate while he sat in his chair sleeping.

"Don't worry though, he was dealt with for murdering Mo. But the weird thing was, they couldn't find the doctor that was treating him. It's like he just disappeared. Dad thinks that the bodyguard killed the doctor too and dumped his body somewhere. They haven't found him yet." They talked for a few minutes longer before Cassie insisted that Rick get some rest. He did so with no arguments or hesitations. Cassie covered him up with the blankets that were on the bed, then turned on the television and sat down in the chair at the table and watched the same news report the old man had been watching in the main office of the motel.

CHAPTER 32

Rick woke the next morning to find his sister gone. She had left him a note with a few more hundred dollar bills, instructing him to get something to eat while he waited for his ride home. She also stated that she would call him when this was all over, but she needs to see justice truly served on this town of corrupt people we call Savannah's judicial system. She expressed her concern for him and asked him not to confront his father about any of this. She also said that she would explain her reasons for leaving when she called him and that she looked forward to going to Miami with her big brother to start a new life where no one knew who they really were. She signed the letter, "**Your new found responsibility**" with a smiley face at the end.

He was surprised that he didn't hear her close the door. But the pain and exhaustion cause him to go into a deep sleep. He sat up in bed and then walked to the door, opened it, and looked around in every direction. No sign of Cassie anywhere. Rick shut the door and walked back over to the bed and sat down. He picked up the phone and called his dad to let him know where to send a driver to pick him up, then hung up the phone. He had a bit of anger in his voice as he talked to his dad, but he really didn't care, as long as he made it safely back to New York.

Feeling a little better, he checked out of the motel and made his way to the little diner that was across the street from where he had stayed the night. He sat at the counter and ordered himself some breakfast. He asked the waitress where the pay phone was after she took his order and gave her a smile. She smiled back and pointed towards the back of the diner where the restrooms were. "It's in between the two johns," she said, as she smiled back.

Rick thanked her and made his way to the back of the diner. He reached in his pocket and pulled the change he had and put it into the payphone and called his dad. He let him know that he was at the diner across from the motel about five miles south of the airport. He gave his dad the name of the diner and what street it was on. After a few more words, Rick hung up the phone and went back to the counter and took his seat. The waitress came back a few minutes later with the food he had ordered. He thanked her again and asked if she could get him a newspaper. She shook her head yes and then turned and walked away.

A few minutes later, the waitress returned with the day's copy of the local newspaper. She handed it to Rick as he ate his breakfast. He took the paper and opened it to the sports section. He pretended to be reading sports highlights when in truth, he was trying to keep a low profile until his ride came to get him safely home. He thought about his sister and wondered how she was doing and if she was really going to meet him in New York. He also thought about how he was going to be able to keep his mouth shut around his dad, now that he knows the truth about what his dad did. His guilt rose in him again and, once again, began to speak loudly in his head. *How can you be mad at your dad when you worked for him? You enjoyed killing all the people he told you to and you never gave it a second thought until now. You know the truth about daddy, and you work for him, so what does that make you buddy?* His guilt yelled. He shook the thought out of his head and looked up from the newspaper he was pretending to read, just has he heard the bell on the front door ring. It would ring every time someone would enter or exit the diner. Rick looked up to see a chauffeur standing in the doorway with a sign that had Rick's name on it. Rick waved to the chauffeur and he walked to the counter where Rick was sitting.

"Are you Rick?" the chauffer asked.

"Yep, and I'm ready to go," Rick replied. "Let me take care of my bill and I'll meet you outside." The chauffeur shook his head, walked to the door, and out towards the car he was driving. Rick walked to the counter and asked the waitress to get his bill. He paid his bill and gave the waitress a nice tip, smiled at her, and thanked her for her services. The waitress smiled back at Rick and invited him to come back anytime, as she says to all the customers. He walked out the door and headed towards where the driver was standing. The driver opened the door for Rick to get in. After that, the driver got behind the wheel and drove off heading north to New York. Rick didn't look back but thought about his old friend A.J. and how he died in the crash. *He always said he would die going out with a bang*, Rick thought to himself and smiled. He leaned his head against the window, closed his eyes, and tried to rest on this long journey back home.

CHAPTER 33

Detective Mitchell walked into the fire station ten minutes after leaving the hospital. He spoke to some of the guys that were there doing house duties, as it is called. This job is mainly for the rookies that were new to the station and that the fire Chief felt weren't ready to handle the job of putting out fires just yet. The detective joked with some of them as he made his way to the fire Chief s office. He knocked on the door, then entered after hearing the Chief tell him to come in. "Hey Chief, you gotta minute?" the detective asked upon entering the room. The Chief motioned the detective to take a seat; he was on the phone with an important call from the coroner's office. The detective took a seat and waited patiently for the Chief to finish his conversation. He looked around the room, admiring all the plaques and awards the Chief and the station had received in the past and the present. Thoughts ran through the detective's mind and he wondered if he could really trust the fire Chief. He wondered if the Chief was involved in all this mayhem. "If he is, he's sure doing a good job of hiding it," the detective heard his mind say as he just watched the fire Chief, as he finished his phone conversation.

Shortly after the fire Chief hung up the phone, he began writing something down in the file he was working on, then closed it and looked at the detective with a friendly southern smile. "Hello detective, sorry for having you wait. I take it you're here to see what we found back at the hangar, right?" the fire Chief asked.

"Yes sir. Most importantly, the bodies you found on the plane. Were any of them of a young girl, possibly age 15 to 17?"the detective questioned.

"Well," the fire Chief said as he opened the file he was just writing in. "First off, we only recovered three bodies off the plane. One for sure was the pilot, he was in the captain's chair and we also were able to identify him from his pilot license that was still intact and in his wallet. It was one of the only things in it that was recognizable; the other was a picture of his family."

Detective Mitchell wondered to himself how it was going to be hard informing the pilot's wife of his death. He was an innocent man in all this. He quickly put the thought out of his mind; he was most concerned for Cassie. She was innocent as well and she was also a key witness to all this political corruption. She could help bring down a lot of people in the city of Savannah Georgia. This is big and he knew that he needed her to corroborate the file and books that Marlie Cooper had given him. He still needed to find out who had actually killer her husband and he knew that she needed closure from this and he wanted desperately to give her that.

"We never recovered the body of any young girl. My men search the plane at great length and the bodies they did find were located in the front of the plane. Sorry detective, but that's all the information that we have at this time. The coroner's office is still trying to identify the other two bodies as we speak," the fire Chief continued.

Detective Mitchell thanked the fire Chief for the information and asked that he keep him updated on any new findings, then turned to head for the door. He reached for the doorknob then paused, turned to the fire Chief and asked a personal favor. "Chief, do you think you could have a few of your men search the plane wreckage once more, just to make sure Cassie's not on the plane? She's very important to this investigation and if she's still alive, then we need to find her and fast," the detective said. "For me? I'll owe you big if you do this for me."

The Chief laughed and then scratched his head before speaking. "You know, before I became a Chief with fire department, I used to be on the Savannah P.D. I worked with your father for seven years. We were partners you know. He was a good man you know and now when I look at you, it's clear you're just like him, dedicated to your job. Sure son, I'll do that for you, no problem. I'll call you with whatever they find, ok," the Chief answered.

"Thanks Chief," Detective Mitchell said, then smiled at the compliment that he was just given and turned to walk out the door before the fire Chief stopped him once again.

"By the way, when are you going to marry that girl? You know the one, your partner. She's a fine girl. Will make you some beautiful babies and everyone knows she loves you, but you two just too stubborn to do anything about it," the fire Chief said as he sat back in his chair. "Better hurry soon before some other young fellow snatch her up."

"Yes sir," was all Detective Mitchell said before he walked out the door and shut it behind him. He was a little embarrassed by the Chief's last statement to him, but he also knew that every word the old man had just said were true. Then his thoughts went to Michele. He did admit to himself that he had strong feelings for her and he knew that she felt something for him, but they *both* knew it was against the rules for them to be a couple and partners, and neither one of them wanted to give up being a police officer or get transferred to another precinct. They both loved working in the city of Savannah. *How could it ever work?* he thought.

Detective Mitchell walked out of the fire station the same way he had come in, passing some of the same people he did when he first arrived. He walked to his car and got in. His mind was racing a mile a minute as he thought about Cassie Walker and wondered how she could have possibly managed to get off that plane with all that gunfire going on. He wondered if she somehow managed to get off the plane and was shot in the process. Maybe she was still at the airport, laying in the fields just off the landing strip hurt or worse, dead. His mind began to race in every direction as he reached for his car radio and called into dispatch to have them send any available cars back out to the airport to check the nearby fields for the possible the body of Cassie Walker. He decided to send out an APB (All Points Bulletin) on her once he made it back to his office; he then drove off heading in the direction of the police department. He would spend a few hours there and then go home for the night with hopes of getting a good night's rest for the biggest bust in the history of the Savannah Police Department that was going to happen tomorrow.

CHAPTER 34

Cassie Walker entered the Savannah Police Station about 7:30am, the day after the explosion at the Chatham County Airport. She was tired from the night's journey back into Savannah. The station was busy, as usual, with new law breakers coming and going and even one guy being disruptive over at the officer's desk, who seemed to be taking his statement from an overnight car crash or something. She stopped by the drinking fountain and took a few sips of water. It was refreshing to her lips, tongue, and throat, and all three seem to thank her in their own way. Wiping her mouth with her hand, she looked around the police station to see who could help her. The first officer she saw was busy on the telephone and writing something down at the same time. The second officer she saw suddenly jumped up from behind his desk and approached the man who was continuing to be disruptive and grabbed him by the collar and said something to him, then slammed him down in his chair so hard that the chair gave a cracking sound. Cassie took a deep breath as she stood there trying to get up enough nerve to approach the officer that had just manhandled some creep for being too loud. She looked around to see if there was anyone else she could talk to, but there wasn't. Wiping the moisture from her forehead, she walked up to the officer and got his attention.

"Excuse me sir, I'm looking for Detective Raymond Mitchell," she politely said, as she pulled the detective's business card out and handed it to the officer. "My name is Cassie Walker, I'm sure ya'll been looking for me." The officer took the business card and glanced down at it. He had already recognized Cassie from her picture they had of her when the missing person's report went out back at the hospital from her abduction. Surprised by her demeanor, the officer instructed her to have a seat and he would contact Detective Mitchell for her. He offered her something to eat and a warm blanket, which she appreciated, then he went back to his desk and contacted the detective.

"Detective Mitchell, I'm sorry to bother you at home and so early sir, but you won't believe who just walked into the station," the officer said with an astonished tone in his voice.

"This better be good," was all the detective said in response.

"Cassie Walker. Sir, it's incredible; she just walked right in sir," the officer said.

"Where is she now?" Detective Mitchell asked, as he quickly sat up in bed and reached for the same pants and shirt he had worn the day before.

"She's right here, sir. I gave her some food and a blanket. She looks pretty worn down and she was hungry. It's like she's been walking all night. She says she's fine though," the officer informed the detective. The detective didn't say anything. He was dressing and had the speaker button pressed on his phone. He listened to the officer speak as he brushed his teeth and washed his face. He walked back into the bedroom and grabbed his phone and jacket and headed for the door. Stopping by the mirror next to the front door, he gave a quick glance and approved himself as being presentable, reached for his car keys and out the door.

"Make sure she doesn't leave. Keep her in your sight till I get there. I'm on my way now. Don't let anyone near her and if any reporters show up, keep them as far away from her as possible. The last thing that poor girl needs is some idiot reporter in her face. I'll be there soon as I can," Detective Mitchell said before hanging up the phone.

Detective Mitchell jumped in his car and headed for the police station. He wanted to call his partner, but assumed that she was still in the hospital and decided against calling her. He made it to the station in what seemed to be record time, leaving his car parked directly in front. He turned off the engine and jumped out, ran up the steps and into the main lobby. Looking around the lobby, he noticed one of the rookie officers flag him down. He walked over to the young officer and greeted him. The young officer informed the detective that he was instructed to take him down to the holding cells once he arrived. They were keeping Cassie there for her safety and questioning her as well. The detective walked into the holding room where they had

Cassie. He looked around the room and asked whose idea it was to start asking this girl questions without proper authority present. No one answered; just silence filled the room, as if everyone had suddenly become mute. It was clear to everyone there, at that moment, that Detective Mitchell was not happy about this informal interview of this young victim/witness and now knowing that the Chief is involved in this operation, he really trusted no one there.

"I need for everyone to leave the room, now," Detective Mitchell said to the officers. The look on his face let everyone know that he was serious and just like that, the officers began to get up from their seats and head for the door.

As the officers headed out in a single file motion, one of the rookies turned and asked the detective in an innocent but curious southern tone. "Excuse me sir, but is it true the Chief is involved in a corrupt scandal? Buzz around the station is that he tried to kill himself because your partner caught him with some young prostitute in one of the motels by the airport. It's also said that he tried to kill Detective Brown to keep her quiet, but she got away. Is this true, detective?" the young officer asked with a look of expecting the detective to answer.

"Get out!" Detective Mitchell barked back at the young officer, which caused everyone to move even more quickly out of the room. Detective Mitchell walked over to the door and slammed it shut. He took a few deep breaths before he turned around and faced Cassie. "What the hell happened to you? Are you alright? The last we heard from you was in the letter you left with the nurse at the hospital. We thought you were kidnapped and maybe even dead. You said that if I was reading that letter, then you were dead. How did you get away?" he asked, trying to calm down a bit.

"Well, it's complicated, but I got off the plane the same way Mrs. Cooper did," she replied.

"Wait, how did you know that was Mrs. Cooper?" he asked.

"I recognized her from the pictures of her and her husband my mom had in her files. She has a little baby too, right? I bet he's a cute little boy." Cassie drifted in another direction with thoughts of the Cooper's baby as she was talking to the detective. "The guys who took me were on the plane when it crashed, so I don't think we have to worry about them anymore. They were a part of this too, working for some guy they called 'Boss'. They took me from the hospital and to the airport. They were planning on taking me to New York, like the other girls they've done that too in the past." Cassie held her head down and rubbed her eyes before speaking again. "Once they take you to New York, there's no turning back." She finished.

"What do you mean by that?" the detective asked, as he pressed the record button of the tape recorder that was sitting on the table along with a pitcher of ice water and a stack of paper cups.

"Think about it, Sir," Cassie said, as she stood up from her seat and walked over to the two-way mirror that was mounted on the wall and began to rub her hair with her hands. "All those unsolved missing persons cases you guys have had, where there's no trace of the girls in the entire state. What do you do when you figure that much out, just stop looking? Once you start to follow the paper trail, all roads lead to New York."

The detective now realized that this little girl knows more than they had thought. He wanted to continue to question her, but decided that he needed his legal forces here to witness this girl's incredible statement. He needed to contact Evelyn Hersher and find out if she was able to get the indictments needed to begin this big take down. He used the phone that was on the table and contacted Evelyn and asked her to meet him at the station. They had found the girl that was on the plane and that she was safe, but had a lot of information. "We need to do this right, no mistakes, so no one gets away, Ms. Hersher. We can now collaborate Cassie's statement with Mrs. Cooper's records she gave to me. We are gonna take down a lot of people on this one. Oh, by the way, she just told me about some kind of transport they did with these girls, taking them to New York City for auction," the detective said.

"If that's true, then this has just become a federal case, and you can call me Evelyn if you like. Most of my friends do anyway," she responded in almost a flirtatious tone, that the detective instantly picked up on.

"Well, ok Evelyn," he replied, almost smiling through the phone.

"How do we do this? I don't want to wait any longer on this. We have to end this today."

"Is there any way you can get me those files and books of John David's? Once you have a statement from the young girl, I'll need that too, in order to get the indictments started. I've already contacted my good friend Pat Hardon in Atlanta, so she knows about this and she's on our side. All she need is all the proper information and she can get the ball rolling," Evelyn explained.

"Getting everything you need will be no problem, it's just that I can't leave just yet. I have to stay and make sure nothing happens to Cassie. I don't want someone to come in and just walk out with her like Charles did with you and Mrs. Cooper," Detective Mitchell said.

"I understand. I did notice that your department has a lot of rookie cops on the job and their ability to pay attention to detail has not quite developed," she commented. The sharp tone of the comment she made offended Detective Mitchell just a bit, but he appreciated her honesty. He did realize that the department needed a few more vets than rookies, but with all the budget cuts they had to endure, he was happy just to have a team of men that may have been young but had heart and courage. He continued to talk to Evelyn a few minutes more as she explained to him the process of properly making these arrests and how careful they would have to be, given they would be walking into court rooms, while some may have trials going on and arresting the judges, lawyers, court reporters, and bailiffs.

"That is the entire court room staff, give or take a few innocent people," he said before hanging up the phone and turned to talk to Cassie. "Attorney Evelyn Hersher will be here in a few. She's from Atlanta and pretty powerful-"was all he said to Cassie before she cut off the detective's words.

"Charles Malone's fiancée? I've seen pictures of her before and I've heard Charles mention her a few times to my mom. They would always talk about his upcoming wedding to her and mom would say how she loved visiting Atlanta and couldn't wait for the ceremony. He always carried pictures of her in his wallet and loved to show them off," Cassie finished her words, then politely came back to the table and sat down.

"Oh. Well, she's on the way here. She's on our side and she will help us get you somewhere safe so that you can get cleaned and live the rest of your life in a sober world. I know none of this you asked for, but you are the key to putting an end to this nightmare." Detective Mitchell reached over the table and held her hands. He looked her in the eyes and saw the hurt and sadness in her eyes from all the years of abuse and drugs that she was given throughout her life. His heart bled for this young girl. He thought to himself about how her life may turn out. He knew that she deserved some kind of happiness and a fresh start.

Cassie pulled her hands away from the detective and slid back in her chair. "If it's all the same to you, sir, when this is all over, I'd like to leave this state. I need to move forward and put the past behind me. I have plans of my own," she said.

"I don't think that will be possible. You see, you're only 17, so that makes you still a minor in this state. So, by law, we will have to place you in foster care until we can place you in a safe foster home or until you are of age to be on your own. I'm sorry Cassie, but that's the best I can do. But I will make sure that you are placed with a real loving family. We will do thorough background checks on the people we send you to live with. Once you turn 18, then sweetie, whatever you want to do with yourself will be all up to you," the detective replied.

"Well, then that won't be a problem, given that my birthday is in three days. So, like I said earlier, I'll be leaving this God forsaken place and never look back," she said in a direct manner. The detective looked at her and just smiled. He thought to himself that this was a very strong willed young lady that knows what she wants. He knew that she would be fine once she left Savannah and no matter where she ends up, she'll have money to live comfortably, being that she is the sole heir to her mother's fortune, with the exception of money that was made for her sex trafficking ring. It would take months to sort all that out, but the detective didn't know that Cassie had her own money and more than enough to keep her safe.

Just as Detective Mitchell was about to ask Cassie another question, Evelyn Hersher walked through the door. She looked about as legal as they come, as far as attorneys. There was an aura about her that screamed she was out for blood, this made her look very attractive. Detective Mitchell looked Evelyn up and down, admiring the way that her dress hugged her, showing off the well-cut form of her body. Her hair was pulled back away from her face, which showed off her beautifully structured cheekbones. The detective, being a man, understood why Charles Malone was so in love with her. She was beautiful, sexy, and classy, all in one.

"Good morning Detective. I take it this is our victim/witness," she said, as she looked Cassie up and down. She extended her hand to formally greet Cassie and gave her a warm and friendly smile.

"It's nice to meet you Ms. Hersher," Cassie replied.

"Please, call me Evelyn, no need for formalities," Evelyn said and then took a seat across from Cassie. "There's a lot of information here that we need, so let's get started. Pat's waiting for my call with names for the indictments. I have the state police on the way to meet with us to review with them who they are going to arrest and where these individuals are located. My plan is to take down everyone involved at once. This way there will be no chance of anyone getting away and by snatching up some of these key players, with any luck, this will lead us to the leaders of this ring."

Cassie laughed as she listened to Evelyn's strategy. She thought to herself of how they already knew who one of the leaders were, but hadn't figured that part out yet. She began to explain to them that her mother was one of the founders of this operation and the other founder lives in New York. He mainly handled the auctions and took care of all *"new shipments"*, as it was called. She explained how this was the word they used when new girls were shipped to New York for auction. She continued to tell them about the routine that was used when new girls arrived and how they were prepared and displayed for men and women to buy them for the night. The highest bidder would win and was allowed to do whatever they wanted to these young girls. Some of the girls survived the night and some didn't.

"What happened to the girls that didn't survive the night?" Evelyn asked, as she wrote down Cassie's statement.

"They went away," Cassie replied. "I'm not sure where, but they did, and all traces of them were erased from the house." Knowing that time was a big factor, Evelyn and Detective Mitchell felt that they needed to act fast. They both looked at each other and then back at Cassie.

"Who is this other founder you mentioned. He lives in New York you said. Can you tell us exactly where he lives?" the detective asked Cassie, who seemed to be willing to give as much information as she could.

"I already told you detective, remember the letter I wrote you. If you still have it, his name is mentioned. I don't know of any last names, they always called him Boss, so that's all I know," she continued.

There was a knock on the door as it began to open. Detective Brown walked in, along with the several officers from the Georgia State Police. Everyone walked in and took a seat with the last person in shutting the door behind him. They were quickly briefed on their findings and who was involved. Evelyn excused herself to make the call to Pat Hardon for the arrest warrants so that they could jump into action. Detective Mitchell walked over to his partner and asked her how she was feeling, giving her a look of displeasure for her being there knowing that she was just released from the hospital.

"Don't give me that look. I'm fine, really. The doctor said that all of the drugs were out of my system and I'm cleared for takeoff," she said, smiling at her partner, then giving him the same look of displeasure for him even thinking that she was not well enough to be there.

"I'm just saying," he replied, then rubbed her shoulder as a sign of relief that she was ok.

"So, I hear that's Cassie Walker?" she asked, changing the subject.

"Yeah, she walked in a few hours ago," he answered, looking down at his partner. He thought about how she could have died when the Chief kidnapped her and in that brief moment, he thought how his life would not be the same if he lost her. She meant more to him than he had ever known and he knew at that very instant that he was truly in love with her. Everyone around them had always known that eventually they would become a couple; it was just a matter of time. He touched her face with a gentle caress and whispered to her the words "I love you".

"Ray," she whispered back before he turned and walked away from her and focused his attention back on the task at hand. Detective Brown just stood in her place and watched her partner walk back to the other side of the room. She smiled and then looked around to see if anyone had noticed. She regained her composure and then took a seat at the table along with everyone else, as Evelyn continued to fill them in on today's arrests.

CHAPTER 35

By 1:00am, faxes for the arrest warrants began to pour in. One after another, warrants for judges, lawyers, bailiffs, and two court reporters were spitting out of the fax machine. Detective Mitchell would be leading the sweep. He instructed everyone to their positions. Detective Brown's team would be in charge of having some of the men go to the offices of some of the lawyers and the judges that don't have court hearings scheduled for today. The second team were to issue warrants to those that were off today and maybe spending time at home. Detective Mitchell stated that he and the state police would go to the courthouse and make the arrests there. Everything was set up and all watches synchronized for one hour from now. This bust was to take place before lunchtime. Everyone left the police station at the same time, heading for their assigned destinations to get in position. No one was to make a move until they all hear Detective Mitchell say the word *Go*. This would take about thirty minutes for everyone to get in position. Everyone was to send word on their two-way radios when they were ready and, when instructed, they were to enter their assigned buildings and retrieve their targets without incident. If all goes right, Detective Mitchell knew he would for sure get a promotion, maybe the newly opened police chief position. Detective Mitchell waited until he had confirmation that every unit was in position and ready to move in before giving the word: "GO!"

Tuesday August 23, 1997 11:00am

When the word was given, everyone sprang into action. Many arrests were made that day, most of the suspects went quietly and without incident. A few of the judges and lawyers were at their homes, playing with their children, working from home, or just relaxing but all were embarrassed by the public humiliation of being arrested and for the reasons why. When Detective Mitchell received word that every indictment was served and arrests were made, it pleased him to know that everything went according to plan. He gathered his team of state police officers and gave them instructions on how the approach would go. Given they were at the courthouse, which was in the center of downtown and lunchtime coming soon, the detective wanted to get this over with as soon as possible. He checked the time on his watch and noticed that it was twenty minutes before noon; he knew that they would have to move fast if they were to collect everyone before the downtown area became crowded with hungry workers going out for lunch and the last thing they needed was a crowd.

He and the rest of his team walked into the main lobby of the courthouse and gathered by the receptionist desk to get a view of the day's schedule for the judges and lawyers they were looking for. Six of the warrants were served with no complications, but the seventh warrant would prove to be a little more difficult than expected because the person that they were after, was a well-known judge in the community, and his reputation would be at danger. The judge that they were after was named Judge William Hart. He was known for his crusades in protecting children from abusive, drug addicted, pedophiles parents or caregivers. He had numerous commercials out advocating protecting the children of the community. He was also known as one of the hardest judges in the city on criminals that commit crimes against young innocent children. The people of Savannah liked him so much that they re-elected him as judge four times. Judge Hart had locked himself in his office and had threatened to shoot anyone who crossed the threshold of his office.

Minutes ticked by as they waited for the judge to come out of the office, but when he refused to surrender, Detective Mitchell knew another action would have to happen and fast, before the rush of people came pouring like rain on their operation. "Judge Hart, we're gonna need you to open the door, sir. Don't make us have to break the door down!" the detective yelled into the office through the door. There was no answer from inside the office. Detective Mitchell instructed some of the officers to go outside to the first floor window and see if they could get a look inside the judge's office to see what he was doing. The officers retreated out the main lobby door and quietly crept around the building to Judge Hart's office, then formed a semi-circle under the ground floor window. Without saying a word to each other, one officer signaled to the other to give a quick look in the window. The office slowly rose halfway up to the right corner of the window and looked in. He shifted his head to the left and then to the right and then back down. Saying nothing at all, the officers backed away from the window before he told them his findings.

"Ok, he's in there standing just to the right of the door with a handgun pointed at the door. He also blocked the door with a desk. Looks like he's not gonna give up so easily; we may need to take him down by force," the officer reported. They made their way back inside the courthouse and gave Detective Mitchell a full report of their discovery, as some of the people that were already in the lobby began to stop and watch the action that was unfolding in front of them. Some people came out of the courtrooms, speaking loudly and watched the judges and lawyers being placed in handcuffs right in front of their eyes.

"Lunch time," the detective said, as he looked at his watch and began to become frustrated with himself for not expecting this to go down this way and needed to get this under control and over with *now*." Judge Hart, we need you to open the door, sir or we will be forced to come in with force. We really don't want to do that, being we are in the courthouse and it's about to be really busy out here with a lot of people and we don't want anyone getting hurt, sir!" Detective Mitchell yelled again through the door. There was still no response from the judge, just silence from inside the office.

As the main lobby of the courthouse became even more crowded with people, one of the officer's noticed a reporter coming out of one of the courtrooms. "Detective Mitchell, here comes the press," he said, as he continued to watch the reporter walk out with a camera crew following.

"Shit," the detective whispered, dropping his head and then raising it quickly; he yelled at the door once more. "Hart, open the door! Let's get this over with now. We got you man, so you might as well give up. Why are you making this so difficult? Now, you know as well as I do that there are only two ways of getting out of this. You can either open the door without any problems or we can break it down; either way, we're coming in."

There was a loud crashing sound that came from out of the office the judge was in. Everyone standing outside the door heard it, then quickly backed away looking puzzled. Shortly after, the news crew ran in the direction of the detective and the state officers, cameras pointing, and the reporter already speaking live of the events taking place. Detective Mitchell signaled for a couple of the officers to intercede before they could reach the judge's door. "Judge Hart, are you alright?" the detective yelled again to the door, then waited to hear a response. Nothing came from inside the office, just silence. Detective Mitchell decided to break the door down and was going to do it on the count of three. "One, two, three!" the detective yelled, and he and the other officers burst through the door with the force of an army.

Once inside, they discovered what had made the loud sound. Judge Hart laid face up on the floor with a gunshot wound to his head. Blood splatter and chunks of brain pieces raced along the walls of his office where he stood and ran downward, as if the blood actually poured out of them. Everyone who entered cringed at the site and backed away from the room. By this time, the reporter and camera crew had full coverage of what was inside the office and wasted no time putting it live on the air.

"This is Stacy Perkins from Channel 3 News with a special report. I am standing outside of the Savannah county courthouse, where just minutes ago, the body of Judge William Hart was just discovered about twenty minutes ago dead in his chambers with an apparent gunshot wound to the head. No word as to what exactly happened at this time, but we will bring the information to you when we receive it. Live from the Savannah County Courthouse this is Stacy Perkins reporting."

The crowd grew larger and larger as the state police began taping off the area of the Judge's chambers. Detective Mitchell instructed some officers to keep the public and the reporters out of the way as he surveyed the surroundings and noticed more news trucks beginning to arrive and set up their equipment. Cameras flashed from every direction as people walked past, taking pictures of the scene, which made the detective angry at the fact that the operation did not go according to plan and now he had the press to deal with. Detective Mitchell walked back into the Judge's chambers and began to question the coroner of his findings, even though he already knew what the findings were. He spoke with him for a few minutes before his cell phone rang, startling the detective. He reached into his jacket and pulled it out, excused himself and answered his phone.

"Mitchell," he answered.

"Ray, it's me. We heard about the shooting over at the courthouse. One of the judge's right?" the caller asked. It was his partner on the other end and he knew it. He knew the sound of her voice like the back of his hand and for a brief moment, he was excited that she had called and felt that he needed to hear her voice to give him comfort and strength to deal with the mess that Judge Hart has now created.

"Yeah, Judge Hart killed himself as we were trying to arrest him. He left his brains all over the wall," he said, as he stood over the judge's body. "We're searching his office now for any evidence that he was actually involved in that operation," he continued. As the detective discussed what they found to his partner, one of the state police officers signaled for his attention. He noticed that the officer had a piece of paper in his hand and was reading what was written on it. The officer handed the paper to the detective as he approached and shook his head. It was a note to the judge, but had no name of whom it came from.

"Detective Mitchell, I think you should see this. Looks like someone else knew the judge's dirty little secret," the officer said The detective took the note and read it: *The sins of the wicked will stand and be punished. This* was all that was written, other than the judge's name on it. This intrigued both the detective and the state officer as they looked at each other with the same look of confusion.

"Hello Ray, are you still there?" Detective Brown asked over the phone. She knew that her partner had been distracted by something on his end.

"I have something strange here," he replied. "We just found a note addressed to the judge, but it seems to be some cryptic shit here," he answered. "It says that the wicked will stand and be punished. What that means, I have no clue," he replied, sounding extremely puzzled by the note.

"That is strange," Detective Brown spoke. There was a tone of bewilderment in her voice as she spoke. "We found similar letters like that in three of the attorney's offices as well. They all are exactly the same, addressed to each one personally and something about the wicked being punished." No one spoke for a few seconds, which seemed like an hour, but was only a few seconds. They were all puzzled by the messages that were found. It was obvious to them all that someone else must have found out about what these people were involved in and sent them each a warning. What that warning was surely wasn't clear at the time. The detective informed the officer that he was going to head back to the station to begin the questioning phase of this sting and also to talk more with Cassie Walker, who was still there under guarded protection. He instructed him to stay and finish up there at the courthouse and then he and his men were to meet him later and also to make sure none of the press standing outside gets in.

After giving the officer his instructions, the detective turned and left the room, headed back to his office and his partner. He had to push his way through all the reporters and their camera crews that were posted outside the judge's chambers, trying to get information on what was going on. He continued his conversation with his partner, telling her that he was on the way to the station and he would see her there, before hanging up and heading to his car. *This was not supposed to end like this. It was to be quick and quiet. Why did that idiot have to shoot himself? There goes that promotion you wanted!* Detective Mitchell's mind yelled at him as he drove back to his office.

The station was overcrowded with people from the arrest, as well as others, and even some reporters that had followed the story all the way to the police station. There were cameras rolling and flashing from reporters and general people trying to get photo shots of the many judges, lawyers, and bailiffs that had been arrested and brought in for booking. This was going to be the story of the year for the town of Savannah and Detective Mitchell knew it. He also knew that this story would make national headlines and he also knew that this was far from being over. In fact, he knew that the FBI would be getting involved once they inform them that this child sex trafficking ring goes all the way to New York City.

Walking into his office, the detective closed the door, then sat down at his desk and held his head in his hands. He was both exhausted and angry at today's events at the courthouse and how that coward of a judge could take his own life like that. *I guess he was more afraid of prison than death*, his head spoke to him again. He thought about those that were arrested and wondered if any of them was willing to cut a deal with the DA in exchange for giving up the ringleader or leaders for that matter.

Moments later, Detective Brown entered into the office with a look of concern on her face. Detective Mitchell could see the look in her eyes and for a moment, just stared at her. "It's like a zoo out there; why you hiding in here?" she asked.

"Just trying to take a moment for myself, before I jump into the middle of all that out there," he answered, only telling her half the truth when inside, he felt like he failed his mission.

"I heard it was Judge Hart that killed himself in his office as you guys were making your arrest," she said. "Is Cassie still here, is she safe?" she continued to question her partner.

"Yeah, she should be down in one of the holding cells. We put her there so that she would be safe and there's guards watching over her at all times, so no one can get in or out. She's free to come in and out of the room but she has security with her wherever she goes," he replied.

Detective Brown sat down in the chair opposite her partner's desk and just stared in his direction. She knew something else was bothering him besides the botched arrest of Judge Hart. She wanted to ask him, but decided against it. Just then, the phone rang, startling both of them. It was Evelyn Hersher on the line. She informed the detective that the FBI got word of the botched arrest at the courthouse and decided to take over. They also got the location of 'Boss' and the rest of his gang and were headed to New York to arrest them. She also told him that they were planning to send men down to Savannah to collect the information that they had on the entire operation and use it to properly see that justice is served. And that they planned to do their own full investigation into Savannah's judicial system and possibly do some firing. "Heads are gonna roll on this one detective, but please don't breathe a word of this to anyone except your partner. You two are in the clear," she finished.

"I see, Ms. Hersher. But where does that leave us? My partner and I?" Detective Mitchell asked.

"They also mentioned that you and Detective Brown had already been investigated and they found nothing on you two, but they did find stuff on some of your men though. They said that a lot of them are involved in some way or another to all this, starting with Chief Berry. All of you work under him and they found that some of them did extra work for your Chief," Evelyn continued.

After finishing his conversation with Evelyn, Detective Mitchell hung up the phone and sighed deeply. He felt as though someone had just punched him in the stomach with a slug hammer from the information he had just received. He looked over at his partner and shook his head before he began to speak. "Doesn't look good babe. The feds are headed here as we speak to take over the whole investigation. She said we have corrupt cops right under our nose and they are coming to bust them. We're in the clear though, she told me, and we are to say nothing to no one," he began.

"Who are they coming to get?" Detective Brown asked as she jumped up from her chair.

"She didn't say, but she did say that some of the guys out there are corrupt. They were doing side jobs for the Chief, who we both know is bigger than a pig playing in mud," he continued. "She also said that it's very important that we say nothing to no one about the feds coming, plus I don't know who to trust anymore."

"What the hell is going on here? How did this go from a murder case to corruption right under our nose? Will we ever know who killed John Cooper? That's what this investigation was supposed to be about in the first place, now we find out that there are fucking child molesters in our own judicial system here in Savannah. Where the hell did we go wrong?" Detective Brown shouted, as she slammed her hand on the desk top and walked towards the door, cracked it open, and looked out. "This is going to be epic," she whispered.

Detective Mitchell thought about Cassie Walker and how she was holding up down in the holding cell. His mind began to visualize the feds coming in and arresting over half his staff of police officers who had sworn to serve and protect this city, but instead, contributed to its crime rates. His thoughts began to tease him saying that he should have handled things better than he did. He was the lead investigator of this operation and he couldn't even figure out who killed the lawyer and let alone, handle the arrests differently.

He slid back in his chair enough to open the top drawer of his desk where he usually had a bottle of whiskey that he would sip from on those stressful days. He reached in for the whiskey when he touched what felt like an envelope. He pulled it out of the drawer and looked it over. Noticing that it was addressed to him, but had no return address or post mark on it, which meant that it had to be hand delivered. He opened the envelope and found a greeting card inside. The handwriting was not familiar to him and it was not signed by anyone, just a note written. Turning the card over, he examined the picture on the front. It was a picture of a clown with a very big frown on his face and teardrops falling down on the side of his face. Below the clown face were the words *Maybe next time*. He opened the card and began to read the letter.

"Funny how reversal of fortune really works. When you think something is going right, it's really going wrong. I thought you were a smart detective, given that your schooling history is outstanding on paper. Yes, detective, I did do the research on you a long time ago. You see, you were chosen for this mission because we did know that once you were tipped off about the whole operation, we knew that you would dig deeper and would come up with something bigger than expected, like discovering treasures that have been buried for a 100 years. I never thought you would drop the ball though. How could you not connect the puzzle pieces, which were laid out for you? I had come to the conclusion that you needed a little help, so I sent my son down there to drop a few clues for you, in hopes that you would pick them up. I have to admit, you almost figured it out, but some of the clues I left for you went over your head. You have to understand something detective, my entire adult life I have dedicated myself to the town of Savannah, only to find that your judicial system is made of all different types of criminals. They all have a past that allowed me to begin my operation in your town. Unfortunately, there was one nosey little lawyer that got too close to ruining my plans and let's just say I needed him out

of the picture. The hit was carried out by my son and he did a fine job of it as well. Almost had his lovely wife too, but Charles couldn't do the job properly and may he rest in peace for that matter. This leads me to pick up where you all dropped the ball. The arrests you pulled off today were outstanding, even the botched arrest of Judge Hart was amusing, but that was just the surface to scratch. My work is bigger than you can imagine and no one will ever be able to stop me. As you see, trying to arrest Ale Gracie would have given you the upper hand and maybe, just maybe, you would have caught up to me by now, but you guys are idiots when it comes to police work. You don't know how to keep your mouth shut when you discover things. I have many of men working for me all over your little town so you will never know who to trust. Gracie was shut up because she was weak and slipped too much, but now, my secrets and hers she did take to the grave with her. This leaves me to one last and final concern, my daughter, Cassie. Yes, I did say my daughter. She's young and innocent, but she also can be very smart. I understand you had her in one of your holding cells. And yes, 1did say had. Another unfortunate thing /for you. Try and understand detective, you guys are not as bright and especially when it comes to witness protection. How is it that you think placing someone in a holding cell would keep someone safe? Foolish southern folks you all are. My daughter will be returning to me within the hour. She was released by one of my men there. No one even bothered to question him when he walked out the door with her and shipped her back to me. Another job well done, detective. You have a lot more learning to do in the detective department if you plan to replace Chief Berry in the near future. Too bad it won't before catching me. That will never happen; you're not yet ready to meet me but just know that one day, we will meet face to face and then you will know the truth and you might even make it back alive."

The message was eerie and very cryptic, which left both the detective and his partner confused. Not sure what to make of the letter and what it meant that they would meet face to face someday, they both decided to keep this information to themselves and try to solve this mystery alone. They could trust no one but themselves. Detective Mitchell stared at his partner for few minutes before speaking. "We need to end this ourselves, no one here can be trusted and we now know which cops are corrupt and we have to-"

The detective's words were cut short by commotion coming from the lobby of the police station. The FBI had just arrived and all hell was breaking loose at that very moment. Federal agents arresting police officers was just as bad as the arrests of all the officials in the judicial system of the great city of Savannah. Detective Mitchell stood at the door of his office with his mouth wide open. He was shocked at the scene which played out in front of him. Some of the officers being arrested were with the force for a very long time and he knew their families, and a couple of the men he even played the role of best man for them. He began to walk toward the main lobby to see the commotion up close and personal when he was immediately stopped by a federal agent.

"Detective Mitchell, you need to come with me back to your office," the FBI agent instructed more than stated. "There are some things that you and your partner need to know." The detective and his partner headed back to his office, followed by three FBI agents. The last one in closed the door and began to inform them of the information they had and to get information from the detective about this case. Their plan was to join the rest of the Federal agents that were already in New York city to make the final arrest of the Boss and the rest of his men and close the case of the *Savannah Crimes,* as it was now called, with credit given to Detectives Mitchell and Brown for their cooperation in this investigation, as well as the Federal Bureau of Investigations.

CHAPTER 36

Cassie looked out at the Atlantic Ocean and inhaled the salty air as she felt all the pressures of the past week release from her body like a weight being lifted off her that had been there for many years. She closed her eyes and pictured herself flying over the ocean like the many seagulls that flew in the sky over both water and the land. She realized that she was alone in the world with a bank account the size of Mount Everest, thanks to her corrupt mother and the two overseas accounts that she had that no one ever knew about, except for herself, of course, and her mother, who was now dead and gone. Trying to plan her next move, she glanced back at her new found brother, who was still sleeping in the second bed in the room, and wondered how he really felt about having just discovered that he has a little sister and especially one that was now a recovering addict, thanks to her corrupt parents. She suddenly began to feel sick at the stomach and felt as if she may puke at that very moment. Her body began to shake as sweat began to run down her face like a leaky faucet that dripped nonstop. Cassie collapsed on the balcony and began to go into convulsions. The noise of glass breaking and things being   knocked down caused Rick to wake. He jumped up with his gun pointed in the direction that he thought the noise was coming from.

Still half asleep and half awake, Rick looked towards the balcony and quickly noticed Cassie on the ground having a seizure. He jumped out of the bed and ran to her side, reaching for her head and holding her as she continued to convulse for a few minutes longer. Fear ran through him as he held his sister's head tightly as he tried to ease her stiffened body. "It's alright, little sis," was all he could manage to get out, as he felt her body began to relax and her muscles loosen from the tense ball they were in just a few minutes earlier. Cassie began to cough as she tried to catch her breath. She began to cry as she realized what had just happened and felt a small hint of embarrassment. She held her brother a little tighter as she sobbed in his arms while he slowly began to rock back and forth. "Let's get off this cold floor Cassie, you need to rest," Rick said, as he stood up and then reached down and picked his sister off the concrete floor of the balcony.

"I'm sorry about this Rick. This is my issue, not yours. I understand if you don't want to deal with all this. Leave, I'll be just fine. I'll just check into a rehab and clean myself up. I never asked for any of this, so it's up to me to get right. After that, I have plans of my own," she said in a weak voice.

"Listen young lady, I know that we just found out that we are blood and all that, after knowing each other for so long, but that doesn't give me a free pass to just leave you, especially in the condition that you are in. If you would let me, I'd like to have a chance to get to know you as my sister, instead of that pesky little brat I remember in my teens," he said with a light chuckle in his voice, as he wiped her face with a towel soaked in cold water that he had retrieved from the bathroom.

"They lied to both of us and your father had you kill my mom. I did love her, even though she put me through hell just to keep her secret. She deserved to be punished for what she did to all those girls, but what I don't understand is that why would your father have you kill her when you knew all along that she was his girlfriend?" she asked.

"At the time, I really was only doing as I was told. That's how dad operates. You do as he says without question. I did find it a little odd that he wanted Gracie killed after dating her for so long, but he just told me that she was angry that he had dumped her and that she was going to report him to the feds for the operation he was running," Rick explained. "Had I known that you were my sister, I would have never done the job. She was always nice to me and I had no beef with her. I was just doing as I was told to help keep my dad out of prison," Rick continued to explain.

Cassie closed her eyes and began to fall into a deep sleep. Rick stood beside the bed and watched his sister sleep. Guilt and frustration began to flow through him like snow melting off the side of a mountain and running downstream at a rapid pace. Sitting on the bed next to where his sister slept, Rick closed his eyes and tried to remember his childhood, mostly the teenage years when he would see his dad with Cassie when they would leave the house, and how she always had a look of dread or fear on her face as she sat in the backseat of the car. Back then, Rick just assumed that she was being some spoiled little brat, mad cause she wasn't getting her way. Now he knew the truth.

The phone rang, startling Rick out of his deep thoughts. Hesitating for a few moments, wondering who could have known they were staying in that particular motel in Miami for that matter. Another thought quickly came to his mind that maybe someone just dialed the wrong room. He smiled at the thought as he picked up the phone and said hello. "Hello son, it's good to hear your voice," the caller spoke. Rick instantly knew that the caller was his father. He dropped the receiver as he gasped deeply from the shock of hearing his father's voice, then picked it up and began to speak.

"How did you find us?" he asked in a low tone as he tried to cover the fear that had swelled quickly in his throat. He began to sweat as he listened to his father speak.

"Have you forgotten who I am? I have connections all over this country and when I need something found, well, you know the rest," Boss replied. "But that's not the real concern here, is it son, and we both know that. You were supposed to return to New York with the girl with you and now I find you shacked up in some filthy motel in Miami of all places. I am going to assume that you hiding out from the cops, being you got out of Savannah; good job on that, by the way. Now that you and the girl are safe, I've sent my driver to pick you two up and bring you home. He'll be arriving within the next couple of hour, so pack up your things and the little drug addict, check out, and my driver will meet you in front of the motel. I'll see you home in a few days son," Boss said and spoke nothing else.

"Things have changed dad," Rick said coldly.

"What's changed? The plan has not changed," Boss replied in a questioning tone.

"Everything has changed Dad. Why did you really have me kill Gracie? She was Cassie's mother and you had me take her out as if she was some kind of crook. And by the way, she's not just some drug addict. I now know how she got this way and it's not her fault. It's the fault of a couple of dirty bastards that had no right to do something like this to a person at such a young age," Rick told his father. Anger grew fiercely inside Rick as he listened to his father try and explain to him the situation with Cassie and the judge. He told him lie after lie in regards to Cassie and her condition, saying that she did this to herself hanging with some of the wrong kids in the neighborhood. As for Judge Walker, he just kept to the same reason he gave to his son when he first sent him on this mission.

"Things have gotten out of hand son, but not out of control. I will make everything alright once you and the girl get back here safely, you'll see," His father said, speaking in more of a softer tone, hoping it would help to comfort his only son.

"Why do you keep referring to her as *the girl?*" Rick snapped back. "Her name is Cassie and you know that, given you helped name her. I know the truth dad, no more lies. I know what you've been up to all those years ago when you would take Cassie shopping for the day, as you called it. Back then, I always wondered why you would never let me go with you too, but now I know. I know it all." Rick caught himself beginning to raise his voice, then stopped talking and took a deep breath before he continued to talk to his father. "Listen dad, we will not be coming back to New York. We are going to make a fresh start out here. I'm gonna help her get clean, then maybe help her get back in school and finish her education. I'm gonna get a job and find us a real place to live, you know, make a new life for the both of us and leave the past behind," Rick stated.

There was silence on the other end of the line. His father spoke no words for a few moments before giving Rick instructions as if he was speaking to one of his employees, instead of his own son. "Just have you and that girl down in the lobby in about twenty minutes, check out, and meet my driver in front of that dirt hole of a motel. We will continue this conversation when you get home. Have a safe trip, son," he replied in a clam and direct tone of voice, then slammed the phone to the receiver. Rick sat with the phone to his ear until he heard the buzz tone began to blur loudly. He dropped the phone onto the nightstand and jumped to his feet. He quickly began to pack up the little belongings they had and went over to the window and looked out. He glanced both up and down the highway but saw no cars passing or pulling into the motel parking lot.

"Cassie, wake up, we gotta get out of here," he quietly said, as he began to shake her awake.

"What is it?" she replied, still in a groggy state and rubbing her eyes to see clearly.

"We gotta go now. Dad sent his driver for us to take us back to New York. I don't wanna do that and I know you don't either, so we need to get out of here now," he said, without looking in her direction as he continued to grab what they had and pack it into a small backpack.

"Wait, Rick," Cassie said, as she sat up on the bed and rubbed her eyes. "I think going back to New York wouldn't be so bad." Rick looked at his little sister with a puzzled look on his face. He stopped packing briefly and sat down on the bed opposite his sister and said nothing, but just looked at her as if he had already known what she was thinking.

"I know what you're thinking Cassie," Rick started to say. "But is this really the answer?"

"Yes," Cassie answered. "He has hurt me for many years, just to keep his and my mother's secret. They were both involved in the sex trafficking of all those young girls. My mom kept it all under wraps because she had a lot invested into this business and she loved your dad. She allowed him to hurt me and she still loved him. She helped him form that whole operation and brought in the most prestigious people in town as clients. She watched and helped him create an illegal empire. She loved him with everything she had in her, but when everything started to go south, he had her killed as if she was nothing. As if she was some piece of trash that got in his way. And of all things, he had *you* kill her without you knowing the truth. So, you see, he lied to you. You have the blood of my mother on your hands and for what?" She walked over to the window but did not open the curtain. She just stared at the curtain as if she was watching a movie on a cable channel. Rick stared in bewilderment at his sister before speaking. He wasn't sure what to say for that matter. Rick stood up and walked over to the window and drew the curtains back to check for his father's driver, but saw no one. He turned and looked at his sister, who was still deep in thought.

"What's the plan sis?" he asked plainly. The look on Cassie's face was sinister, almost as if one of the devil's workers had entered her body. She just continued to stare at the curtains in a trance, consumed with her own thoughts. "Cassie, can you hear me?" he asked, as he waved his hands in front of her face. He noticed the expression change on her face, as if someone else had taken over her body. She smiled a wide, devilish grin before speaking. Rick also noticed that her voice had become slightly different, deeper than her natural voice. A cold chiller rose in the air, as if someone had turned the A/C all the way to max. Rick rubbed his hands together and began to blow into them to warm them when he noticed that suddenly, he could see his own breath. Cassie smiled an evil smile as she began to speak, her voice sounding even deeper than before. Her eyes were wide and black, and her skin looked almost frozen. Something had for sure taken over her and was now speaking through her.

"Fear not son, I will not harm you. Your sins have been forgiven and I know that you were just following your father's orders. You have a new purpose now and that is to make sure she is safe. No harm will come to you or to her. As for your father, I can't say the same. He thinks he can get away with this. My blood will not have been spilt in vain. Oh, Big Boss will never see this coming." Cassie walked over to the chair next to the small table in their room and sat down. Rick saw that she was still in a trance like state and he watched her as sat staring straight ahead.

"Who are you?" Rick asked to his sister, knowing full well that this was someone other than Cassie. "What have you done with her?" Cassie turned her head slightly and stared directly at Rick and then spoke again.

"John David Cooper." she replied. "Remember?"

Rick jumped up from his seat and gasped, as if the room had suddenly lost all oxygen. He instantly remembered who John Cooper was and fear ran through him like water. He backed up to the wall on the other side of the room before he spoke. He opened his mouth to speak, but no words came out. "Don't be afraid of me. It is not for me to harm you. I only want the revenge that is due to me and you are not the one that I seek. It is your bloodline that I look for. You will help me get what is owed to me, whether you want to or not, that is your punishment," Cassie said. She stood up and walked over in the direction of her brother. She reached out her hand and touched Rick on the shoulder. Her hand felt like ice on his skin and then began to suddenly burn. Rick dropped to his knees from the pain before letting out a yell. Cassie released her hold on him then turned and walked over to the bed and stretched across the bottom. She closed her eyes then took a deep breath. She spoke one more time before falling into a deep sleep. "We will go to New York and pay Boss a visit. And I will take his soul to hell and drop it off on the Devil's door."

CHAPTER 37

The driver pulled up in front of the motel Rick and Cassie were staying and parked in front of the main door, turned the car off, but did not exit. He waited inside the car as instructed by Boss. Rick looked out the window and noticed the grey sedan parked in front of the building. He quickly closed the curtain and turned and looked in the direction of his sister, who was still on the bed staring at the ceiling. "It's time to go," Cassie said and rose to her feet. She still had the ghost of John Cooper inside her and it was obvious to Rick that he was in full control of his sister now and for some reason, he trusted this vengeful spirit that inhabited the body of Cassie. She walked to the door of the motel room and reached for the door handle. Before she opened the door, she turned and looked in the direction of her brother. She stared at him with cold, black eyes and began to speak. "I have spared your life, for you are blind, but if you interfere to save your father, then I will surely punish you as well. Am I clear?" she spoke in that same strange voice she had when the spirit of John David Cooper decided to inhabit her body and use her as a vengeful tool. Rick said nothing as he followed this spirit that was inside his sister as she headed outside and towards the main office of the motel so that they could check out.

After that, they both walked out and headed for the car parked in the lot, waiting for them. The driver recognized Rick, then exited the car and headed for the back door. He greeted Rick with a smile. "Good to see you alive and well Sir," the driver said as he smiled at Rick. He then turned and looked in the direction of Cassie. His eyes widened as he looked at her with a surprised look. "I didn't expect to see her looking so healthy. I thought she'd be in full withdrawal mode by now."

"Looks are deceiving," Cassie said, without turning her head to address the driver. No one spoke anymore words. The driver opened the back door of the sedan and motioned for them both to get in. He closed the door behind them and walked towards the driver's door, got in, and drove off. The ride back to New York City was long, which gave both of them time to think. Well, at least it gave Rick time enough to think of what just happened a few hours ago. He looked over at Cassie, who just sat there staring straight ahead, still in her trance like state. Rick wondered what the spirit was thinking or if it was thinking at all. He wondered why John Cooper's spirit decided to spare his life, when he was the one who pulled the trigger and took the life of this high powered attorney.

Boy, high powered he sure was, to have the ability to come back from the dead and seek revenge on those who wronged him. He also had the ability and compassion to forgive of the one who wronged him. What did he mean, I have another purpose? This is some freaky shit, he thought to himself.

Cassie shifted her head in Rick's direction and stared at him with those same cold, black eyes she had back at the motel. The corner of her mouth curled in the shape of a smile that was surely devil and then spoke. "Your purpose will be known when this is all over. A vengeful soul will never rest until *justice is* served and compassion and forgiveness is what is ordered. Rest now, you will need all your strength," she said before closing her eyes and taking a deep breath.

"So, you can read my thoughts?" Rick asked, but received no answer from Cassie or John Cooper. He knew his sister was in there somewhere and he felt for some strange reason that this spirit or whatever it was could be trusted, but for how long?

"Trust," the spirit spoke in a very deep but low voice and those were the last words to come from John Cooper for the duration of the drive. Rick stared at Cassie, still amazed at her ability to read his mind for a while, before turning his head and staring out of the window. The afternoon sun was high in the air as he watched cows and horses all seeming to be enjoying themselves in the summer heat. He drifted off to sleep feeling a sense of dread and fear for what was going to happen when they finally reached New York. He also felt the need to trust in this spirit that inhabited his sister. He remembered the spirit telling him that he had a purpose to take care of Cassie and he believed this spirit when he said that he would not let anything happen to either one of them. And for the first time in weeks, this thought made him feel a small amount of safety and he tried to rest as he was instructed. One thing was for sure, he knew was that death was coming for his father and there was nothing he could do to

stop it. He tried to remember the good times that he had with his dad as a child growing up, there wasn't very many, but the few memories he did have were good. He also remembered all those times when his dad would favor Cassie over him. Neglecting him and favoring this little girl that wasn't even his real blood, so he thought. To know his father kept *that* secret from him all these years and for him to find out now that he is a man, and also to learn about the abuse inflicted on her and for so long, caused Rick to anger inside.

"Rest," the spirit inside Cassie said to Rick with her eyes still closed. There was silence after that for the duration of the trip.

CHAPTER 38

Rick woke to the sound of car horns and taxi drivers yelling profanities out their windows. The driver announced that they would be arriving at his father's mansion in about thirty more minutes and then welcomed Rick and Cassie home. "Thanks," Rick said, wiping his eyes to clear his vision as he looked over in the direction of Cassie, who was now staring straight at the roof of the car, eyes wide open and still as black as coal. He knew that the spirit of John Cooper was still inside of her. The noise of the outside world around them seemed to get the attention of Cassie, who turned and began to stare out of the window as if she recognized her surroundings.

"Good morning Cassie?" Rick said to his sister, who was still staring out the window. He wasn't sure if she heard him so he repeated himself, but a little louder this time.

"Have your driver find the nearest pawn shop," she demanded.

"I know you're still in her, so I know you can hear me talking to you. Maybe he did some terrible things and you want to punish him for it, but don't think for a minute I'm going go buy the gun you're going to kill my dad with. He is *still* my *dad,* in case you forgot," Rick stated sternly.

Cassie turned and began to stare in Rick's direction. He watched in disbelief as her eyes began to turn from black to their normal color, and for a brief moment, Cassie was back. Rick reached over and hugged his sister as she began to whisper softly in his ear. "Please, he will send my soul to hell, if you don't cooperate," she said as squeezed Rick and then suddenly lunged forward, as if someone had just walked up to her and stabbed her in the back with a very large kitchen knife. She moaned in pain, but no blood was on her back.

"Cassie, what is it? Are you alright?" Rick asked in the most concerning way as he lifted her head out of his lap and wiped her hair from her face. "Oh my God, are you alright?" he asked once more, looking into her face. She smiled an evil grin at him as she sat back in her seat. Her eyes had turned that deep, dark black he remembered from back at the motel. Fear crossed his face as he sat and watched this spirit jump in and out of his sister and speaking to him.

Still smiling, she began to speak again. "I am growing tired of you, but you are her protector and how can you protect her if you are the reason she's destroyed? Her heart grows weaker with every minute I remain in her body, so if you want to save her, keep disobeying me and I will bring her soul to the gates of hell myself and leave her there to rot for eternity," Cassie said, but clearly Rick could see that Cassie was quickly gone.

Rick instructed the driver to stop by the nearest pawn shop and got out of the car, along with Cassie. He gave the driver a twenty-dollar tip to wait and tell his father nothing of this side trip. The driver just smiled and shook his head. Rick and Cassie walked into the pawn shop and returned a few minutes later. Rick instructed the driver to continue his route to the mansion and within minutes, they were home.

The driver pulled into the large driveway of the gated mansion surrounded by guardsmen with very large guns. He pulled up to the main entrance where two men dressed in black suits waited for the car to come to a stop. One of them walked forward and opened the door on Cassie's side of the car. He helped her out of the car and did the same for Rick, then escorted them both inside after shutting the car door. They walked down the long hallway until they reached the last door on the right. The guard informed them that Boss was waiting for them on the other side of the door, then quickly turned and walked away, bumping Rick on the shoulder as he rushed past.

"Remember that you are not to try and stop anything you see in here or you will die with your father," the voice of John Cooper came rolling out of Cassie as she reached for the door knob and turned the handle. Rick felt his heart rise into his throat as fear began to take over him, causing him to instantly feel sick at the stomach and wanting very badly to vomit where he stood. Instead, he took a deep breath and followed his sister into the office. He slowly shut the door behind him as he turned to see his father sitting behind his desk, looking as if he was the king of the world.

"Welcome home son," Boss said in a sarcastic tone of voice. "It's good to know you're safe, even if the mission was a major failure. Your mission son," Boss then paused his words and stared at Rick for a few moments, giving him a look of disappointment.

"You don't seem too pleased to see your only son dad, you would think a parent would be more grateful to know that their only child was safe and sound. Oh, but am I really your only child?" Rick flared the words at his father, obviously angry at him.

"What is that supposed to mean?" Boss questioned. Cassie walked over to one side of the large desk where Boss sat and began to stare at him with cold, black eyes that seemed to instantly turn red as blood. Boss gasped deeply as he jumped back in surprise as he watched Cassie's eyes change. Unsure of what he had just witnessed, Boss reached into one of the desk drawers and pulled out a revolver and pointed it in the direction of Cassie. "Back off, you crazy little shit," Boss said, holding the gun in visibly shaking hands.

"What's the matter dad? Don't you recognize your own flesh and blood?" Cassie said, as she stepped closer to him. "You are a very evil man and you will pay for what you have done."

"I don't know what you're talking about. What makes you think you're my kid? And if you think I had something to do with your mother's death, you're wrong. I was just as surprised as you were. I happened to love your-"

Boss's words were cut short as Cassie lurched towards him, grabbing him by the head and began to squeeze. Flashes of visions of young girls being snatched off the streets and stuffed into vans, cars, and trucks as they kick and scream for their lives popped into his head. Images of these girls being beaten, raped, tortured, and even killed flooded his mind, causing extreme pain. He managed to pull himself away from Cassie's hold and rushed backwards, hitting the wall. Cassie walked towards him as he yelled for her to stop or he would shoot, but she continued forward as if she heard nothing he had said. Her face twisted into an evil grin that changed the look of her face. She stopped directly in front of Boss and let out a devilish scream that pierced the ears of both Rick and Boss, causing both of them to cover their ears and fall to the floor. Cassie reached down and grabbed Boss by the head again and lifted him off the floor, suspending him in mid-air. Boss screamed from the pain and from the visions overtaking him, once again of the brutality that he was responsible for and then of the murder of John Cooper that he had arranged to keep the man from talking. Visions of Cassie came to him when she was a child and of all the things he allowed to happen to her and of the things he had done to her himself, just to keep her from telling the wrong people of the bad things he was involved with and of the numerous acts of crime that she witnessed as a teen and how he drugged her and would allow men to commit all sorts of sexual acts on her.

The room began to fill with darkness as the sounds of someone banging on the door began to come from the hall. Screams and cries came from every direction as the sounds of gunfire rang through the entire mansion. Police sirens came from outside, surrounding all sides of the mansion. The banging grew louder as the voice of Savannah P.D. came from through the door. Boss struggled to free himself from Cassie's grip but to no avail; her hold was too much. Pain ran through his head running down his back like a branding iron. He screamed from the pain as he reached for her eyes and pushed as hard as he could into her sockets. Cassie released her hold on him as he dropped to the floor. He crawled on his hands and knees towards the door as Cassie stood rubbing her eyes. She quickly turned and looked in the direction of Boss, who was slowly inching for the door where the police were on the other side. His mind began to speak loudly, saying that he would be better off behind bars than to endure any more of this torture.

Suddenly, the room was quite. No sounds from outside the door could be heard. Rick stood up from his chair and ran over to where his sister stood. He put one hand on her shoulder as he softly called her name. She did not respond to him as she stood still and quietly gazed in the direction of Boss. "Cassie, what is happening?" Rick yelled.

"Back away Rick. Do not interfere. They are coming for his soul now," she replied, pushing him to the side. He could clearly see that she was not in control of her own body at this moment. He knew John Cooper was inside of her now and he was full of rage, hatred, and revenge. He had summoned the dark forces from hell to come and take redemption on his father for all of his sins and crimes against those he had caused harm to. Rick backed off, slowly moving into a corner and dropping to his knees, covering his eyes, not wanting to bear witness to the evil coming. Screams from hell seemed to come from behind the walls of the office as the room grew darker.

Boss had reached the door by this time but was unable to open it. He banged on the door and cried for help from the police in the hall, but it was as if they could not hear his pleas. Cassie grabbed Boss by the ankle and pulled him towards her as he kicked and screamed like a toddler who was having a temper tantrum. The screams from the walls became louder and louder as the walls began to shake and crumble. Moans from thousands of souls cried out in pain and misery from the burning flames of hell. Boss begged Cassie to release the hold she had on him but all she would say is that punishment would be eternal and that he must pay for his sins. More cracks came from the walls as plaster began to fall like a hail storm. The wall began to open slowly as dark shapes started forming from the smoke and flames that were building up behind them. Boss pulled away from Cassie as she held her grip tighter on him.

"Let go of me bitch," Boss said, reaching forward and grabbing a handful of her hair and pulling her to the floor. They began to tussle on the floor as Boss continued to try and free himself from her grip. Just then, another loud crash came from the back part of the office.

"Freeze, nobody move!" Detective Mitchell yelled as he stepped into the room with his partner close behind. They both stopped in their tracks at the sight of what was happening in the room.

"What the hell is going on here?" Detective Brown asked, as she followed her partner into the room. Suddenly, the door slammed shut behind them as furniture began to fly about the room, crashing and breaking everything. Detective Mitchell was struck in the back of the head by a flying vase, knocking him out cold and hitting the floor hard. His partner raced to his side, kneeling down to check his pulse. He was still alive and breathing. She reached and pulled her gun from the holster and pointed aimlessly in all directions, afraid of what was happening in front of her eyes. Looking down at her partner, she held his head gently in one hand as she watched the struggle between Cassie and Boss as they tussled around the room. The figures from the wall began to take more of the form of some evil creature. It had the shape of half a man and half a goat. It had an evil face with teeth as sharp as razors with blood dripping from each one. It had a hungry gaze in its eyes and was heading in the direction of Boss and Cassie.

"Oh my God!" Boss screamed as he saw the creature coming closer and closer.

"God can't help you now. Your day of redemption has come," Cassie replied, as she began to drag Boss towards the creature. The creature let out a loud, horrifying scream, raising its arms and reaching out for Boss. Detective Brown sat frozen from fear of what was taking place in front of her. She held her partner tight as she motioned towards the front door of the office in the attempt to open it to allow the rest of the police force inside the room, but to no avail. She looked down towards her feet and realized that her leg had been trapped by one of the large tables that toppled over in all the commotion. Feeling helpless, she pulled out her radio and tried to contact anyone that would answer, but the only response she received was the sound of screeching and loud noise.

Overcome with total fear now, Detective Brown closed her eyes and began reciting the Lord's Prayer over and over as she heard the screams from the creature grow louder. The smell of sulfur filled the air in gusts of winds coming from the walls. Boss yelled once more as he gave one final tug of his leg and freed himself from Cassie's hold. He rose up from the floor and tried to run for the door but the creature reached out and grabbed him by the neck, lifting him off the floor. Boss screamed a high pitch yell that had the tone of horror that had never been heard before. Rick launched in the direction of his father, but was quickly thrown against the wall on the far end of the room, knocking him out cold. Cassie turned her head and looked across the room to where her brother now lay unconscious.

A looked of concern flashed briefly on her face then quickly disappeared and was replaced with the rage and hatred that was previously there. She began to speak in a language unknown she had never spoken in before and instantly, the wall in the middle of the room opened wider. Boss begged for the creature to spare his life but it did not listen to his pleas. He shook and wiggled, trying desperately to free himself from the clutches of this beast, but the more he moved, the tighter the creature would hold. Flames shot from the walls like lightening during a bad storm, setting the room on fire. Furniture began to burn quickly, spreading the fire from one chair to the next, then the desk and bar began burning like motionless fireballs.

Detective Brown realized that she needed to get her and her partner out of there before it was too late and they would die as well. Her mind started to race, showing her visions of what her future was supposed to be and who her future was supposed to be with. This gave her the courage and strength to free herself from the rubble and edge her and her partner slowly towards the door in back of the room where they had originally entered. She made it to the secret back door of the office and pushed with all her might to open it. Her strength was weak from the pain of her leg being crushed, causing her to only be able to push the door just a crack.

"Someone help. We're stuck inside!" she yelled and tried to listen for a response. She turned and looked back just in time to see this creature strike Boss across the chest, opening it up like a surgeon performing heart surgery on one of his patience. Blood spilled out of him like an overflowing river racing downstream. Boss gave out another painful scream, causing Cassie to reach into his mouth, grab his tongue, and began pulling it out of his mouth until she was holding it in her hand. Smiling at him, she told him to burn in hell before the creature walked towards the wall where it originally entered from. The screams from hell began to chant in unison, as if singing praise to the creature for its success in capturing another doomed soul of man. The sounds of pure fear came from Boss as he continued to plead for this creature to not take him to hell as it inched closer and closer back to the wall that entered into hell. Dark spirits came floating out of the wall, greeting the creature home and ravaging Boss' flesh as he passed each of them. The flames surrounded them as the creature continued walking through the wall, holding Boss on one of its claws as if he was some kind of prize it was claiming.

With eyes wide open, Boss gave out one final scream before they both disappeared into the flames and the walls began to close. Silence and darkness filled the room and nothing moved for a few moments. Suddenly, light filled the room in bursts of sunshine, welcoming the end of this real life nightmare. The smell of fresh air poured in like a spring rain and the darkness was no more. Detective Brown looked around the room and noticed Rick in the far corner of the room beginning to sit up, moaning and holding his head from the pain of smashing it against the wall. She also noticed Cassie, who was standing still facing the wall that Boss had just been carried through. She spoke no words and no movement came for a few moments.

Suddenly, she turned her head and looked in the direction of Detective Brown, causing a chill to run down the detective's spine. The detective pulled out her gun and pointed it in the direction of Cassie, who was slowly walking towards her and her partner. "Don't be afraid of me. I am not here for you. This was not supposed to be witnessed by you or your partner, for that matter, detective. That is why you must not speak of this to no one, for it would not be understood or believed by anyone you tell. You must forget what you saw here to save your life and the life of your soon to be husband," Cassie said, looking down at Detective Mitchell and smiling slightly, then fixing her gaze back to Detective Brown with the same smile.

"If I don't speak of this, what will I tell the people standing on the other side of that door?" she asked, pointing in the direction of the main entrance where the rest of the Savannah P.D. was still trying to gain access.

"You will tell them nothing for you will have anything to tell," Cassie replied. She kneeled down and took the detective by the hand. She instructed her to trust her, which seemed to be a difficult task for the detective because she clearly understood that she was looking at Cassie Walker, but there was something else inside her, controlling her every movement. Reaching her other hand forward, she placed it on top of the detective's head and ran it slowly and gently down her face and instantly, the detective was asleep. Cassie laid the detective down on the floor then stood up and walked over to Rick, who was still groggy from the fall but was conscious. She reached down and helped Rick to his feet.

"We must go now," she said, then helped her brother towards the back entrance of the room and disappeared through the door. A loud crash came from the front door as the police finally gained access into the office. Police officers came rushing in with guns pointed in every direction, covering all corners of the room quickly. FBI agents followed the officers into the room and immediately found the detectives unconscious on the other side of the room and called for the EMT. Searching the room, the officers reported back that there was no sign of Boss anywhere. The federals agents instructed them to seal off the room and to let no one come in or out except for officials.

"Where the hell did he go?" one of the agents asked the lead agent. "We had proof that he was here in his office. There's no way he could have escaped without being caught. How could he just disappear without a trace?" he continued.

"I'm not sure, but I'll bet those two might know what happened here. Once they come to, we'll have the chance to ask," the lead agent said, looking in the direction of the detectives. "Where the hell are those EMT's?" he yelled, heading out the door and looking down the hall.

CHAPTER 39

Three days later, Detective Mitchell awoke to find Detective Brown at his bedside, holding his hand and smiling that pearly white smile that made his heart melt each time she smiled at him. He squeezed her hand slightly as her voice became clearer to his ears. "Good morning sunshine. Did you have a nice nap?" she asked, smiling at him and gently stroking his forehead. She was not in uniform today, which was a bit different for her. She wore the most beautiful, long, yellow maxi dress that seemed to hold every curve perfectly with just the right amount of cleavage showing but not too much. Her hair was hanging down gently laying across the edges of her shoulders, instead of the usual bun she wears. She was beautiful.

"How long have I been out?" he asked.

"Three days. Doctors said you took a really bad hit to the head, which caused your brain to swell. But they said you'd be ok and would wake up from this, but I never thought it would take you this long," she said, still smiling at him.

"What happened? Did we get Boss?" He asked. Detective Brown's smile faded as she shook her head, indicating they didn't succeed in their mission. She informed him that there was no trace of Boss anywhere, but the FBI is still questioning that notion because they said that they have proof that Boss was inside the room.

"Unfortunately, no other witnesses were in the room with the exception of you and I and we both were unconscious, so they're not questioning us for now. They hoping we remember something," she told him.

"Where's Cassie?" Detective Mitchell asked.

"I got a phone call from her a couple of days ago. She says that her and her brother are fine and were no longer in the state. I asked her if she knew what happened that day because I do remember her and her brother being there in the room when we first arrived. She told me that a letter had been sent to the FBI's lead investigator giving full detail of what took place that day and also of where all those girls that weren't rescued in the double raids could be found. The letter also stated who really killed Attorney Cooper and why."

"What about Marlie Cooper? Is she safe?" He asked more anxious, while trying to sit up.

"Relax, Marlie is fine. I mean, she knows the truth as well and somehow she feels vindicated," Detective Brown replied. "She also said that she was leaving Savannah for good. Too many bad memories I guess."

"When did you talk to her; did she say where she was moving to?"

"No, she just said to let you know that she would be fine now that she has some closure to her husband's death. I talked to her a couple of days ago while you were out of it. She said that she wanted to start a new life for her and her son and that staying here in Savannah would just prolong the healing she's facing, and that it would be best for her to leave the memories behind her," Detective Brown answered.

Detective Mitchell leaned back against his pillow and tried to ignore the pounding headache he had. He looked at his partner and smiled at her, while gently running a finger across her bottom lip. He thought of how beautiful she was and how happy she makes him feel when she comes around and about how his life would not be the same if she was not in it. His heart began to beat faster as he felt his mouth open and words come out that even he himself had not expected to say, at least not at that moment. "Marry me Michele," he said, looking her directly in the eyes. Detective Brown gasped at the words she just heard. Her heart seemed to jump up into her throat, causing her to not be able to speak for a moment. Tears formed in her eyes as she just sat at his bedside and smiled. "Well woman, will you have me or not? I know I'm not much but I will be that man that you need in your life to be your protector, your lover, and your friend. I want to make a family with you and raise them together. It's always been you, Michele. I can't explain it, but from the first day you came to the department, somehow, something inside me knew you were the one but I was just being too stubborn to realize it," he said, smiling at her.

"Yes," she said as tear ran down her face. They embraced for several moments kissing and holding each other in the most sensual manner that aroused them both. They made love there in the private hospital room.

THREE WEEKS LATER

Marlie stared at the now empty room that was once her husband's home office. Memories of many long nights he spent in here working on case after case came flooding her head. Tears welled in her eyes as she took a deep breath, turned out the lights, and closed the door of the office. She walked into the kitchen and looked out the bay window at the garden she had planted many years ago when she and John had just started out as newlyweds. "Saying goodbye is hard to do," Evelyn said, as she walked into the kitchen where Marlie was. "But I think a fresh start would be best for you and John Jr."

"Yeah, I know, but this is where John and I planted our roots. We started our family here and wanted to grow old here as well. He wanted more children. Maybe three or four, he would always say. I'd just laugh at him and say that he's not the one that has to carry all those babies and how would he like having a wife with a body all stretched out from bearing children," Marlie replied, wiping tears from her eyes. "I'm really gonna miss this place."

Evelyn walked over to Marlie and gave her a hug. Neither one of them said anything for a few moments before looking at each other nor smiling. They understood each other's thoughts without words. "We should be going now, Marlie. Our plane leaves in an hour. And you know how traffic can be heading towards the airport. John Jr. is already in the car and asleep," Evelyn said.

"Sure. Just let me lock up and I'll be right out. You go ahead and get in the car. I'm on the way out," Marlie said, as she picked up her purse and keys. She walked over to the light switch and flipped the knob down, then turned and walked down the hall towards the front door. She turned around to get one last look at her house and say one final goodbye when she noticed a light shining in front of John's office door. The light was bright but did not hurt her eyes to look at. Staring at it for a few moments longer, Marlie walked towards it until she was close enough to see a figure standing inside the light. The figure did not have a shape yet, but was forming into the shape of a man as Marlie came closer and closer. She stood there looking at the image until what she recognized made her gasp. "John," she said surprisingly.

"Hello, my love. I am so happy to see you," John replied.

"How is this possible? Oh John, my love," she said, reaching out to hug him, then realizing she could see right through him.

"I just wanted to say goodbye and that I will always watch over you and John Jr. I will always be there for you. But I need for you to not allow grief to consume you. Yes, you will hurt for a while, but I want you to promise me that you will move on with your life and be healthy. Raise John Jr. to always give respect and he will be well respected in return. I want for you to be happy, Marlie. I am so proud of you for finding my killer but I am most proud of you for forgiving my killer. He is a young man who deserves a second chance to see for himself that his life can be more than what he expected. Cassie will watch over him and he will watch over her. They will be just fine. Everything is in order now and justice will be served. I can rest in peace knowing that you will be strong enough to move forward with your life and raise our son to be healthy and whole," John said.

"I promise I will John," Marlie said, as she watched her husband's ghost fade away into mid-air, then disappear into the morning light. Tears filled Marlie's eyes as she stood there for a moment longer, trying to hold on to the moment as long as she could. The sound of the horn blowing outside hurrying Marlie along startled her enough to cause her to move her feet. She turned and walked back to the front door, this time reaching for the doorknob and turning it. She opened the door and a gust of wind seemed to come from behind her, rushing through her and out the door.

"Goodbye John," Marlie whispered as she smiled. She walked out the door and shut it behind her without looking back. She locked the door, took a deep breath, then turned and walked towards the car that was waiting to take her, Evelyn, and John Jr. to the airport and to Atlanta. Evelyn had found her a house down the street from where she lived and had put a down payment on it for her. Marlie reached for the door handle of the car to open it when something caught her eye. Standing over by the old oak tree where the swing hung that they once sat in rocking John Jr. to sleep on many of those warm summer nights, she saw her husband's ghost one last time as he stood waving at her then turned and walked away into the day's sunshine, then he was gone. Marlie took a deep breath then exhaled. She said her final goodbye then opened the door of the car and got in. The car slowly pulled down the driveway, turned left and up the street, headed to the freeway for the airport and off to Marlie's new life.

BIOGRAPHY

Growing up in Akron, Ohio life was not easy, but it was always good. I grew up the youngest of seven children; with a single mother that worked tirelessly to support us. Being the youngest child I was cared for by my one sister and five brothers while mom provided all of our needs. Money wasn't plenty in our household so we made the best with what we had and was always thankful for it. As a teen, I spent a lot of time reading all kinds of books from romance to comedies, but most of all; I have a deep love and passion for mysteries and thrillers! You know the kind that keeps you on the edge of your seat and up late nights not able to put it down. I continued this passion well into adulthood. I developed a hobby for writing starting in high school, using it as a way to express my feelings. My mom always told me as a youth that if I ever felt that you could not talk to someone about my feelings than write them down on paper. I always took that piece of advice to heart. At 13 years old my mom bought me my first diary and told me to use it as a way to express my feelings and it would always make me feel better, and she was right. I used that diary daily writing all kinds of poems, dreams, wishes and letters to myself not realizing that I was developing a talent for writing and I never thought it would take me anywhere. In my adulthood I continued writing as a hobby mainly writing poetry about what was taking place at that moment of just a simple thought I was having at that time. Cleaning out the garage one day a few summers ago, I came across an old notebook that belonged to one of my sons from his old high school days. I noticed that the book was completely unused, so I kept it thinking that I'd use it for something one day and set it aside for future use. I picked up that notebook one day and started writing my first book that I am now sharing with the world. It was not an easy journey getting to where I am. This past year alone has been the challenge of a lifetime for me almost losing not only one special person in my life but two special people. My Son and my Mother both faced death this year and with God's grace and mercy both walked away from death healthy and whole. And I am most thankful that I was able to care for the both of them, while working, maintaining my home and completing this book. The events of this past year of my life has proven to be my struggle to greatness and has also shown me that I can reach my goals no matter what comes my way. I've worked in the dental field for the past 22 years and have currently lived in Las Vegas, Nevada for the past 12 years. I am blessed to have a good man by my side for the past 23 years that has always been there for me and encourages me to pursue my dreams and never give up. Completing this book is my dream come true but having my book published is my bonus. If you ever heard the statement "Being in the right place at the right time," and wondered if it was possible? Well it is. It actually happened to me with my writing. I was at a wedding in 2014 of a friend of mine and during the reception I met a few people that seemed to have similar interest as I did. I began talking about my writing hobby and how I had recently finished my first book and was working on my second book but never dreamed of having them published out of fear of rejection. That's when I was given information about a book fair that was coming to Los Angeles and being that LA is not far from Las Vegas, I was encouraged to attend. I called the telephone number that was on the information paper given to me and inquired about this book fair that was coming in a few months and if there was any way possible for me to come network myself with hopes of picking up a publisher or even information on how to self-publish my work. Needless to say that at the end of my conversation with the person who answered. I had come to find out that I was actually speaking to the

CEO of Bright Beginnings Publications, and she was interested in me and my work. She asked me if I could submit a few chapters of both my books so that she could review them and she would let me know if they would fit into her vision of the types of books she wants to publish with her company. Three days after submitting my work to her, she contacted me and offered me a book deal. That was the start of my new career in writing. I do hope you enjoyed reading this as much as I enjoyed writing it.

Check Out Other Smoking Hot Books From Bright Beginnings Publications

A Taste of Honey

AMAZON'S BESTSELLING AUTHOR
SONYA K. BOONE

www.ingramcontent.com/pod-product-compliance
Lightning Source LLC
Chambersburg PA
CBHW060805120626
46557CB00001B/92